The Freeuse Proposal

A Spicy Age Gap BDSM Series

My Freeuse Party Temptation
My Secret Freeuse Affair
My Freeuse Entanglement

April Cross

Paperback ISBN: 978-1-960162-46-5

Book Cover by Paper or Pixels

Contents

My Freeuse Party Temptation

Book 1

April Cross

CHAPTER 1

"Red or green?"

The woman who introduced herself as Bianca when I entered the mansion raises her eyebrow and looks down at two baskets of ribbons—one with green ribbons, and the other with red.

Without hesitating, I say, "Green, please."

It's a freeuse Halloween party and green means I'm open to anything tonight, including anal—the red, no anal. Go big, or go home, right?

The scent of Bianca's flowery perfume wafts towards me as she smiles, and my body tingles as she ties the ribbon around my wrist. I'm wet and ready for whatever experience awaits me.

My mind wanders, imagining having sex with a stranger, as I hand over my phone and purse. Bianca stows them in the row of small lockers behind her. The metal door clangs shut as she turns back to me. "You're number 91. I'll be here when you're ready to collect your stuff."

I adjust the tiny skirt of my slutty Queen of Hearts costume and the bustier top. My damn tits keep almost popping out. I don't know if anyone will actually recognize what I'm supposed to be since I look nothing like the Queen of Hearts from any version of Alice in Wonderland that I know of, but my red and black checkered outfit and golden crown is enough to satisfy me. I also get a kick out of not coming dressed as a slutty Alice, since my name is Alice.

Not that what I'm wearing matters—I'm here to get used. A green ribbon makes it perfectly clear. I just need a rough pounding tonight, and I want all my holes stuffed.

Bianca calls out, "Have fun!" as I head down the hallway past her.

Somewhere in the mansion is Willow—my best friend. She arrived before me because the ride share car taking me to the party got into a fender bender. No one was hurt, luckily, but I had to wait to give a statement to the insurance company over the phone about what happened. Once we got everything settled, another ride share car came to pick me up. Willow's been here for at least an hour and I bet she's ten cocks in by now. I've got a lot of catching up to do.

I barely make it into the living room before a guy wearing a wolf mask walks up to me and grabs me around the waist. "The perfect slut, I want you." His voice is husky and full of promise.

I grin at the tall stranger, thrilled someone already wants me. I hope he doesn't disappoint. This is the first freeuse party of Cherry's that I've attended, and from what I've heard, they're supposed to be epic.

Plus, I just want to be mindlessly fucked and forget about my troubles. I have to move out of my apartment right before Thanksgiving with no money saved to pay a deposit on a new place. After I suck on a few cocks and maybe get a couple of orgasms, I can forget my life problems.

My wolf man guides me over to the back of the couch. Two men are seated on it while being straddled and fucked by a pair of women wearing nurse costumes. The women both have brown hair styled the same and similar builds, so I'm guessing the matching outfits were deliberate.

The scent of sex fills the air as the wolf bends me over the back of the couch. I grip the side, practically leaning over one guy. When the wolf lifts my skirt up, he discovers that I'm not wearing any panties. His fingers prod into my pussy as if he's testing to see if the oven is warmed up.

He doesn't need to worry…it is.

The nurse bouncing on the lap of the guy in front of me tips my chin up and kisses me deeply. Wow wait, I can be used by women? Do I want this?

While our tongues dance together, a gentle heat in my core lets me know that I'm definitely okay with making out with the nurse. She tastes like coffee, and I moan into her mouth as the wolf slams his cock into me. This is going to be an amazing party.

The wolf grunts with each thrust, and my tits spill out from the top of my revealing outfit. The other nurse lifts my breasts and bends down to suck on my nipple while the first continues to kiss me. I've never kissed a woman, let alone messed with two women, and the feeling is extraordinary. I'm not interested in women under normal circumstances, but I'm ready to embrace all the pleasure tonight.

Suddenly, I realize I'm in the middle of an orgy. How did this happen? I've barely been here five minutes and I've got two women's mouths on me and some guy fucking me. I came here thinking I'd be a whore, but this surpasses even my wildest expectations.

The woman kissing me is pulled away and squeals as the guy she's fucking takes control and forces her onto her knees on the floor. The other woman still twirls her tongue around my nipple, and the suction at my breast makes my clit pulse as the wolf drills into me at a steady pace. I can already feel an orgasm building, and I close my eyes, welcoming the bliss.

Only it doesn't happen.

The wolf groans and blows his load, and when he pulls out, I realize he had a condom on. He slaps my ass and lowers my skirt, and the nurse stops sucking on my breast to concentrate on the guy she's riding.

Disappointment fills me as my wolf strides across the room to find more prey, and I shakily rise to a standing position. Leaning against a wall, I try to catch my breath. Shit, I actually wanted the guy to not be wearing a condom. I want to be so full of cum tonight, it's dripping out of me on the car ride home.

Yep, I'm a slut.

My frustration vanishes when I lock eyes with an attractive older gentleman sitting in an armchair across the room. He's dressed as a pirate with a patch over one eye, and his salt and pepper hair glimmers in the light. He's studying me with an unreadable expression on his face, but even from this distance, I can see the bulge in his pants. I think someone enjoyed watching me with the nurses and the wolf even if his face doesn't show it.

My lips are still moist and puffy from the kissing, and my clit throbs. I want that pirate to fuck me next. He might be older, but they say older men know how to please a woman, right? He looks like he won't leave me without giving me an orgasm.

My breasts are still exposed from my costume, but I ignore the fact as I saunter towards the pirate. For some reason, I'm desperate to be the focus of his attention.

He remains seated but watches me the entire time. The lines around his mouth deepen as if he's holding in a smile. When I stop in front of him, he tugs me onto his lap, so I'm sitting across him with my legs hanging off the side of the chair.

I giggle as he fondles one of my breasts. His rough, yet strong, touch sends delight through my body while he toys with my nipple. His intense gaze mesmerizes me, and I look into his warm hazel eye. The eye patch makes him look even more dashingly handsome.

When he speaks, the combination of his Scottish accent and speaking like a pirate thrills me. "Hi there, lassie. What's your name?"

Yep, I could listen to him talk all day. I snuggle closer against his chest. "I'm Alice."

He runs a hand through my blonde hair affectionately. "Alice, eh? It suits you well. You seem rather lost, Alice."

Noting that he's staying in character and using his 'pirate' voice, I feel like a little slutty misfit despite being dressed as a murderous queen. "Yes, I am indeed lost. Could you give me a ride, Captain?"

The words sound flirty in my head, but when they come out of my mouth, they sound dumber than I intended. I should stay away from flirting. I'm much better at being direct and just telling someone to fuck me.

But my awkwardness doesn't stop him from kissing me, and as his mouth brushes against mine, his free hand slides up my skirt. Mmmm, this is great. I spread my legs eagerly, and he heads straight for my wet pussy.

"It's all right, lass. I'm going to give you a ride on my ship," he says with a grin.

I'm self-conscious since everyone around us can hear, but I get over it as he slips his finger inside me. The immediate zing of pleasure makes me moan. Oh wow, that's nice.

"I'd like that," I purr in my sexiest voice and snuggle deeper against his chest, burying my face into the rough fabric of his shirt. He smells like oranges, and I like the scent too much to wonder why. I breathe deeply and relax.

The sounds of fucking and laughter from the party around us fade into the background, leaving just the two of us in this intimate moment. As his fingers continue to tease me, I can feel my body growing more sensitive, the tension coiling tighter and tighter within me.

I close my eyes and listen to the party noises around us as his fingers slide in and out of me. His thumb circles my clit, and I moan softly as I surrender to the moment.

All thoughts melt away, and I focus on the sensations as I rock against him, sliding up and down, creating a delicious friction against my clit. All I think about is the magic his nimble fingers are creating as delicate swirls of euphoria ripple through me. I want him to get his cock out and fuck me right here, right now.

I start feeling dizzy, and when he inclines his head and whispers into my ear, my insides clench. "That's a good lass. Let yourself come for me, Alice. Be a good, obedient girl."

His words tip me over the edge. Waves of pleasure wash over me, and my muscles squeeze around his fingers. When he withdraws, I sigh happily, still hiding my face in his shirt. Maybe I'm not just a slut–I'm a pirate's treasure, too. And that realization, more than anything else, makes me smile.

When the sexual fog clears, I remember we're at a freeuse party, and out in the open. I peek around the room and several people are watching us. A rush of embarrassment hits me, and I can feel myself blushing—and also my pussy waking up again. I guess that slut likes a little humiliation.

I wiggle my ass against his erection, and he tweaks my nipple hard enough to make me gasp in pleasure.

"Behave," he growls, and then ruins his harsh treatment by gently stroking my face and kissing me softly.

"Yer a good lass, Alice. I want to feel your sweet pussy clamped around my cock."

I can tell he broke character a little, and I grin stupidly at him, unable to hide my glee. "Yes, captain, yes!"

The night is still young, and I'm ready for him to fuck me for as long and as hard as he wants.

Chapter 2

The pirate helps me off his lap, and he leaves me briefly to pick up my crown off the floor by the couch. Oh, oops. I didn't even notice it fell off. I brush my fingers through my hair self-consciously before he fits the crown on my head. I'm still fuzzy from my orgasm, and I want to give him as much pleasure as he gave me.

He swiftly removes his belt, and I giggle at how silly this all is. I'm with an older guy whose name I don't know, and willing to do whatever he wants. My heart races as he glances at me, his piercing gaze making me laugh even more. Oh shit, I hope he doesn't think I'm laughing at him. This guy could be old enough to be my father, and I'm desperate to fuck him. This is not how I expected my night to go. I assumed there would be a pile of guys on me by now.

He trails his fingers along the green ribbon at my wrist, and my breath quickens. Is he going to fuck my ass?

"Kneel." His voice holds a predatory edge, and he's dropped all pretense of being a pirate.

His words trigger something deep inside me, and I'm powerless to do anything but obey. I slowly lower myself onto my knees in front of him, ready to service him in front of the crowd. I'm surprised at how much I want to give this to him.

The pirate seizes my wrists, pulling them tightly behind my back to secure them with his belt. As he binds me, I glance around the room and catch the eye of a man by the bay window. He smiles, raising his glass in acknowledgement. My gaze shifts to the pirate as he steps in front of me and pushes down his pants, revealing an impressive cock. I doubt I'll be able to take all of him in my mouth.

But I'm determined to try.

He puts his hands on my head, avoiding the crown, and guides my mouth closer to him. With my wrists bound, all I can do is use my tongue to lick the salty pre-cum on his cock from the base to the tip. I lavish it with plenty of saliva and swirl my tongue around the end, focusing on the underside right beneath the head. He groans and guides himself deeper into my mouth. I work my throat around him, adjusting to the size, and when he's finally buried to the hilt, he rocks his hips.

Holy hell, he can fit! I'm surprised at how he's able to get in all the way. It's tight, but I feel like a world-class cock-sucker for accommodating his full length.

The pirate's scent, a combination of that orange smell and his own unique musk, fills my senses as I taste his skin. It's a heady mixture that lingers on the tongue, and I like it. I could suck on this guy all night and be happy.

I try to breathe steadily, but I don't quite have a handle on it yet. Each time he pulls most of the way out, my body takes over, sucking in a deep breath. Being bound and at his mercy triggers something primal in me, something that bypasses thought and taps into pure instinct.

I'm a slut who loves being used, and in this moment, it's all I want to be.

I look up at him as he slowly fucks my mouth. There's something comforting about not being in charge, and trusting this older guy to make the decisions and take care of me. My mouth is full and stretched, but he's not being rough. I relax into his hold on my head and let him have my mouth while my body hums with desire.

"What a good girl, letting me use your mouth while all these people watch. You like it, don't you?" he asks as he strokes my cheek almost tenderly while still guiding me on and off his cock with the other hand.

I moan my agreement as he moves faster. I want him to fill my mouth with cum until I can't swallow it all. But before he can finish, he pulls away, leaving me desperate for more. I watch as he adjusts himself, my eyes following the outline of his erection as it disappears into his pants.

I'm left kneeling with my tits still hanging out of my dress. I see a few other couples having sex, while another woman glances over at me appreciatively. When the pirate pulls me up, he kisses me. His lips are hungry and possessive, his tongue exploring my mouth with a passion that mirrors my own. I close my eyes and lose myself in the sensation, forgetting about the crowd around us and focusing only on him.

This guy has an unfamiliar power over me. All he did was call me a good girl and give me an orgasm, and suddenly I'm ready to follow him around all night and be his personal fucktoy.

He breaks off the kiss and rests his forehead against mine. When I open my eyes, lust is written all over his face, and he asks, "You ready for me?"

His breath is warm, and I whimper from being so turned on. I don't know if it's the authority he projects or his incredible kiss, but I'd do anything for him to finish what he started.

I whimper in response, my need so intense that I can barely think. "Please," I beg.

He turns me around towards a hallway and I can tell that's the direction he wants to go, but before we take a step, he whispers into my ear, "I'm tempted to take what that green ribbon is offering."

My eyes widen, and I shiver at the thought of him fucking me in the ass. Isn't that what I wanted when I chose the green ribbon? I might sometimes think I'm shy, but I really want all my holes filled tonight—and now I want my pirate to be the one who fills them.

He grins. "You like the idea of getting that cute little butt of yours stuffed full of my cock?"

I manage to nod. My mind is cloudy from being so horny. "I've only done it once..." I struggle to find the right words, then decide to just say exactly what I'm thinking, "I want you to do whatever you want to me. Please?"

That sounds a lot less desperate than it feels, and he kisses my neck, close to my ear, and whispers, "That's exactly what I wanted to hear."

Does this mean he's going to fuck my ass? God, am I going to have to beg for it? Tonight is turning out to be better than I ever imagined, all because of the sexy pirate with a Scottish accent.

"First," the pirate says, "you must do as I say."

I grin with excitement. "Aye aye, captain!"

He removes his belt from my wrists and loops it through his pants. I vibrate with yearning as I watch him, and his lips twist into a knowing smile as he leads me down the hallway to a dimly lit gaming room. The scent of leather and cigar smoke fills my nostrils as we enter. There's a gaming table to one side, surrounded by four guys playing poker, but the pirate leads me to a large leather couch in the middle of the room.

"Get on your hands and knees and stick your cute little butt out. Let me get a good look at that pretty hole."

He pushes me down onto the couch, and I can feel the coolness of the leather against my knees. No one has ever talked to me this way, and having an older guy I don't know saying these things to me somehow makes it filthier.

I blush as I hold on to the backrest of the couch and realize I'm facing the guys playing poker. They've abandoned their game and are watching us with interest. My body lights up with pleasure, knowing they're about to get a graphic show as I get fucked.

My pussy throbs, the anticipation of the pirate fucking me is driving me crazy. I want him to take me, to make me scream in ecstasy. He pushes up my skirt, fingers tracing up and down my wet slit. I moan, and the watching men are suddenly forgotten as my head drops, crown tumbling onto the sofa cushions. The teasing is exquisite, each touch sending a jolt of sensation through me. I'm so sensitive that I might come all over his hand at any moment.

When I feel a finger pressing against my asshole, I arch my back and instinctively move against him. He removes his finger and a sharp spank on my ass startles me, making me squeak in surprise.

"Stay still and quiet, Alice."

"Sorry, captain," I mutter, my face flushing with embarrassment.

He puts his finger against my ass again and pushes it in. The pressure feels good and I hold myself still. Is he going to replace his finger with his cock? Fuuuck, I want that.

He laughs gently. "That's right, baby. Hold still for me."

I keep silent as he carefully probes my ass. Once he seems satisfied that I can take his finger, he slides a second one inside. This one burns and stings, but before I can move or make a noise, he bends down and bites my ass.

I yelp at the sudden pain in my flesh as my ass clamps down on his fingers, which only intensifies the burn. Then his lips glide along my skin as he kisses where he bit me.

The burning turns to pure desire, and when I tilt my head to look at him, he's smiling as he uses his other hand to rub my clit. Oh, god. His nimble fingers play with my pussy while his other hand is busy stretching my asshole. It feels amazing.

I pant as he works his fingers in and out of me. The joy builds, and when he increases the speed of his finger on my clit, the dam cracks and the tension in my belly releases. I cover my mouth with one hand to muffle my cries as my body convulses. Euphoria rockets through me as my orgasm robs me of my senses, and all I can focus on is the bliss.

When my climax dies down, he removes his fingers and flips me over so I'm on my back. He kneels between my legs, pushing them wide open. If I wasn't so blissed out, I might feel vulnerable in this position. My skirt is at my waist, and my tits are hanging out—but he's given me too much pleasure to care. My skin feels sensitive everywhere, and I can still feel the ghost of his fingers in my ass as my whole body trembles.

"Ready?"

His deep voice entrances me, and all I can do is nod. He takes his cock out and rolls a condom onto it, and I bite my lip to stop myself from telling him to fuck me raw. I really want him to fill me with his cum so I'll be dripping on the way home, but it's better this way.

He doesn't say another word as he pushes his cock into my pussy in one long thrust. Oh god, even though I had him in my mouth, he feels bigger than I expected. He stretches me out, and it feels so fucking good.

I gyrate my hips, encouraging him to fuck me harder. He withdraws until just the head of his cock is barely inside me, and slams into me again. My tits bounce with every powerful thrust, and I revel in the raw intensity of his movements. I tip my head back and close my eyes as rapture swirls in my core. This is a guy who knows how to fuck.

He keeps going, increasing his speed, and I tighten around him in pleasure. I've never been fucked like this, and I wish this guy didn't have to disappear after tonight. He grinds against me, his length massaging my inner walls as he fills me completely. I lose myself in the sensation, crying out with every thrust.

He brushes his fingers against my clit and I'm thrown into another wave of pleasure. The pressure is too much, and I explode all over his cock. He growls with approval and slides his hands under my ass, lifting it up so that I'm tilted and my breasts bounce even more.

When he's almost there, he bends over and latches onto my nipple. The suction from his mouth sets me off, and I come all over his cock again as he pulses his own release.

He pulls out and tugs me up for a kiss, his mouth crushing mine as I lean against him. This guy seriously just fucked me senseless. I'm not sure I could even walk at this moment.

When he stops kissing me, he retrieves my crown from the couch. He settles it on my head again, and kisses my nose affectionately.

"Now you're the perfect slut, and such a good girl."

Perfect? I'm a mess, but I'm happy and content as I slump onto the couch and close my eyes. If he wants to fuck my ass, he's gonna have to just roll me over and take it. I don't think I can hold myself up.

He sits down next to me and I snuggle against him, enjoying the faint scent of oranges again.

He rubs my shoulder. "Relax a moment, but then I have to go get you some water."

Hmmm? Yeah, I could use a drink. "Okay, thanks."

I melt into his side and drift. I'm not sure how tonight could get any better, but it's still pretty early, so once I regain my strength, maybe I'll be ready for more.

Chapter 3

After a few minutes, he stands up and helps me adjust my dress, and then straightens his pirate costume. The guys playing poker clap and before I know it, my pirate pushes me to their table and bends me over it. He pulls up my skirt again and slides his fingers inside my pussy.

I gasp from delight when he growls, "You guys want to see her come again?"

"Fuck yes," one of them answers.

I close my eyes and relish the feeling of his fingers pumping in and out of me. Bracing my hands flat on the gaming table, I moan loudly and feel like a complete slut. The pirate rubs my clit as he continues to finger fuck me. I'm still overly sensitive, and my breathing gets more erratic as the pressure builds up again.

I'm a trembling mess and I cry out, "Ohh, fuck!" as my orgasm hits. My legs buckle, and the pirate holds me steady, still stimulating my clit as the pleasure peaks multiple times. I'm only vaguely aware of the surrounding guys, clapping and cheering him on as I writhe over the card table.

After the euphoria subsides, he lifts me into his arms. My brain is scrambled from being well plundered by the pirate and I can't even think straight. He carries me down the hallway, presumably toward the kitchen for that drink he mentioned. Before we get there, though, he stops and gently sets me down, turning me to face him.

"I'm Leo, by the way. Nice to meet you, Alice."

I stand there with my mouth agape, stunned by his unexpected introduction. Something about knowing his name makes this feel more real, less like a fantasy. At least now I won't have to think of him as 'the pirate' forever.

"Hi, Leo. It's nice to meet you, too."

He's holding the hand with the green ribbon on it, and he fingers the edge of the silk with his other hand. "Do you still want what this ribbon represents?"

He's staring intently at me and my legs tremble. Just him mentioning fucking my ass has my heart pounding with excitement. God, I want that.

"Yes."

I feel like I should say more, but I can't bring myself to ask for it. Fortunately, Leo doesn't make me.

He cups my cheek in his hand. "But do you want it with someone other than me?"

His eyes capture mine, and I find myself lost in their depths. The thought of someone else fucking my ass tonight seems impossible, almost absurd.

"No, only you," I whisper, the truth of it resonating through me.

When he smiles, warmth blooms in my chest. I feel like a princess in a fairy tale, but one where the prince is deliciously dangerous and the happily ever after involves silk ribbons and exquisite torture. The power he holds over me should be frightening, but instead, it feels like coming home.

He tugs on the ribbon, untying it with deliberate slowness, his eyes never leaving mine. "Then we don't need this anymore, do we?"

I'm breathless and can't speak as he slips the ribbon into the pocket of his trousers.

"Let's get a drink and find a private room. I want a proper look at that tight little hole before I take it for a spin."

My eyes widen and he bends down and kisses me gently, as if we're in a scene in a romance movie. My heart flutters as I lose myself in his arms. This is not how I expected my night at a freeuse party to go, but I'm really not interested in anyone other than Leo.

He breaks off the kiss, and we continue our trek through the mansion. When we get to the kitchen and I look around, it's a sea of people fucking over all the surfaces. The wolf from earlier has his tongue buried deep between the legs of a brunette dressed up like a nun. There's a woman dressed as a pixie getting railed over the table by a train of guys, and a guy on his knees on the floor enjoying his mouth being used by several other men.

Should I be shocked by the blatant sex everywhere? I'm not that experienced, and I've never been a part of an orgy before—which this party definitely has become. It's wild and fabulous, but it makes me glad I found Leo. He makes me feel safe.

Taking his arm, I huddle close as he retrieves two bottles of water from an ice-filled tub. He opens one and hands it to me, ensuring I take a few sips while he does the same. When we leave the bustling kitchen, I'm uncertain of our destination but follow his lead up the stairs. We pass several occupied bedrooms, and I can't help but wonder about the activities taking place behind those closed doors—likely similar to the uninhibited scenes playing out downstairs. My anticipation builds as we finally locate an empty room, and I'm eager to step inside.

The moment the door closes, Leo draws me into a hard, bruising kiss. I can tell he's impatient to fuck me again, and I match his passion, trying to show him how much I want him. My clit throbs, hungry to feel his thick cock inside me.

As his tongue twines with mine, he unzips my dress. Helping him, I push it down my arms so it can pool on the floor at my feet. His hands run across my naked skin, and I flush, wanting him to touch me everywhere.

When he lifts his mouth from mine, he steps away, looking me up and down with an appreciative gaze. I feel an uncomfortable vulnerability being naked in front of him while he's fully clothed. My nipples harden and I can feel my face grow pink from embarrassment, but at the same time, I enjoy being admired and it turns me on even more. Being at a freeuse party allows me to embrace my inner slut. I'm never going to see Leo again, so there's nothing to stop me from being bold to get what I want.

As he removes his eye patch, the full intensity of his striking features is revealed. His silver-fox good looks accentuates the age gap between us, giving me a jolt of naughty pleasure. His gaze is fixed intently on my pussy, and I slip my hand between my legs, aroused by the raw hunger in his eyes. I moan when my fingers brush against my clit.

"I want to be a good, obedient girl for you. What do you want from me?"

He licks his lips, and when he speaks, his voice is rough. "You know exactly what I want, don't you?" His words send a thrill through me, and he continues. "Turn around and spread yourself wide for me. Bend over and touch the ground so I can get a good look."

His words send me into a frenzy. Jesus, how is he doing this to me? I do exactly as he commands, my body responding to the gruffness in his voice.

I widen my stance a little and slowly reach towards the floor. The carpet is soft under my fingers, and I feel the slightest strain behind my knees—my high heels aren't helping. I feel like a filthy slut, and I revel in it.

I tremble with excitement as I wait for him to touch me. I hear him removing his clothes, and every second he makes me wait is exquisite torture. When his fingers press into my pussy, I gasp in pleasure. I'm not sure how I got so lucky to find him at the party, but he really does know how to please a woman.

Leo continues to finger me. "Mmm, you're so wet for me. Do you like having your wet little pussy played with?"

"Yes," I peep out softly. Yes, I fucking do, especially when he says stuff like that. It makes me want to do whatever he commands.

He stops fingering me for a moment, and I hear a bottle cap flick open. My heart races as I realize it must be lube—this is really happening. Though I shouldn't be surprised, given that my hands are on the floor and I'm spread open for him. Something about that small sound makes everything feel suddenly, intensely real.

A cool liquid drips down on my ass that makes me shiver. His firm hand presses against my lower back, bending me further as his fingers tease the rim of my ass, spreading the lube around.

"Ohhhh, my god!" My pulse races as he works one lubricated finger into my ass. I focus on my breathing, trying to relax.

"Dirty girls deserve rewards. Are you my dirty girl?"

When I don't respond, he stops moving his finger. Fuck! He wants me to answer him? How can I form words when he's making me crazy with desire?

He continues to not move his finger and I finally find my voice. "Yes, I'm your dirty girl."

My words come out weakly, and it makes him chuckle as he starts finger fucking me slow and steady again. Mmmm, yes, this is more like it. How is he so good at knowing what I need?

My mind feels foggy and I close my eyes, losing myself in the bliss. A moment later, he adds another finger, and I suck in a sharp breath. He gently thrusts in and out, and the painful stretch quickly subsides, replaced by pleasure. His fingers thrust a little harder, and it feels like he's loosening me up.

"I'm going to take care of you tonight."

The lust in his voice is unmistakable, and I can barely contain my need for him to bury himself in my ass. His fingers pump into me again and again, and I don't think I can hold back any longer. All I can think about is him filling me with his cock.

When he removes his fingers, I whimper my protest and my knees feel like jelly.

"Get on the bed, lass. On your hands and knees," he commands. "It's time to fuck that ass."

Thank god, he's finally going to give me what I want. The sound of a foil wrapper tells me he's getting a condom on. I kick my heels off and stumble to the bed, crawling to the center. I stay on my hands and knees, wiggling my ass and looking over my shoulder at him as he climbs onto the bed.

He holds me steady by the hip as he positions himself behind me. I feel the head of his cock press against my asshole while his other hand reaches around to gently massage my pussy.

"God, your wet pussy drives me wild. I could shove my dick into it whenever I want. Would you like that?"

His voice is rich and powerful, and I moan in joy. "Yes, use me whenever, wherever. As often as you like. Make me yours."

I feel like a filthy slut, but I can't help myself. I'm overwhelmed with desire and have no control over my actions.

With a groan, he sinks his thick cock into my ass slowly, the mixture of pleasure and pain coursing through me as he works himself in deeper. When he's fully seated, I gasp from the intensity of the sensations. I've never been filled like this before, and my brain is mush.

Leo pauses. "Breathe, Alice. Good girl. Tell me when I can move."

I wait, taking a few more deep breaths as I relax. I knew he had a gigantic cock, but I didn't realize how it would feel inside my ass. This is the fullest I've ever been.

After a few moments, I whisper, "I can take it now."

He takes me for my word and pulls back. The second his hips thrust forward, stars burst along my vision as pleasure races through my body. The feeling of his cock moving inside me is almost mind-blowing.

He grasps my hips firmly and picks up speed. I clench around him in delight as he pounds into me.

"Head down," he groans, and I quickly lower my elbows to the mattress, spreading myself wider for him. "Now be a good girl and touch yourself."

He doesn't have to tell me twice. I slip my hand between my legs, circling my sensitive clit. Oooh, god, I'm going to come like this.

I rock back against him as intense pressure builds in my core. Everything he does makes my body respond, and all I can do is moan with every spike of pleasure. He shifts his angle and I rub my clit harder. When his cock pushes all the way in again, I cry out as waves of ecstasy roll through my entire body.

I'm a bundle of nerves and pleasurable energy while he fucks me through my orgasm, and rasps, "You're such a good girl. I'm about to come."

I play with my clit again, my pussy slick with desire, and I cry out as he speeds up his movements. The sound of flesh slapping together echoes around the room, and it sends me over the edge again. Lights sparkle along the corners of my vision as euphoria makes my mind blank.

I ride the waves of bliss as he plows into me several times before burying himself balls deep as he explodes. The intensity of it all wipes me out, and I collapse on the bed, unable to hold myself up any longer.

When he pulls out, I shift my legs to lie down on the mattress. My body trembles from my orgasm, and I shudder in bliss. Holy shit, that was amazing.

I'm not sure how much time passes as I come down from my high, but I feel him leave the bed for a moment and go into the adjoining bathroom. When he returns, he climbs onto the bed behind me and helps me roll onto my side so we're spooning with me as the little spoon.

"That was fantastic," I purr dreamily.

He rubs my side and my hip, and the attention from him is a balm to my soul. He kisses my shoulder. "We have plenty of time, just drift."

He's right. I don't know the exact time, but I can hear the party is still going strong. I close my eyes and murmur, "Sounds good," and let myself bask in the afterglow of my orgasm.

Chapter 4

When I wake up, I'm facing him and Leo is studying me with a soft expression on his face.

I smile up at him and squirm closer. His heat warms me, and I wrap my arm around his chest and give him a kiss. He presses me back until he's on top of me. As our lips part, I gaze up into his handsome face, and desire floods through me once more.

I hum from joy as he kisses his way down my body, starting at my mouth and moving down my neck before licking my breasts and sucking on my nipples.

The pleasure spikes, and I wiggle beneath him, the anticipation building. He runs his tongue down the valley of my breastbone, continuing to lick a line down my tummy. My insides quiver, and I dig my heels into the mattress and claw at the comforter. I hold my breath when he dips his tongue lower and runs it up the length of my slit, tasting me.

Oh god. I want more.

I exhale loudly when he sucks on my clit, and I surrender to the intense pleasure. My world shrinks to focus on what he's doing to my pussy. The pressure in my core builds as he holds my thighs apart, worshiping me. It doesn't take long before my orgasm rushes through me, and I press my lips together to stop myself from screaming in pleasure.

The warmth slowly fades, and I blink away the spots in front of my eyes to see Leo snuggling against me. I melt into his side, resting my head against his chest. The party is still noisy and chaotic outside our door, the promise of a million exquisite delights awaiting, but I don't want anyone but Leo. I'm sated and don't think I have enough energy in me to find more people. Plus, I had all my holes filled. That was my goal for the evening.

I'm suddenly feeling shy and uncertain what to say to Leo. Do I just get up and thank him for the great fuck and say goodbye? A huge part of me wishes I was going to see him again, but I bet he thinks I'm way too young for anything more than a one-night stand. I would ask him...but what if he says no? At least he helped me forget my troubles for a while tonight.

I finally work up the courage to speak. "I might be done with the party," I say with a yawn. "This has been a crazy night. More fun than I expected."

Leo kisses the top of my head, and I swear I hear a smile in his voice when he replies, "Me, too, lass. I'm feeling quite knackered. Shall we clean up and gather our things?"

I murmur my agreement, and he helps me off the bed. I wander into the bathroom with my clothes, feeling lightheaded and wonderful. As I clean up and make myself presentable, I think back on the night. God, I can't believe I was brave enough to wear the green ribbon and let a guy I just met fuck me in the ass. Willow is going to freak out in a good way when I tell her what happened. I hope she's having as much fun as I am.

After leaving the bathroom, I find Leo already dressed. He draws me in for a deep kiss that sends pleasure coursing through me. My mind races with thoughts of seeing him again. I don't want this to be it. Tonight was so amazing, I'd totally fuck him again. Since I'm single, why shouldn't I enjoy more encounters with this handsome older man who knows exactly how to please me?

But what if I hint and he doesn't take the bait? Oh god, that would suck.

When our lips finally separate, he gestures towards the door. "Shall we get out of here? Do you have a ride home? If not, I could give you one."

Ooooh, this might be my chance! "I was going to call for a ride, but I'd love one from you, if you have time."

He brushes his fingertips against my cheek as he studies me. The smile that slowly forms makes me melt inside, and he speaks with his deep Scottish accent I adore.

"I would like to get to know you better, lass. What do you say about a wee adventure with me?"

My smile is so big that my cheeks hurt. I wrap my arms around him and give him a long kiss. I have a feeling my night isn't over yet. I stop kissing him and murmur, "An adventure with you sounds lovely."

He takes my hand and we leave the room, navigating the hallway full of half-naked people. I've completely lost my shyness when we cross paths with people fucking, and I have no problem staring at a couple having sex against the wall.

On the main floor, I see several groups of people engaged in orgies. There's a circle of guys with women and other men on their knees giving them blow jobs, and there's a pile of people off to the side fucking. Holy hell, thank god I found Leo. I'm not sure I'm ready for that kind of wild abandon. I look around for Willow, but I almost feel relieved when I don't see her in any of the piles.

Bianca is still there at the entrance, and we quickly get our stuff from the lockers. Right before we say goodbye to her, Leo says, "Bianca, I'm driving Alice home. You know my full name. Can you mark it down on your list that she left with me?"

Bianca smiles. "Sure thing, Leo," and scribbles something on the guest list.

As we walk outside, I'm puzzled. What was that all about? Leo glances at me and he can see the question on my face.

"It's for your protection, lass. You shouldn't leave parties with unfamiliar guys, or if you do, make sure someone knows."

My eyes widen, and I stumble over nothing. My crown flies off my head into the grass. He quickly steadies me so I don't fall flat on my face and then he retrieves my crown. I blush as I take it from him and set it on my head.

"Jesus, you're right. I can't believe I didn't think of that! This is all so new to me, and it all sounded so fun in my head, but the party was more...intense than I expected. Like, a lot of people are actually hardcore."

He takes my hand and I thread my fingers through his, leaning closer as we walk to his car. "Then it's good we found each other. I wasn't sure if I was going to fuck anyone tonight. I thought I'd just have fun watching until I saw you."

That explains the lack of urgency I felt from him originally and why he didn't fuck me immediately. My heart warms at the thought. I wasn't just a convenient hole. He actually really wanted me.

After a short walk, we reach his SUV parked a block away. He opens the passenger door, and I climb in, settling into the comfortable seat as he makes his way to the driver's side. He doesn't start the engine, and instead turns to me with an earnest expression.

"I want to be direct with you," he says. "I've enjoyed our time together tonight, and I'd like it to continue. Would you be interested in spending the night at my place? If you're not comfortable with that, I completely understand and I'll take you home."

Holy shit! He wants me to sleep over. He's waiting for my reaction, and I lean over, knowing that it puts my cleavage on display, and smile at him. "I'll go to your place, but only on one condition."

My tits are practically spilling out of my costume and his eyes are drawn to them. When he focuses on my face again, he returns my grin. "What would that be? Something my pet desires sexually?"

My nipples harden and my brain goes fuzzy. Shit, what is this guy doing to me? I blurt out my demands before he makes me forget them. "I want another orgasm tonight, and I want you to make me breakfast in the morning."

His smile becomes predatory, and I squirm in my seat. Oh god, I can't believe I just said that! Who am I to be demanding he give me an orgasm and make me food?

"Are you going to be a good girl for me?"

Mmm, fuck. I'll be the best girl if it gets me more pleasure, but I can't help teasing him. "Maybe."

He arches an eyebrow at me and starts the car. "Buckle up. Do you know what happens to bad lassies when they misbehave?"

I'm giddy at the turn of events, and I laugh. "No, what happens to them?"

The desire written all over his face makes me want to bend over and suck on him right here in the car. Instead, I quickly buckle my seat belt.

He reaches over and cups my breast, brushing his thumb over my nipple. The friction makes me whimper at how good it feels. When he pulls his hand back. I make a noise of disappointment. He ignores my obvious neediness as he says, "Bad girls get punished, lass. They get spanked for misbehaving."

Bliss swirls in my core as my pussy throbs. Shit, I'd take a spanking from him.

"So, will you be good for me, or are you going to be naughty?"

I decide to have some more fun with him. "If I'm good, will I get another orgasm?"

He pulls onto the road and there's amusement in his tone. "You'll get as many orgasms as you want, my pet...and breakfast."

I sigh with happiness. This sounds perfect, though I might see if I can get a spanking, too. Something tells me I'd love him making my ass red. I'd probably end up begging him to fuck me.

He rubs my knee before putting both hands on the wheel. I like that he touches me a lot, and I relax in the passenger seat, enjoying the beautiful decorations of the surrounding houses. I briefly wonder where his house is as I head towards an unknown future.

I don't know what we're going to do or what he has planned, but I trust him and I'm looking forward to spending more time with him.

CHAPTER 5

Eventually the warmth of the car and the sound of the road puts me to sleep. I don't know how much time passes, but I wake up when we're entering a garage attached to a massive house. It has room for several cars and then some. There's an RV, a small trailer, and an expensive sports car in it. The metallic clang of the garage door echoes around me as I rub my eyes to make sure I'm not dreaming. Who needs this many vehicles?

When he shuts off the car and comes around to open the door for me, he takes my hand and kisses it before leading me into the house. It's modern, immaculate, and huge. The kitchen is beautiful with stainless steel appliances that gleam in the light, and a huge island with a marble countertop that feels cool and smooth under my fingertips as I run my hand over it.

As we move through his house, the furniture looks like it belongs in a magazine, each piece perfectly arranged and polished. Hell, this dude is rich...and trusting. He doesn't know me any better than I know him. I could fuck his brains out and rob him blind. Somehow I know he won't hurt me, and I'm a good person so I'm not going to take advantage of him either.

He stops in the living room and kisses me softly as I wrap my arms around his neck. The warmth of his body feels wonderful against mine, and that mix of oranges and musk fills my nostrils. I really like this man. He makes me feel safe, no matter how crazy that sounds.

He gazes at me with such affection that it makes my heart squeeze with joy. "Are you sure you want to spend the night, lass? I want you to have fun, not be bored with an old man."

I giggle as I run my hand along the nape of his neck and up into his hair. It's soft and thick, and he tilts his head to enjoy the feeling of my fingers against his scalp.

"I doubt you'll bore me, Leo. You're the best part of the night."

His eyes light up at the compliment, and he bends down and kisses my cheek before taking my hand and guiding me towards an ornate spiral staircase. Jesus, I don't feel like I belong here with him. I live in one side of a duplex that has seen better days, and I won't even be there for long since I have to move out in a couple of weeks. Ugh, I was trying to forget about that for one night.

As we reach the second floor, I notice the faint scent of lavender coming from the bedroom as I follow him in. The bedside lamps cast a warm glow, and I can see the faint outline of the city lights through the large windows. The bed is huge and the comforter is turned down. The crisp, white sheets look incredibly comfortable. It's going to be like spending the night in a fancy hotel.

He wraps his arm around my waist and I lean against him. His voice rumbles through his chest. "Relax. You're here to enjoy yourself. I want you to be a good girl and come so hard you can't remember your own name. Do you think you can do that for me, lass?"

I love how he keeps calling me lass. "Yes," I breathe out, finally allowing myself to relax into his embrace. "This is better than going home to worry about my troubles."

His fingers trail lightly over the hem of my skirt as he nibbles at my neck, sending shivers down my spine. "What troubles?"

Oh shit, what should I tell him? I try to sound casual. "I have to be out of my place before Thanksgiving and I don't know where I'm moving yet. Everywhere I've looked is too expensive."

He kisses my neck again. "Let me help you out of that costume, and then we'll shower together. The water will help you forget everything."

Somehow I think it's his cock that will make me forget everything and not the shower, but I hold that thought to myself as I remove my costume slowly like a striptease, drawing it out. The look of raw desire I get from him makes it worth it. I've never had anyone look at me like he does, or treat me with such kindness. I'm going to enjoy tonight and not worry about the future.

Once I'm undressed, he quickly takes off his costume as well and throws it in a wicker laundry basket. The moment I see his cock again, my pussy throbs. I really want him inside me.

"I know that look, lass, but patience. First, a nice, long shower."

He leads me to the connected master bath and turns on the water in a massive shower that could easily hold four people. I give him a coy grin as I walk past him and test the water from one of the shower heads—there's one on each end of the shower. It's already hot—and I'm not surprised. He's probably got a fancy tankless water heater that instantly heats up. I step in and close my eyes as the warmth cascades over my body. The sound of the water is soothing and I let out a contented sigh.

My peace doesn't last long. He grabs me, pinning me against the cool tile, and I gasp in surprise. He kisses me passionately, his cock rubbing against my mound. His aggression causes my neediness to skyrocket and I mewl with frustration when the kiss ends. I'm wound tighter than a spring, and all I can think about is getting his cock in me again.

I pout at him, but he smiles and lathers a loofah in body wash. It smells like oranges, and I almost melt from pleasure at the familiar scent. He takes his time washing me, even my hair, before rinsing me off. When I make a move to grab his cock, he pushes me away and turns me around to smack my ass once.

"Behave," he warns, and my pussy flutters in delight from his tone.

He quickly washes himself with the orange soap and rinses off. My ass tingles from the one smack and I desperately wish he'd given me more.

He turns off the water and guides me out of the shower, grabbing a towel to dry me off. I giggle. "Shouldn't I be the one drying you?"

He laughs and finds another towel to wrap around his waist. "If I let you dry me, you might get carried away and try to have your wicked way with me, lassie. Let me take care of you first. Just enjoy it."

He winks at me and I feel like I'm a compliant puddle of goo. It's a strange sense of contentment. "Okay, you can take care of me," I say, giving in to his charm.

Once I'm dry, he leads me into the bedroom and has me sit in a chair while he brushes my hair. The gentle rhythm of the brush lulls me into a trance, and I sigh happily as he combs it.

I feel boneless, and I close my eyes, losing myself in the soothing sensation. He places a soft kiss on the top of my head, and I peek up at him in gratitude.

"Does this feel good?" he asks, and I nod, still feeling lazy as the brush works wonders on me.

His touch is gentle and caring, making me feel cherished. And as I sit there, letting him take care of me, I realize that I'm really enjoying being with him.

When he's done brushing my hair, he moves in front of me and caresses my cheek. The firmness of his fingers feels good as he runs his thumb across my jawline. The scent of his body wash tickles my nose, and I feel like I'm under his spell.

"Do you like me being dominant over you?" His rough tone sends a thrill through me. My pussy throbs as I recall the dominance he displayed at the party, and I want it again.

The pressure between my legs grows, and I swallow nervously, uncertain how to answer. I love the way he's making me feel, but I don't want to sound so needy.

His eyes glitter with amusement and he steps even closer and threads his fingers into my hair. He tugs, pulling my head back. When he leans down and takes possession of my mouth, my mind races. Holy hell, how does he know what I like when I don't even know it myself? I've never reacted this strongly to a guy, and I'm ready to give him whatever he wants.

He releases my mouth and smiles down at me. "Answer me, lass. Do you want to be my good girl and obey me?"

The pleasure he gave me earlier flickers in my mind. I want him, and I want to be his good girl.

I nod my head and say softly, "Yes, please."

He looks pleased with my answer and pulls me out of the chair, leading me over to the bed. The plush carpet beneath my feet makes me feel like I'm walking on pillows, and I appreciate the luxuriousness of his bedroom. I didn't set out to snare a rich dom, but I'm going to enjoy my time at Leo's house.

"Then get on all fours on the bed," he demands, and I nearly swoon at the dominance in his voice.

I can't take my eyes off of him as I watch him open the drawer of his nightstand and take out a condom. As he opens it and rolls it over his thick cock, my mouth goes dry. I better do as he requested if I want to get fucked. I scamper onto the bed, spreading my knees wide and resting my forearms on the mattress so my pussy is stretched open to his view.

He growls from behind me and my hips automatically rise up to him in response. I want him. I need him. My pussy clenches in anticipation as he grips my ass and kneels behind me on the bed. He kisses down one ass cheek, giving me little bites on the soft flesh. I gasp from the sensation, the pain mingling with the pleasure to create a heady mix that makes me moan.

"Leo…" I wiggle my ass, hoping he'll get down to fucking me.

He drags his tongue over my pussy lips and then focuses on my clit. My insides quiver, the intensity almost too much for me. I lose myself to the pleasure as I speed towards an orgasm.

When he pulls his mouth away, I mewl in complaint. I'm so close, why did he stop? I look over my shoulder just in time for him to slam his cock into my pussy. Hunger blazes in his eyes, and the force of his movement makes me gasp as my eyes roll into the back of my head from bliss.

My pussy stretches around the thick length of him as he drills into me. I cry out his name, and he presses me into the mattress as he buries his cock deep inside me. It feels incredible, and I pant from the overload of ecstasy racing through my veins.

He fucks me furiously, hitting a spot so deep inside me that I feel like I'm flying. The pleasure is overwhelming, and my body begins to shake from the intensity. His breathing is ragged as he speeds up, his hips slamming against my ass. I can feel his cock stretching me wide, and the sensation is both painful and pleasurable.

When he reaches between me and the mattress, pressing his hand against my clit, my entire body clenches in response as I come undone. I scream into the comforter as white lights sparkle behind my eyelids.

"Oh god!" I cry out as he whacks against my pussy, chasing his orgasm. The room spins and I shatter with another climax. My pussy clenches around his cock, and he continues to fuck me. I can feel his cock throbbing inside me, and I know he's close. With a loud roar, he slams into me one last time as he explodes. He jerks against me a few more times, and then collapses on top of me.

I'm content to simply enjoy the weight of him. I feel sated, safe, and utterly cared for. What I wouldn't give for this to last forever.

He eventually rolls off of me and I cuddle against his side so I can rest my head on his chest. I lazily kiss his nipple as he strokes my back. My energy is depleted, and I can't even keep my eyes open anymore.

I hear his chuckle as he removes his condom and drags a blanket from the edge of the bed to drape over us. As I relax into him, he whispers.

"Sleep, sweet Alice. I'm going to enjoy having you as my pet. Rest, so I can have my wicked way with you again in the morning."

Mmm, that sounds wonderful. I snuggle closer to him, the scent of oranges and the steady rhythm of his heartbeat lulls me to sleep as I drift away.

Chapter 6

Warm sunlight gently coaxes me from a delicious slumber. I blink slowly, savoring the exquisite satisfied ache from between my legs. Strong arms tighten around my waist and I melt against the solid wall of Leo's chest, reveling in this seemingly perfect moment. I feel cherished, protected, wholly content.

"Good morning, my sweet girl," Leo rumbles, nuzzling his face into the sensitive crook of my neck. His stubble scrapes me lightly, and I shiver as all my nerve endings awaken. It's been a long time since I've woken up in someone's arms. I could get used to this.

I give a tiny smile, knowing he can't see it. "Mmm...morning." I wiggle against him suggestively, delighting in his soft moan as I brush against his growing hardness. I play innocent and keep my tone light. "Sleep well?"

"Like a rock, with you in my arms." He nibbles my earlobe, voice still gravelly from sleep. "You wore me out. I'm not a young man anymore."

I roll over to face him, trailing a finger down his chest and enjoying the light covering of hair that accentuates our differences. "You certainly kept up with me just fine. More than fine." Images of our passionate night are burned in my brain, and I blush. "I may never walk straight again."

Leo chuckles, a deep, sexy sound. He catches my hand and brings it to his lips, kissing each finger. "Believe me, the pleasure was all mine. You're exquisite when you let go." His hazel eyes darken with remembered lust. "I could feast on you for days."

My heart flutters wildly at his words. I open my mouth to respond when he puts a finger over my lips and says, "Let me make you breakfast. Relax here."

Leo presses a quick kiss to my palm before sliding out of bed and shrugging on a plush robe. "To be continued," he promises with a heated look.

I stretch languorously, enjoying the decadent feel of the smooth sheets against my naked body. I can't remember the last time I felt this pampered. It's heavenly.

Since I'm not sure how long he'll be gone, I get out of the comfy bed with regret and take a quick trip to the bathroom to freshen up and brush my teeth. He has an unopened toothbrush on the counter that I assume is for me. How often does he have women over if he keeps extra toothbrushes for them? I push the thought aside. I don't want to ruin my mood.

I'm back in bed by the time Leo wheels a cart into the room, the delectable scents of rich coffee and something sweet making my mouth water. He lifts silver domes with a flourish, revealing a gourmet spread: fluffy scrambled eggs speckled with herbs, glistening bacon, flaky golden croissants, fresh strawberries, and dainty glasses of orange juice. A red rose in a crystal bud vase adds an elegant finishing touch.

"Breakfast in bed? You're spoiling me," I say, propping myself up against the pillows.

"You deserve to be spoiled." Leo settles next to me, handing me one of the glasses of orange juice.

I take a sip. "Delicious. Thank you."

He smiles. "I aim to please." Picking up a fork, he gathers some fluffy egg onto it and holds it to my lips. "Open up."

I obey and he slips the fork into my mouth. Flavor bursts across my taste buds—creamy eggs seasoned with a hint of garlic, chives, and cheese. I let out an appreciative groan. "Oh my god. I could get used to waking up like this." The words slip out unguarded.

Leo's eyes soften. "I'd like nothing more than to wake up with you every morning. Feed you, worship this gorgeous body..."

My pulse quickens at his tender words. I want that too, so badly I ache, but doubt trickles in. As much as I'm relishing this blissful escape, we've only just met. This passionate fantasy has an expiration date.

Leo notices my change in demeanor. "What is it, lass? Where did you go just now?"

I hesitate, focusing on my juice. I don't want to taint our time together with real world worries. But his eyes are so earnest and caring, I feel the truth spilling out.

"It's just...I have some things I have to figure out. My living situation, for one." I worry the edge of the sheet between my fingers. "Like I said, I have to move out by Thanksgiving."

He feeds me another bite of egg. While I'm chewing, he asks, "You don't have any idea where you're going to move to?"

I swallow the bite of eggs, avoiding eye contact. "Not yet. There's a complication I have to take care of first."

"Complication?" His voice is sharp, and I wish I had never brought the subject up.

I shrug uncomfortably. "I haven't found a new place I can afford, I'm going to look around some more."

Warm fingers cover my fidgeting hands. "I want to help, Alice. Please, let me take care of the rent for you. At least until you get on your feet."

My head snaps up, eyes wide. "What? No, I couldn't possibly accept that. We barely know each other. It's too much, and I don't know when I could pay you back."

"I want to do this for you," he says gently, squeezing my hands. "It would be a gift, not a loan. No expectations."

I search his face, seeing only open affection and sincerity. Tears well up and I have to blink them away. "You're too good to be true," I whisper. "I don't deserve you."

"Yes, you do. You deserve everything your heart desires." He cups my face, thumbs sweeping my cheekbones. "Now humor a man who has more money than he needs. Let me do this for you."

Emotion swells in my chest, stealing my breath. How is this man even real? Did the universe plop me into his lap last night because I needed help? "Okay," I say softly. "Thank you."

His answering smile warms me. He leans in, capturing my lips in a searing kiss that quickly makes my head swim and all thoughts of my troubles scatter. We lose ourselves in each other again, the breakfast tray pushed carelessly aside. Leo maps every curve and hollow with reverent hands and mouth, bringing me to dizzying peaks over and over until I'm a quivering mess.

When he finally slides his cock inside me, I cry out his name like a prayer, seeing galaxies explode behind my eyelids. I've never felt this intense, soul-deep connection before. I cling to his shoulders, meeting his powerful thrusts–desperate to make this exquisite feeling last.

After another amazing orgasm, we lay tangled together as our breathing slows. In the hazy afterglow, it's easy to imagine this is more than one weekend. That he'll invite me over occasionally for a wonderful few days.

I know this bubble we're in right now will pop eventually, but I push those thoughts away and just enjoy his solid warmth and offer of help. I feel boneless and utterly happy. It's a perfect moment where nothing exists but us.

For however long I can hold on to it.

CHAPTER 7

I survey the piles of boxes strewn across the floor, and sigh as I contemplate how I'm going to get them all packed up in time. I should sort through my closet and decide which pieces to donate. But instead, I keep daydreaming about the Halloween party and Leo.

I really got lucky the night I met him. He gave me a mind-blowing experience, and he's paid the deposit plus three months' rent on my new apartment. A part of me still feels like I shouldn't have accepted the money, but I'm also a realist. How often does fate hand you an opportunity like this? My pride isn't worth living on the streets.

It's been two weeks since the freeuse party, and I can still feel the delicious sting of his palm against my ass and the rumble of his approving growl vibrating against my neck. He played my body like a finely-tuned instrument, drawing out sensations I never dreamed I was capable of feeling.

I've replayed every moment a thousand times—the way I melted under his commanding touch, the intense pleasure. He pushed me right to the brink and held me there, quivering and desperate, before

I shattered apart. Why can't every guy be like that? No man has ever made me feel so alive, so exquisitely feminine and desired. Craved.

Just the thought of submitting to Leo again makes me restless. He and I have been texting over the last couple of weeks, but he hasn't tried to hook up with me again. Every conversation with him has an underlying flirtatious heat, and just thinking of him makes me giddy. If he asked me to come over, I'd beg him to fuck me and it has nothing to do with the money he paid for my apartment. I'd be a slut for him again, no matter what.

The chime of an incoming text jolts me back to reality. Ooh, is it Leo? My heart races as I fumble with my phone. Leo's name is on the screen, a thrill shooting through me as I open the message with trembling fingers.

LEO: I have a proposition for you, sweet Alice. Call me.

Ten little words. A proposition? What could he possibly...No. I cut off that train of thought before my imagination runs away from me. There's only one way to find out.

My body was already on a low simmer and now I'm fully turned on. Please be something sexual. I want to feel his cock pounding into me again instead of just daydreaming about it.

I hit the call button and raise the phone to my ear, trying to calm my rapid breathing. He answers on the second ring.

"I'm so glad you called." His Scottish accent is a velvet caress, wrapping around me and tugging at something deep in my core. I'd do whatever this guy asked of me.

"Hi," I manage, inwardly cursing the slight tremor in my voice. "What's this proposition?"

"Straight to the point. I like that." His low chuckle sends shivers racing down my spine. "How often have you thought about the Halloween party?"

Heat floods my core and I squirm in place, thighs pressing together. Just hearing his voice has me wet. "Often," I admit softly.

There's satisfaction in the deep rumble of his voice. "I've been thinking about it constantly—how responsive you were, the little moans you made as you came."

God, that's so hot. I have to stifle one of those moans just hearing him talk about how much he enjoyed them. How can he just say things like that so casually? I'm used to partners who fumble awkwardly through their dirty talk, not this smooth confidence that leaves me weak at the knees.

"Which brings me to my proposition," he continues. "Come stay with me until the new year. For the next few weeks. Be mine completely—my freeuse submissive to do with as I please. Let me guide you deeper into this world of pleasure. I want to take you apart and put you back together until you forget where you end and I begin."

The air leaves my lungs in a shuddering rush. Oh fuck. I actually sway on my feet, desire slamming into me like a tidal wave. Live with him? Submit to him and put myself at his sexual mercy? It's insane. Reckless. Dangerous.

And I've never wanted anything more in my entire life.

My body is already aching with the desire to obey, to please him. To feel that blissful escape that only his dominance provides.

"I...wow. Leo, that's..." I trail off, swallowing hard. My thoughts are whirling, torn between caution and craving.

"If you want to think about it, I understand," he says, voice gentling. "I know it's a lot. I don't want you making this decision lightly. But Alice..." He pauses and I hear him take a slow breath. "I haven't been able to get you out of my head. The way you trusted me, the sounds you made, how utterly exquisite you were when you let go...I need to experience that again. I want to take you further."

My brain blips out and all I can think about is letting him do whatever he wants to me. I've never had a man speak to me like this, and I want to give him everything–and then beg him to take more.

"Okay," I hear myself saying. "Yes. I'll do it. I'll come stay with you."

"Good girl." Those two words are a dark purr of approval that makes my toes curl involuntarily. "I'll pick you up tomorrow evening. Pack for every occasion...and if you're fine with it, I will hire a moving company to take the rest of your stuff to your new apartment."

"Yes, sir." I hear myself say, and then I blush furiously.

He murmurs, "I'll see you tomorrow," and hangs up.

I stare at the phone in my hand, trembling all over. Am I crazy? Weeks of being his live-in submissive, at his beck and call, his to command and control.

It's thrilling and terrifying and I've never felt more alive. Doubts try to creep into my mind, but I firmly shove them aside. For once in my overly-cautious life, I'm going to take a risk. I'm going to embrace this wild, sensual side of myself that Leo has brought out. If I don't take this opportunity, I am going to regret it for the rest of my life.

I want this.

I don't know exactly what's going to happen, but I'm ready to submit to my deepest, darkest desires. I'm going to place myself in Leo's masterful hands and see where this leads.

Look out, Leo. Your willing little submissive is on her way...and she's going to blow your mind...somehow.

Laughing at myself, I start throwing my sexiest clothes in my suitcase. This is going to be a thrilling adventure.

My Secret Freeuse Affair

Book 2

April Cross

Chapter 1

My palms are sweating around my suitcase handle, and I've changed outfits three times. I finally settled on a plaid skirt, wool thigh highs, and chunky boots. Sexy without trying too hard. At least, that's the hope.

Holy hell, I can't believe I'm actually doing this.

It's been two weeks since the Halloween party, and I keep replaying it. Leo commanding me to kneel. How he rasped "good girl" in my ear. The way he used me until I couldn't even remember my own name. Now I'm standing outside my duplex, looking at it one last time before spending December completely his, then moving into my new apartment in January.

The rumble of an engine makes me look up. A sleek black SUV pulls to the curb, and when Leo unfolds his tall frame from the driver's seat, I forget how to breathe.

It hasn't been that long since I last saw him, but somehow, I'd forgotten how devastatingly sexy he is. His salt-and-pepper hair gleams silver in the afternoon light, and those chiseled features make me want to lick him from jaw to collarbone.

He's in his late forties to my twenty-four, and that gap has never been more visible, or more appealing. The lines around his mouth deepen as he takes me in, warm hazel eyes raking over me like he's already deciding what to do to me first.

He hasn't even touched me, and I'm already wet.

"There's my sweet lass." That deep Scottish rumble does things to my insides, and I press my thighs together. "You look good enough to eat."

My cheeks flame. "Hi Leo."

Two weeks of anticipation and that's the best I can come up with? I should really leave the flirting to people who are actually good at it.

He stops just short of touching me, close enough that I can smell his familiar scent of oranges and something spicier underneath. My body recognizes it immediately, and my pussy clenches. Just from a smell. I'm pathetic.

"Nervous, lass?" he asks, not unkindly.

I peek up at him through my lashes. "A little. But excited too."

His grin widens, satisfaction glittering in his eyes, and then I'm crushed against his chest, wrapped in his arms. I melt into him instantly, breathing deep. A shiver runs through me.

"My eager little kitten." He chuckles, clearly feeling my reaction. "Ready for me to make you purr?"

"You can try, Sir." Something about knowing I'm going to be his for weeks makes me braver, like I can push a little without fear of losing this.

Lust flickers behind his eyes. "Careful, Alice. If you're a bratty little tease, I'll put that mouth to better use."

The warning makes my breath catch, and I bite my lip to keep from whimpering. Holy hell, I want whatever he's willing to give me.

He must see it in my face because he smirks and gives me a knowing look that makes every filthy thought in my head completely transparent. "In the car, lass. Let's get you home so I can play with my new toy properly."

Home. The word resonates through me as I slide into the leather seat. I've still got my job at the retail store, so it's not like I'm Cinderella and he's my Prince Charming. Luckily, my boss was understanding about me taking the month of December off. Apparently being willing to work every holiday season for the past two years earned me some goodwill. And for a few weeks, I'm going to enjoy living in luxury and being Leo's freeuse toy—whatever that means, whatever he wants it to mean.

As we pull away from the curb, Leo's hand settles on my thigh. His touch sears through the thin fabric of my skirt.

"I trust you followed my instructions and got tested?"

"Yes, of course." I try to keep my voice steady, but it's difficult with his fingers tracing patterns on my skin, inching higher with each pass. "Came back all clear."

"Good lass." His approval does something stupid to my chest. My shoulders relax even as my body winds tighter with anticipation. "I got tested too. I want to feel every inch of your tight pussy with nothing between us."

Oh god. My pussy floods. I squirm in my seat—yep, my panties are a lost cause. "I want that too," I whisper, my voice coming out husky. "I want to feel you come inside me."

He groans, fingers digging into my thigh. "Christ, baby. Keep talking like that and I'll pull over and take you right here."

I'm tempted to push him further. But I want our first time without barriers to be somewhere comfortable, somewhere I can really feel every inch of him. So I just smile innocently and let my legs fall open a little wider.

He squeezes my thigh. "Before we get to my place, we need to talk about something important."

The shift in his tone makes me sit up straighter. "Okay."

"At the Halloween party, things were controlled. Bianca had your information, there were rules in place. But this arrangement is different. More intense. So we need to establish safewords."

Thank God he's the one bringing this up. I've read enough online to know safewords are important, but I had no idea how to ask without sounding like a weirdo. "I've heard of those. We can use the stoplight system, right?"

"Aye, that's right." His thumb traces circles on my inner thigh, the gesture turning me on even while it calms me down. How does he do that? "Red means stop everything immediately. Yellow means slow down, we need to talk or adjust. Green means you're good and want more. Can you repeat that back to me?"

"Red to stop, yellow to slow down and check in, green for good. And you'll actually stop if I say red?"

"Always, lass. The moment that word leaves your lips, everything stops. Your safety and comfort come first."

The certainty in his voice makes my chest tight. "Thanks for explaining that."

"You don't need to thank me for basic decency, my sweet." He lifts my hand to his lips and kisses it. "But I need you to promise you'll use them if you need to. Don't try to push through something that doesn't feel right just to please me."

I nod, meaning it. "I promise."

"Good girl." The praise sends warmth flooding through me. "Now, where were we?"

The rest of the drive is sweet torture. He caresses my inner thigh in slow, maddening circles, each pass getting closer to my pussy until I'm practically vibrating with need. I'm shamefully wet, and it takes everything in me not to shift my hips so his hand lands where I really want it. Judging by the smile on his face, he knows exactly what he's doing to me.

When we finally pull into his massive garage, I almost sigh with relief. The cool air hits my overheated skin as we get out, but that relief doesn't last. Because now I'm here. In his house. His territory.

Completely at his mercy until the new year.

He takes my coat and hangs it in a closet before giving me a quick tour to remind me where everything is. It's all beautiful, but it's also strangely impersonal. The kitchen is gleaming white, and all the furniture is perfectly arranged like it belongs in a magazine. I can't imagine curling up on that pristine leather couch or leaving a dirty dish in the spotless sink. His lifestyle is so far removed from my cramped duplex. Even the air smells like money and professional cleaners.

But then he takes me up the spiral staircase, opens a door, and everything changes.

Rich jewel tones and inviting textures everywhere. The plush carpet is soft beneath my feet, and the king-sized bed is heaped with silky cushions and throws that look impossibly comfortable. It's sensual and indulgent, and I realize with a start that this isn't his bedroom. He's given me my own space.

"You like it." It's not a question. He's watching me take it all in.

"It's beautiful." I trail my fingers over the oak dresser before turning to face him. "But not as beautiful as you."

The words sound silly the moment they leave my mouth, but I don't have time to cringe because desire flares in his eyes. He pulls me to him, one hand fisting in my hair as he tips my head back for a searing kiss. I open for him immediately, moaning as his tongue sweeps possessively into my mouth. He tastes like mint, and I want to kiss him until I'm drunk on him.

He walks me backwards until my legs hit the mattress, his lips never leaving mine as he pushes me down and covers my body with his. I arch up to meet him, relishing his weight pinning me in place. His hardness presses against my pussy through our clothes, and I rock against him instinctively, chasing the delicious friction.

He groans against my throat, pressing open-mouthed kisses along the sensitive skin. "Christ, I need you. I need to feel your sweet pussy around me. You're all mine until New Year's."

"Yours," I gasp, tilting my head to bare more of my neck to his hungry mouth. "Yours, all yours..."

"Damn right you are." He bites down in emphasis, and the sharp sting makes me gasp, but then his tongue is soothing the spot and I'm melting into the mattress. "My sweet, filthy lass. I'm going to make you feel so good, you'll never want to leave this bed."

He shoves my shirt up, and his large hands on the bare skin of my stomach make my entire body buzz with anticipation. Holy hell, maybe he really could keep me here forever. As long as he keeps touching me like this, I wouldn't complain.

My bra is a front-closure, and he pops it open, baring my breasts to his gaze before pushing my skirt up to my waist. I should be self-conscious with him still fully dressed, but all I am is turned on and desperate to have his cock inside me again.

"Look at you." His voice has gone rough, his Scottish accent thickening in a way that sends heat pooling between my legs. "Like a bloody dream, and all mine to play with."

He skims his hand over my panties, pressing firmly against my pussy, and I moan and rock up against his palm. Fuck, I need him inside me. But I also like being teased. If I'm his freeuse toy now, he gets to choose what he wants to do with me. And there's something delicious about that.

His hand cups my breast, fingers pulling my nipple into a stiff peak. The pleasure builds as he plays with me. I've been so stressed and busy packing to move that I haven't given myself an orgasm since the party. At this rate, I'm going to explode the second he slides inside me.

"Please..." I pant, hips rolling restlessly against the bulge straining his pants.

"Shh, I've got you, lass." His voice is tight with hunger as he undoes his pants. "I'm going to give your needy little pussy what it wants. I'm going to stuff you so full."

I love his dirty talk. Every word out of his mouth makes me certain I'm exactly where I'm supposed to be—spread open beneath him, desperate for whatever he wants to give me. As soon as his cock is free, he's settling between my legs, and anticipation coils tight in my chest.

But instead of pushing inside me, he kisses down my stomach, trailing his mouth lower until his breath ghosts over my throbbing pussy. I let out a noise of frustrated surprise. "Leo, please, I need you to—"

He cuts me off by pushing my panties aside and dragging his tongue in one long, slow lick up my slit. The sensation nearly sends me jackknifing off the bed, and I cry out, hands fisting in the expensive bedding. Fuuuck. He's licking me like I'm the most delicious thing he's ever tasted, groaning against my flesh like he can't get enough.

He laps and sucks, spearing me open on his tongue until I'm a writhing, incoherent mess. My thighs are shaking, my spine arching off the bed, every nerve ending lit up. He works me mercilessly, keeping me teetering on the edge with teasing flicks one moment, then driving me out of my mind with targeted suction on my clit the next. Over and over until I'm clawing at his hair, my whole body drawn taut. I'm going to shatter. I'm right there, right—

And then he's surging up my body, replacing his tongue with three thick fingers as he captures my wail with his mouth. He kisses me deeply while he finger-fucks me, curling against that perfect spot inside me. I can taste myself on his tongue, and the filthiness of it pushes me over the edge. I explode with a muffled cry, pleasure rippling from my core through every limb.

He keeps finger-fucking me through the aftershocks, and I shiver and clench around his fingers as waves of bliss wash through me. When he finally slips them free, I ache with emptiness.

But then he replaces his fingers with the tip of his cock, and I forget how to think.

"Christ, look at you." His voice is raw. "So bloody perfect and dripping wet for me."

When he pushes in, I cry out at the sweet stretch, my body yielding easily to his thick cock. And oh god—no barrier. Just him, hot and thick and bare, stretching me open until I can feel every ridge, every vein sliding against my oversensitized flesh. It's so much more intense than before. I can feel him everywhere.

"Jesus, so goddamn tight." He bottoms out with a groan, and I'm impossibly full. This is what I was missing.

I close my eyes and let the bliss overtake me as he fucks me with shallow thrusts. He keeps talking dirty, and his words wash over me—about my greedy pussy and how perfect I am around him. Every syllable settles deeper into my bones.

"Oh god, why do I like this so much?" The question tumbles out before I can stop it, but I'm too far gone to be embarrassed. "Everything you say makes me want to give you more."

His answering groan is almost pained. "Because you're mine, lass. And you were made for my cock."

I moan and cling to his shoulders as he sets a deep, driving rhythm, hitting that magical spot inside me on every thrust. The wet sounds of our bodies and our ragged breathing fill the room. We're still mostly clothed—his shirt unbuttoned but on, my skirt bunched at my waist, my bra pushed aside. It's urgent and desperate and perfect.

I wrap my legs around him, hooking my chunky boots together behind his back so I can pull him in deeper. He rewards me with a groan that rumbles through his chest. Holy hell, I could live in this moment forever.

Every nerve ending is alive, my skin sizzling everywhere it meets his. I'm drowning in sensation, being swept away. He could fuck me like this forever, and I'd never want him to stop. This is what it means to be his, and to surrender so fully there's no space left for doubt.

I can feel my second orgasm building, my entire body tightening as he pounds into me. White-hot pleasure licks up my spine, and I cry out, "Oh god...oh god..." as I hover on the edge.

"Look at me." The command makes my eyes fly open, and I meet his burning gaze. "Keep those pretty eyes open and come on my cock, lass."

That's all it takes. I scream as my body goes taut, my pussy clamping down on him as waves of molten pleasure crash through me. I hear Leo groan as he follows, and holy hell, the feeling of him pulsing inside me, filling me with his cum, sends another wave of aftershocks rippling through my body.

I cling to him and ride out the tsunami until I'm boneless and shaking. When I drift back to awareness, Leo is slumped over me, his face buried in my neck.

"My sweet lass," he mumbles eventually, lifting his head to grin at me. His eyes are soft and hazy. "You're going to kill me with that sweet pussy of yours."

"Me?" I laugh breathlessly, still twitching with little aftershocks of pleasure. "I can't think. You broke me."

He looks far too pleased with himself. "Fucktoys don't need to think. I'll keep you mindless and tied to the bed while I use you as much as I want."

"Promises, promises," I tease, snuggling deeper into his embrace with a contented sigh. His plan sounds pretty appealing, honestly. A few weeks of this? I could get used to it. I could get used to a lot of things about being his.

"Oh, lass..." His chuckle is low and wicked. "I always keep my promises."

I shiver and hold in a smile. He can't scare me with a good time. I'm ready to be his toy and do whatever he wants, wherever he wants, however he wants.

It's going to be a hell of a holiday season. My pussy is already writing thank-you notes.

CHAPTER 2

The next morning, Leo sits me down on a stool at the kitchen island while he makes breakfast. I'm deliciously sore from last night. He fucked me multiple times before we finally slept, and every shift on the seat reminds me exactly how thoroughly he used me.

He sings sea shanties while he scrambles eggs, his voice a pleasing rumble. The sound makes me smile. There's something about his confidence and age that makes me feel both young and safe.

"You seem happy this morning, pet," Leo remarks, sliding a plate of steaming eggs and crispy bacon in front of me. His eyes crinkle at the corners when he grins, and my chest flutters. It feels natural to be sitting here with him while he sings and cooks, and the thought catches me off guard.

"I am happy," I admit, taking a bite of the perfectly cooked eggs. Holy shit, these eggs are incredible. I moan around my fork like it's indecent. "How could I not be after last night?"

He chuckles, pouring us both coffee. The scent of oranges—his signature—mingles with the fresh brew, and I breathe it in like an addict. That combo already makes my brain go fuzzy.

"What do you do for fun, lass? Outside of work?"

The question catches me off guard. Fun hasn't been a priority in years. Not since my parents died when I was young, or after my aunt—who raised me—passed right after high school graduation.

"I used to paint," I say finally. "Nothing serious. I wanted to take classes in college but couldn't afford them. Now there's no time. Or space." I shrug. "I'll get back to it someday."

"What did you paint?" His eyes light with genuine interest.

"Abstract stuff mostly. Playing with color." Heat creeps up my neck. "It's silly."

"It's not silly." His tone leaves no room for argument. "Creativity matters."

We sip our coffee in comfortable silence until his posture shifts and becomes more focused.

"Now, lass. There are some things we need to discuss about our arrangement."

I straighten immediately. "I'm listening."

He leans against the counter, coffee cup in hand. Even relaxed like this, he radiates authority. "While you're here, I have expectations. Rules." He pauses, his gaze holding mine. "First, whenever we're home, I choose what you wear. Or I keep you naked and accessible."

My pussy throbs despite how sore I am. Down, girl. "Yes, Sir."

He nods approvingly. "Good girl. Second, you're not to touch yourself or come without my permission. Your pleasure belongs to me now."

I squirm on the stool, anticipation building between my legs. Holy hell, how am I supposed to keep my hands off myself when he says things like that? The ache is already starting, just from his words. "Yes,

Sir," I agree, desperate to please him even though I know it's going to drive me crazy.

"Lastly," he continues, setting his mug down and walking over to me. He tips my chin up, and the intensity of his gaze steals my breath. "You'll always be honest with me about your feelings and your limits. I can't push your boundaries if I don't know what they are."

I swallow hard under the weight of his stare. "I promise, Sir. I'll be honest with you."

He smiles and kisses me softly. "That's my good lass. Now, finish your breakfast. We have a big day ahead of us."

As I eat, Leo explains that he wants to take me to an upscale sex club downtown where he's a member. A place where people socialize and indulge in public play. My stomach does a backflip. A sex club? Part of me wants to hide under the covers, but if he thinks I'm ready, I want to try.

After breakfast, Leo draws me a bath. I watch as he tests the temperature with his fingers, and something about that simple gesture makes my throat tight. He helps me undress, and when I sink into the water, I let out a contented sigh as the warmth envelops me.

Leo kneels beside the tub and begins to wash me with a washcloth, his hands gliding over my body with possessive care. "Tonight, at the club," he says, running the washcloth along my collarbone, "I want you to wear something that makes you feel sexy with no panties. But remember, you're mine. No one touches you but me."

The thought of being on display sends heat curling low in my belly. I bite my lip. "Yes, Sir."

When I get out of the bath, Leo wraps me in a soft, fluffy towel. As he dries me off, I can see the hunger in his eyes, but he steps back with a soft smile.

"Go get dressed, my pet," he commands. "I have some business to attend to, but I'll be back for you at five. Be ready."

I didn't expect him to take me to a sex club, but this might be my only chance to see one. I'm curious what will happen, and more than a little nervous about being watched.

Chapter 3

When we step into the club that evening, I'm completely out of my depth. The place looks like sex wrapped in velvet. Burgundy curtains, dark wood, chandeliers that make everyone look gorgeous.

People dressed in elegant clothes laugh and chat at the bar or sit in booths. I can feel their curious eyes on me. Appraising.

I move closer to Leo instinctively. He places a reassuring hand on the small of my back, his palm warm through the thin fabric of my dress. Leaning down, he murmurs in my ear, "Remember, you're mine. No one will touch you without my permission."

I nod, pulling in a deep breath. He'll keep me safe. I'm wearing a purple dress that hugs my curves and shows off my cleavage, paired with heels that make my legs look amazing. I feel sexy, but all the eyes on me make me feel vulnerable too. But isn't that part of the point? To be seen, to be desired, but to belong only to Leo?

As if reading my thoughts, he says, "Everyone here has consented to be part of this environment, lass. To watch and be watched. That's the agreement when you walk through those doors. No one is here by accident, and everyone knows exactly what kind of club this is."

Something loosens in my chest. This isn't like being caught doing something shameful. Everyone here chose to participate in this particular kind of pleasure.

Leo guides me to the bar, his hand never leaving my back. He orders us non-alcoholic drinks per the club rules. As we wait, he caresses my shoulder and neck. A subtle, possessive touch that doesn't go unnoticed by those around us. I catch the envy in some of the men's eyes nearby, and it sends a thrill through me.

Drinks in hand, Leo leads me to a booth in a secluded corner, and he slides in beside me. I sip my fruity drink and giggle when I think about how different my life is right now from what it was two days ago.

"Nervous?" Leo asks.

"A little. But I trust you."

His smile softens, and he leans over to kiss me gently. "Good girl. Now let's have a little fun."

He slides his hand under the table, resting it on my knee. His thumb traces a slow circle on my skin, and he leans close, his breath warm against my ear. "I want to touch you right here, lass. With all these people around. Is that something you want?"

My pulse kicks hard. I nod, not trusting my voice. If I open my mouth right now, I might moan.

"Words, pet. I need to hear you say it."

"Yes, I want that."

His smile turns predatory. "Good girl."

Slowly, he begins to move his thumb upward, pushing the hem of my dress with it. I tense, my eyes darting around the room, but no one seems to be paying us any attention. His fingers reach the apex of my thighs, and he rubs gently over my bare pussy—no panties, just as he demanded. Pleasure jolts through me.

Holy hell. I grip the edge of the table. "Leo," I whisper, unsure what I'm asking for.

"Shh, my pet." His fingers continue their torturous teasing. "Let me control your pleasure."

I try to relax into his touch. He slips his fingers between my slick folds, stroking through my wetness. I press my lips together, stifling a moan as he circles my clit. Just enough pressure to make me squirm but not enough to satisfy.

This is insane. I'm getting fingered under a table at a sex club like I'm ordering appetizers. What does that say about me? My pussy votes that I stop overthinking it.

"Such a good girl," he praises, his voice husky near my ear. His accent thickens slightly. "So wet for me already."

I whimper, my hips moving slightly, seeking more friction. He chuckles softly. His fingers still.

"Not yet, my sweet lass. We're just getting started."

He withdraws his hand, leaving me aching and needy. I watch as he brings his fingers to his mouth, sucking my juices off them with deliberate slowness, his eyes locked onto mine the entire time. It's filthy. I can't look away.

"Delicious," he says, a wicked gleam in his eyes. "I think it's time we explore more of the club, don't you?"

My heart pounds as I slide out of the booth on shaky legs. Leo takes my hand, steadying me, and leads me deeper into the club. My thighs are slick and every step reminds me of how desperately I want more.

We pass through a curtained doorway into a larger room filled with plush seating areas. The walls display artwork depicting various scenes of erotic play—bodies intertwined, faces contorted in pleasure.

"This is the main play area," Leo explains. "Here, people can indulge in their fantasies more openly."

Holy shit. Couples and groups everywhere, doing everything from making out to—yeah, that's definitely a blowjob happening on that couch.

A woman across the room catches my eye. She's on her knees, head thrown back in obvious pleasure while her partner whispers something in her ear. She looks utterly lost in the moment, and I recognize the surrender in her expression. That's what I must look like when Leo takes control.

Is that what I want? To let go like that in front of strangers?

My pussy throbs, answering the question before my mind can.

Leo guides me to an unoccupied couch in the corner, where we can observe without being too conspicuous. He sits down and pulls me onto his lap, his arms wrapping around me protectively. I lean back against his chest.

"Watch," he says, his breath warm on my ear. "See how they give and take pleasure."

I do as he says, my eyes drawn to a nearby scene. A woman is bent over a spanking bench, her wrists and ankles secured with soft leather cuffs. Her partner stands behind her with a flogger in his hand. He runs the tails over her bare skin before he begins to strike.

Each impact makes her cry out, her body tensing and then relaxing. Her partner pauses, caressing her gently, pressing kisses to her reddened skin before resuming. Their dynamic is mesmerizing.

Would I want that? I watch her face transform with each stroke—pain turning into pleasure turning into something that looks like she's left the planet. My breath comes faster just watching.

Leo's hard cock presses against my ass through his pants. He shifts slightly beneath me, his hand sliding under the hem of my dress to caress my thigh. I squirm against him, seeking more.

"Do you like what you see, my pet?"

"Yes." My breath hitches as his fingers trace the edge of my bare pussy. "It's intense."

He hums in agreement and slips his fingers between my slick folds to stroke my clit. "Would you like to feel the bite of the flogger?"

I hesitate. The idea is both terrifying and exhilarating. "I...I think so. Maybe. I want to explore."

"That's my brave girl." His voice is warm with approval as his fingers circle my clit. Pleasure jolts through me. "We'll start slow and explore your limits. But for now, let's focus on this."

He increases the pressure, moving his fingers in quick circles. It's difficult to stay quiet as the pleasure builds. I'm dimly aware of the people around us, but all my focus narrows to Leo and his fingers on my clit.

I'm being fingered in a room full of people, and instead of shame, all I feel is a desperate need to let go completely.

"You're allowed to come, my sweet lass."

His words push me over the edge, and I climax with a soft cry, my body convulsing as waves of pleasure crash over me. Leo holds me tightly, his fingers slowing but not stopping, drawing out every shudder and tremor until I'm boneless against him.

Leo's display of dominance hasn't gone unnoticed, and there are murmurs of approval as I come down from the high. Pride hits me out of nowhere. I just came in front of strangers and enjoyed it.

I like belonging to him so completely that he could do this to me anywhere. A month ago, that thought would have horrified me. Now it just makes me want more.

Leo's voice is warm with satisfaction. "You're my good girl. You did so well."

He removes his hand from between my legs. I watch through heavy-lidded eyes as he licks his fingers clean again. The sight sends lust zinging through me, even though I'm still trembling from aftershocks.

"Are you ready to explore more?" he asks, a wicked gleam in his eyes.

A slow smile spreads across my face at the thought of more. "Yes, Sir. I'm ready."

Leo helps me to my feet. My legs are still unsteady, and he keeps his arm around my waist as we move through the club. We enter a smaller room with various implements hanging from the walls—floggers, crops, paddles, and other toys I don't even recognize. A few other groups of people are engaged in their own play.

Leo approaches a table displaying an array of sleek objects. He picks up a small, bullet-shaped vibrator and holds it up. "Have you ever used one of these?"

A blush rises to my cheeks. "Yes, but never in front of anyone before."

"Well, we'll have to remedy that."

He turns on the vibrator, and it buzzes softly. He touches it to my arm, and the sensation sends a jolt of desire through me as I imagine what it will feel like between my legs.

"You're going to use this while I watch. But you aren't allowed to come without my permission."

Butterflies swirl in my stomach. The thought of performing for Leo thrills me, but I also feel shy about doing it in front of other people. What if I look ridiculous? What if...

"Go on, my freeuse pet," he encourages. "No one here is judging you."

I pull in a deep breath and accept the vibrator from him. When I glance around the room, everyone is absorbed in their own pleasure. Leo watches me eagerly when I turn back to him.

Slowly, I lift the hem of my dress, revealing my bare pussy. I slip the vibrator down my body, the cool metal against my flushed skin making me shiver. I tease myself, running it over my inner thighs, circling closer to my aching pussy.

When I finally press it against my clit, I moan in pleasure, rolling my hips in sync with the toy.

"You're beautiful," Leo says, his voice rough. "So sexy and all mine."

His words spur me on, and I increase the pressure against my clit. My orgasm builds, the tension coiling deep within me. I'm close, so close.

And then Leo's hand is on mine, taking the vibrator from me. I whimper in frustration, looking at him with pleading eyes.

"Not yet, my sweet. I control your pleasure, remember? And I want to be the one to make you come."

He turns the vibrator off and slips it into the pocket of his pants. My attention drops to the noticeable bulge in his pants. I did that. My inner slut preens.

"Come with me," he commands, taking my hand.

I don't know where he's taking me, but I'm so turned on I don't care. As we weave through the club, we pass people in various scenes of play, but he doesn't pause. He knows exactly where we're going.

We enter a dimly lit hallway lined with doors. Leo stops at one and turns to face me. "This is a private playroom. Inside, I'm going to make you come, my pet. But remember, you only come when I say so."

I nod, my heart pounding with anticipation. "Yes, Sir."

He opens the door, revealing a room with textured red walls. The floor is laminate, great for easy cleanup, and in the center is a large four-poster bed draped in red silk. My eyes widen at the array of toys and restraints laid out on a nearby table.

Leo closes the door behind us, and when he turns to me, there's a dominant hunger in his eyes. He cups my face gently. "Before we begin, lass, you remember your safewords?"

I nod, my voice steady despite my racing heart. "Red to stop, yellow to slow down, green for good."

"That's my good girl." His thumb traces my lower lip. "I want you to use them if you need to. Promise me."

"I promise, Sir."

"Good. Now, strip for me. Slowly."

My hands tremble as I reach for the hem of my dress. I pull it up slowly and Leo's gaze follows the movement as I reveal more skin. I slip the dress over my head and let it fall to the floor. I stand before him in just my heels and fight the urge to cover myself. I want to please him, and the appreciative gleam in his eyes tells me that I am.

"Beautiful," he murmurs, circling me. "Now lie back on the bed. I want to taste you."

I obey, climbing onto the bed and spreading my legs for him. The silk is cool against my overheated skin. He kneels on the mattress, his hands running up my thighs, and I whimper.

He lowers his mouth to my pussy, and the first touch of his tongue sends a jolt of pleasure through my entire body. He explores every inch of me, licking and sucking, as I moan. I fist my hands in the bedding, trying to hold back my orgasm as the wet sounds of his mouth on me fill the room.

If someone had told me that being a freeuse toy meant this much attention on my pleasure, I wouldn't have believed them. But here I am, melting under his mouth. I'm not complaining.

He slides two fingers inside me, curling them to hit that perfect spot, and I cry out, my body trembling. "Please, Sir," I beg. "Please let me come."

He lifts his head, his fingers still fucking me. "Not yet, pet. You can take more."

He reaches into his pocket with his free hand. I hear a buzzing sound, and then he presses the vibrator from earlier against my clit. Holy hell. I arch off the bed, my hips bucking at the intense pleasure.

"Oh god," I moan, my body writhing beneath him. "I can't...I can't hold back much longer."

"You can, my sweet. And you will."

I grit my teeth as my body trembles from the effort of holding back. The pleasure is so intense it borders on pain, every nerve ending screaming for release. Just when I think I can't take it anymore, Leo turns off the vibrator and withdraws his fingers. The sudden emptiness is its own kind of agony, leaving me shuddering and hollow.

"Good girl," he praises, his voice thick with desire. "Now, I'm going to fuck you. And you're going to come all over my cock. Understand?"

The room spins, and I'm so mentally fuzzy that I'm babbling. "Yes, Sir, please, please, fuck me, I need—can't—please, I'll do anything, just please—"

Leo sheds his clothes quickly, revealing his rock-hard cock. My mouth waters at the sight. He positions himself between my legs and rubs the head of his cock against my pussy.

"You're so fucking wet. You want this cock, don't you?"

"Yes," I moan, rocking against him and trying to make him slip inside. "Need it."

He grasps my hips to hold me still. "Beg for it. Tell me how much you want it."

"Please, Sir," I whimper. "Please, Sir, I'm desperate for your cock. I need you inside me, need you to fuck me hard. I'll be so good for you, please. I need to come on your cock, need you to fill me, please."

"Fuck, you beg so beautifully." He slams into me, and I cry out, my back arching.

He doesn't give me time to adjust, immediately setting a driving rhythm that has me seeing stars. Each thrust sends waves of pleasure coursing through me.

This is what I was made for. The thought surfaces unbidden, but it feels true.

"God, you feel so good," he says roughly. "So tight, so wet. Fucking perfect."

I moan, my nails digging into his shoulders as I meet his thrusts. The wet sounds of skin slapping together and our ragged breathing fill the room. My orgasm builds again, the tension coiling tighter and tighter.

Leo captures my mouth in a fierce kiss. His tongue mirrors the movements of his cock, claiming me, possessing me completely. I'm totally at his mercy, and I love every second of it.

"Come for me, my pet," he commands, breaking away from the kiss. "Come all over my cock. Now."

His words send me crashing over the edge. I scream his name as my body convulses with the force of my orgasm. He continues to fuck me, drawing out my pleasure until he explodes. With a final, deep thrust, he groans, his cock pulsing inside me as he fills me with his cum.

I'm still shuddering when Leo rolls off me and pulls me into his arms. I snuggle against his chest and giggle from pure euphoria. Holy hell, that was incredible.

"You did so well, my sweet," he murmurs and kisses my forehead. "I'm so proud of you."

I smile, basking in his praise. "Thank you, Sir. I loved that. All of it."

He chuckles. "And I loved watching you. You're so incredibly sexy when you surrender."

We lie there for a while in the quiet aftermath, our bodies cooling and our heart rates returning to normal.

Eventually, Leo sits up, pulling me with him. "Come on, my pet. Let's get cleaned up and go home. I have more plans for you tonight."

I give him a playful grin. "More, Sir? I'm not sure I can handle much more."

There's a wicked gleam in his eyes. "Trust me, you can. My freeuse toy is mine to use as much as I want."

A jolt of pleasure ripples through me as we get dressed, and a sense of belonging settles over me that I didn't expect. I might not be part of this world permanently, but tonight I discovered several things about myself.

I like being watched. I like surrendering. I like being his.

And I can't wait to see what else he has planned.

CHAPTER 4

I wake to Leo's fingertips trailing up my spine. I'm naked, and I shiver at the tickling sensation. A slow smile stretches across my face as I remember the thrill of being watched last night.

He really knows how to treat a girl.

"Morning, lass." Leo's lips brush my shoulder, and the familiar scent of his orange body wash wraps around me. "How do you feel today?"

I roll over to face him, my body aching pleasantly. "Mmm, amazing."

Something warm flickers in his eyes. "I'm glad you enjoyed it, pet. Your willingness to explore impressed me."

My chest does that stupid fluttery thing again. "I trust you complete-ly, Sir. I know you won't push me too far."

"And I won't." His voice carries the weight of his promise. "Now, I have something for you."

He pulls a black credit card from the nightstand and hands it to me. My eyes widen when I see my name embossed on it in silver letters. "What's this for?"

Leo chuckles and tucks a strand of hair behind my ear. "It's for you, my sweet lass. Go out today and buy whatever catches your eye—clothes, shoes, jewelry, anything that makes you happy. Consider it a reward for being such a good girl."

I hesitate, running my fingers along the smooth edges of the card. It feels heavier than a credit card should. Like accepting it means something I'm not ready to name. "But...I can't accept this. It's too much."

His expression softens, and he cups my cheek with one large hand. "It's not too much, lass. I enjoy spoiling you, and I plan on taking immense pleasure in removing whatever you buy from that delectable body of yours."

My face goes hot, but I'm grinning like an idiot. "Well, when you put it that way..."

He laughs, and the sound rumbles through his chest in a way that makes my stomach dip. "That's my good girl. Now, no limits. Buy what makes you happy."

I kiss him before I can think too hard about the feeling ballooning in my chest. "Thank you, Sir. I won't disappoint you."

I mean it, too. And not just about the shopping. When did pleasing him become the thing I think about before I fall asleep? When did "good girl" start hitting harder than an orgasm? I shove the thought away before it gets too real.

We climb out of bed, and Leo stops me with a hand on my arm. "Wait, lass." His tone shifts, becoming commanding, and my heart thumps. He presses his body against mine from behind, and oh god, I can feel how hard he is, his cock thick and insistent against my lower back.

"I need you first." He pushes me toward the nearest wall. I gasp, bracing my hands against the cool surface, and his foot nudges mine apart, spreading my legs wide.

"So fucking sexy." His hands slide up to cup my breasts, kneading them possessively, thumbs circling my nipples until they peak. "My sweet, eager lass needs to start her day with a pussy full of cum."

Holy hell, that's filthy. I love it. I want to tell him I'm only this eager because I enjoy him taking control, but all I manage is a whimper. He pulls on my nipples again, and the sharp pleasure-pain zings straight to my clit.

With a final pinch that makes me squeak, he presses me flat against the wall. I have to turn my head to rest my cheek against it.

The blunt head of his cock presses against my entrance for one breathless moment, and then he sinks into me with one firm thrust.

"Fuck, you feel so good." He groans against my neck and sets a relentless pace. Fuuuck, and I moan as each powerful thrust scrapes my nipples against the wall, sending electric shocks of pleasure through me that make me clench around him.

His hands roam my body like he's claiming every inch. This should feel degrading, right? Instead I feel wanted in a way that makes my chest ache.

He grabs a fistful of my hair and pulls my head back. I cry out at the sharp tug.

"You're mine," he rasps. "Mine to fuck, mine to use, mine to control. Say it."

My head spins, thoughts scattering as pleasure builds with each thrust. "Yours...oh god, yours. Yours."

Holy fuck, that's hot. I'm just a hole he can use for his pleasure. He's taking what he needs, and I'm loving every second of it.

His body tenses as his cock swells. He's close. I clench around him deliberately, wanting to make him come.

He thrusts deep one final time, shuddering, and his groan is primal as jets of warm cum bathe my insides. Oh, fuck. Suddenly, I realize I'm not going to come and I whimper.

He stays there for a long moment, pinning me to the wall, his chest heaving against my back. When he pulls out slowly, I shiver as his cum and my own wetness trickle down my thigh.

He turns me around, his hands steadying me, and kisses me softly. When he pulls back, his eyes search mine. "Are you okay, lass?"

I open my mouth to say yes automatically, but something in his gaze stops me. My hands won't stop shaking. The ache between my thighs borders on painful, and when I try to swallow, my throat is too tight. I blink, but wetness still pricks at my eyes.

His whole demeanor changes in a heartbeat. "Hey. Look at me." His voice is gentle. "Do you want to stop? We can end this right now."

I take a shaky breath. My chest rises and falls. The ache between my thighs pulses with each heartbeat. But underneath the desperation, underneath the need that's been building—what do I actually want?

My fingers curl into my palms. My throat works.

"No." The word comes out steady. "I don't want to stop." Heat crawls up my neck. "I want...I want you to keep control. Please, Sir."

His eyes change, and the intensity softens at the edges. His hand comes up to cup my face, thumb brushing my cheekbone.

"You're sure?"

I lean into his touch, my body answering before my words do. "Yes, Sir. I'm okay. I want this."

"That's my good girl." He kisses my forehead tenderly. "I know you're aching for it, but that orgasm belongs to me. You'll wait until I decide to give it to you."

"Yes, Sir." The words come out shaky but certain.

He hugs me, holding me close for another moment. "Go clean up now, and then you're off to pamper yourself. I have work, but I'll be thinking about you all day." His voice drops lower, rougher. "And knowing you'll be desperate to come but can't touch yourself."

Heat floods through me. "Yes, Sir."

He gives me one more quick, hard kiss that leaves me breathless. "Good. Now go on."

I head to the bathroom on unsteady legs. In the shower, I let the hot water cascade over my shoulders, washing carefully. When the soap slips between my thighs, I gasp and jerk away from my own touch. Too much. Everything is too sensitive. I finish quickly, focusing on the body parts that won't make this worse.

Afterwards, wrapped in a towel, I notice the way each step creates friction. The way sitting down sends a pulse of desire through my core. I smile despite the frustration humming under my skin. There's something oddly pleasurable about walking around unsatisfied because he decided I would be.

In my bedroom, I find a simple black dress laid out on the bed. No panties.

Holy hell. My thighs clench. He picked this out. Decided for me. I grab the dress, already turned on. There's probably something I should unpack about why I like this so much, but I don't care. For these few weeks, I just want to be his.

The mall feels surreal when I know I can buy whatever I want. His credit card burns a hole in my pocket as I drift toward the high-end boutiques. I'm aware of how I must look with my blonde braids and chunky boots. Like I raided a teenager's closet rather than dressed for designer stores. I half-expect someone to stop me and ask what I'm doing here. But no one does. The salespeople smile and offer help, treating me like any other customer. With a strange flutter in my chest, I realize I look like I belong here—or at least, like I belong to someone who does.

I run my fingers over silk blouses and cashmere sweaters. What does it mean that spending his money doesn't make me feel guilty? That I want to buy things he'll enjoy taking off me? Without his credit card, I would have agonized over every price tag. Now I'm selecting items based on how Leo will react when he sees me in them.

I'm changing. The realization settles over me, impossible to ignore. I try on a deep blue silk dress in the fitting room, and it transforms me into someone I barely recognize—sultry and confident. My eyes are bright, and there's something different in the set of my shoulders. I'm more alive. More certain of what I want. I like this new version of me.

Once I decide to buy the dress, it gets easier to go wild. By the time I'm done at the boutique, I've got an impressive haul—the blue dress, a skintight red number that'll make Leo lose his mind, and several other pieces I know will end up on his bedroom floor. The total makes my eyes widen, but I hand over the card without hesitating.

I consider heading to a lingerie store next, but then a better idea strikes me. I should buy a sex toy that Leo can use on me.

My body flushes as I make my way to an adult toy store tucked in a discreet corner of the mall. I've never bought a toy with the intent of someone else using it on me—let alone with someone else's money—and my pulse kicks up as I step inside.

The store is beautiful, with displays that look more like modern art installations than a sex shop. A woman with a friendly smile guides me to a wall of vibrators in jewel tones, and I spot one immediately. It's beautifully designed, curved like a wave with a smaller nub for clitoral stimulation. It's a deep, luxurious purple.

I imagine Leo's eyes on me while I use it. Better yet, him controlling it, deciding when and how much pleasure I get. The thought makes me squeeze my thighs together.

"I'll take it."

She packages it discreetly, and handing over the card feels easier than ever.

When I leave the toy shop, I pass an art supply store and pause at the window, eyeing the display of paints and brushes. With Leo's card in my pocket, I could finally buy quality supplies. But that feels different than buying clothes he'll enjoy removing. Art supplies feel too much like I'm taking advantage. I move on.

I skip the lingerie shop for now and find a bench, pulling out my phone to text Willow.

Alice: Yo, want to go lingerie shopping with me soon?

I need some girl talk. Maybe it's time to tell her what's really going on with Leo. She responds almost immediately.

Willow: Sure, when and where? I need something sexy too.

I work out the details with her, smiling to myself. She doesn't know it yet, but I think Leo's going to end up buying her that "something sexy."

By the time I leave the mall, shopping bags dangling from both hands, I'm ready to get home and find Leo. Hopefully he'll be ready to use me again.

I think I'm becoming addicted to him.

The thought should worry me more than it does.

CHAPTER 5

Anticipation thrums through me as I walk into the house, eager to show Leo what I bought. I find him in his study, poring over paperwork, but he looks up as I enter. His eyes light up, crinkling at the corners, and a smile tugs at his lips.

"Ah, my sweet lass is back." He leans back in his chair. "Did you have a good trip?"

I set my bags on the floor, unable to keep the grin off my face. "I had a wonderful day. Thank you again for the credit card. I bought some things I think you'll like."

"Oh, really?" He raises an eyebrow. "Don't keep me in suspense, my pet. Show me."

I reach into one of the bags and pull out the blue dress I tried on earlier. The silk catches the light as I hold it up for him to see.

Leo's gaze darkens, hunger flickering in his eyes. "You're going to look stunning in that. But I must admit, I'll enjoy peeling it off you even more."

I blush and continue, pulling out the red skintight dress next.

A low sound rumbles in his chest. "Are you trying to kill an old man like me?"

I'm not sure how old he really is, but it makes me giggle. "You're not that old." I hesitate, then reach into the toy shop bag. "And this thing..."

I pull out the vibrator, open the box, and hold it up. The deep purple silicone gleams under the study lights, and my pulse hammers against my ribs.

His eyes sharpen with intrigue. "Oh, is my pet wanting more toy time?"

I nod, feeling bashful at being this blatant. "I thought it could be fun...for us."

He walks around the desk to stand in front of me. "You're full of surprises," he says, brushing a finger along my jaw. "And this just confirms that you're perfectly suited to be my freeuse toy. I'll enjoy seeing you use it."

My breath hitches. "You want to watch me?"

"Yes, and if you're a good lass, I'll even let you come."

I suppress a groan of desire. "When do you want me to use it, Sir?"

He brushes a thumb over my lower lip. "Tonight. After dinner. I want you to remember the anticipation. Each time you hold back, it'll make your release that much sweeter."

"Yes, Sir." The words feel thick in my throat.

He steps back, his tone shifting to authority. "Now, go put your purchases away and take a shower. When you're done, meet me in the kitchen. I have plans for us before dinner."

After cleaning up, I put the black dress back on with nothing underneath since Leo didn't tell me to wear anything else. I find him at the kitchen counter, chopping vegetables and singing softly. The scent of herbs and garlic fills the air.

He looks up as I enter and smiles. "Just in time. I have a task for you. Something to keep you entertained while I cook."

Nervous energy coils low in my belly. "What do you want me to do?"

"I want you to give me a show. Strip for me, and let's see how well you can follow instructions while I prepare our meal."

Holy hell. A thrill races through me. I grasp the bottom of the black dress and peel it upward slowly. Leo watches intently, his eyes filled with hunger as the dress slides over my breasts and shoulders, then drops from my fingers to the floor.

Standing there completely exposed, I meet his gaze. "Is this what you wanted, Sir?"

His lips curl into a wicked grin. "Turn around."

I obey, shivering under the weight of his gaze. The cool kitchen air prickles against my skin.

"Lovely," he breathes. "Now, bend over the counter with your ass facing me. I want you to touch yourself, but you aren't allowed to come."

This is deliciously filthy. I bend over the counter, leaning on one elbow and gliding my fingers down to my pussy. The first touch makes me shudder. A low sound comes from behind me, almost a growl. My thighs tremble. The knowledge that he's right there, seeing everything, sends electricity through every inch of my skin. I'm performing and indulging all at once.

"You're a beautiful sight, my pet. Take your time and let me enjoy this."

His appreciation gives me confidence. I tease my clit, circling my finger slowly, careful not to get too worked up. Knowing he can see how wet I am makes me want to give him the best show I can.

I hear him move to the stove and add the vegetables to a skillet. I can't resist peeking over my shoulder, and there's a noticeable bulge in his pants.

"Eyes forward, my pet." His voice carries an edge that makes my core clench.

I snap my gaze back to the cool marble under my forearm. His voice fills my thoughts as I sink a finger into my pussy and start fucking myself.

"Good girl." The words roll over me like warm honey. "Now, take your fingers out and taste yourself."

My hand shakes as I follow his command. The sweet and musky taste on my finger makes a pulse of desire roll through me.

"Now slide your fingers back in. Don't go too deep. I want you to edge yourself."

I whimper as I do what he says, pushing two fingers inside and slowly fucking myself. I moan softly as the pleasure builds, my hips rocking against my hand.

"You're doing so well." I can hear the smile in his voice.

My breathing speeds up. I'm so close. Every instinct screams to chase the release, but forcing myself to wait makes everything more intense. I rock my hips and gasp at the jolt of pleasure.

When I speed up and I'm teetering on the edge, Leo suddenly commands, "Stop."

I whimper as I force myself to stop.

"Hold that feeling. When I'm ready, I'll decide how to reward your patience."

My face burns as I stand and turn, leaning against the counter. I don't know how much longer I can take this without coming.

"Do you want me to do anything to help get dinner ready?" The quicker dinner is over, the sooner I get more playtime and, hopefully, an orgasm.

Leo glances at me over his shoulder with a playful smile. His salt-and-pepper hair is slightly mussed, giving him an adorably relaxed look.

"Aye, lass. Set the table for us." His voice takes on that commanding edge I'm learning to crave. "Do it carefully and line everything up perfectly. All the details matter, my pet. I don't want to see anything crooked."

A thrill runs through me at his order. If something's not perfect, will he punish me? The idea makes me ache. I'm half-tempted to fail on purpose. But I need to come tonight too badly to risk it, so I play along.

"I'm on it, Sir!"

I gather the plates, cutlery, and glasses. My hands shake slightly as I position each fork exactly parallel to the knife. Why does the angle of a spoon suddenly matter? I glance at him. He's watching me, arms crossed, expression unreadable. Because he can. Because I'm his toy now, and he'll use me however he wants—even for this. My breath comes shorter. I adjust a glass that was already straight, hyperaware of his eyes tracking the movement. The room feels warmer. My thighs press together as I reach for the napkins, but it doesn't help the ache building there.

"Very good," he praises once the table is set, and I beam at his approval. "Now, pour some water for us."

I reach for the pitcher, pouring our drinks carefully while Leo watches closely. Every command he gives, no matter how simple, feels like an erotic act in itself.

Leo dishes food onto our plates and sits at the head of the table. I sit across from him.

"While we eat, I want you to think about how after dinner, if you beg sweetly, I'll let you come. If not…"

He lets the sentence hang in the air, and I shiver in delight. "Yes, Sir."

The food he made is delicious, and we chat about casual things, the words flowing easily between us. Now and then, Leo slips in a flirtatious comment, his eyes glinting with warmth that makes my body hum. He's attentive, almost like he's my boyfriend, but I shouldn't think that way. I appreciate that he makes me feel valued, and not just a fucktoy around the clock. I occasionally catch his gaze drifting, lingering on my bare skin. He's keeping me in a constant state of arousal, and eating naked at the table gives me a naughty zing.

"Are you enjoying being my obedient pet?" he asks.

I pause, wanting to answer honestly. "It's incredible, Sir. Your attention…I love it. I didn't know I could want to be controlled like this."

"And it's only going to get better, lass." The promise in his voice makes my stomach tighten.

When we're finished eating, Leo stands up, gesturing for me to stay seated as he gathers the dishes. "You've done wonderfully, my pet. Now, it's time for your reward."

Is it going to be his cock? Please let it be his cock and an orgasm. Before I can jokingly ask, he says, "Go fetch the purple vibrator you bought today."

I hurry to the bedroom, quivering with anticipation as I retrieve the toy.

Returning to the dining room, I present the vibrator to Leo, holding it out in both hands like an offering. He takes it from me, and the brush of our fingers sends sparks through my body.

"Good girl." His voice is a low rumble that makes my insides melt. "Now come over here and sit on the table in front of me."

He pushes his chair back, leaving enough room for me to stand before him. "You're going to use the toy while I watch, but you aren't allowed to come."

"Yes, Sir." My body is already thrumming with need. The thought of pleasuring myself literally right in front of his face is mortifying and thrilling.

I perch on the edge of the table, spreading my legs without being told. This obedient, needy mess is a far cry from my usual self, but I love this version of me.

He hands me the purple vibrator. "Use this until I tell you to stop. Give me a show."

I take the toy, its silicone surface cool against my flushed skin.

"Go on." Leo settles back to enjoy the view. "Make yourself ache for me."

I spread my legs wider, my pussy still slick from the earlier attention. The vibrator buzzes to life, and I shiver before it even touches my pussy. I tease myself, running it over my inner thighs, circling closer to my pussy.

When I finally press it against my clit, I gasp. The sensation is almost too much after being denied all day. But it's fucking incredible.

Leo's eyes are locked onto the toy as I twitch and gasp. "That's it, lass. Bring yourself to the edge."

I moan, arching my back as I slide the toy lower, teasing my entrance. My pussy clenches, hungry for more. I ease the vibrator inside, moaning as the delicious vibrations hit that perfect spot.

"Oh god," I sigh, working the toy in and out. "It feels so good."

"I bet it does." His voice is rough with desire. "Your pussy's swallowing it up like it's starving. Faster."

I obey, picking up the pace. The vibrations light up my entire body, building familiar tension low in my belly. My hips rock to meet each thrust of the toy, and I whimper, "Please?"

Leo leans forward, his eyes dark with lust. "Not yet. You're not desperate enough."

I whine in frustration, but do as I'm told, easing off as I'm about to tip over. It's sweet torture.

"Please, Sir?" My free hand pinches and rolls my nipple. "Please let me come. I'll do anything—just please."

He stands and quickly pulls his cock out of his pants, looming over me with a wicked grin. "You don't get to come unless it's all over my cock."

He takes the vibrator from me and presses on my shoulder, forcing me to lie back on the table. I expect him to set the toy aside, but he presses the tip against my clit. I arch my back and cry out as the intense pleasure almost makes me catapult over the edge. Oh god, what happens if I come without permission?

He keeps the vibrator pressed firmly against my clit as he sinks his cock inside me. I throw my head back with a strangled cry, my body spasming.

The intensity ramps up so fast I can barely breathe. It's too much—the vibrator buzzing relentlessly against my oversensitized clit, his cock stretching me, the denial that's been building all day crashing into this sudden overwhelming flood of sensation. My vision blurs at the edges.

For a split second, panic flutters in my chest. The word yellow hovers on my tongue, my brain screaming that I can't handle this, that I'm going to shatter into a million pieces.

But then Leo's free hand finds mine, threading our fingers together and squeezing. That single grounding touch pulls me back from the edge of panic. I'm not drowning—I'm flying. The sensation shifts from overwhelming to transcendent, and I realize I can do this. I want this.

I squeeze his hand back, a silent confirmation, and his approving groan tells me he understands.

"That's it, lass," he rumbles, his voice thick with pride. "Stay with me. You can take it."

And I can. Holy hell, I can.

"Christ, you're so wet," Leo groans as he pulls out and then sinks back into me, balls-deep.

I can only whimper in response, too lost in pleasure to form words. The buzzing against my swollen clit combined with his thick cock filling me up is pure bliss. Each thrust sends shockwaves through my body. The wood of the table presses against my spine, and it's all I can do to keep myself in the moment without spiraling out of control.

He sets a relentless pace, the table shaking with the force. "Such an obedient little fucktoy."

My inner muscles flutter around him, desperately clenching as I hover on the razor's edge of release. But I can't come. Not until he says. It's not just my body surrendering. It's every part of me I've kept locked away, offered up to him.

"Please, Sir." My voice cracks with desperation. "I need to come. Please let me come on your cock."

"Shh, not yet, my pet." He leans down to capture one of my bouncing nipples in his mouth, sucking hard.

I buck beneath him. "Please, please, please."

I don't know how long I can hold off. Every thrust sizzles my brain.

"Aww, is my poor fucktoy desperate?" He somehow manages to fuck me even deeper. "Does she need to come so badly she's willing to beg for it?"

"Yes! Yes, I'm begging!" Tears leak from the corners of my eyes from frustration. "I've been begging!"

"Do you want me to fill you up until you're dripping with cum?"

"Yes! Oh god, yes!"

"Then beg for it like you mean it."

"Please!" The scream tears from somewhere deep. "Please let me come. I need it! I need you! Please, Sir, I'm begging you! Let me come!"

"That's my good lass." His groan vibrates through me. "You beg so prettily. Come for me. Now."

On cue, my whole body seizes, back arching clean off the table as the most intense orgasm of my life crashes over me. I convulse violently, my pussy clamping down on Leo's cock as wave after wave of pleasure ripples through me. It wrecks me.

"Time to fill this pussy." Leo hammers into me through my contractions. His cock pulses inside me, flooding me with his cum, and the sensation only intensifies my climax. I come again, blinded by the sheer force of it.

I have no idea how long I'm spasming beneath him, lost to the all-consuming bliss radiating through every cell.

When I finally start to come back to myself, Leo hovers over me with a satisfied smirk as he watches me tremble through the aftershocks. My chest heaves.

"Thank you, Sir," I manage to whisper, my body still shivering. His cock is still buried deep, and I can sense the wetness of our combined release dripping out. This table is going to need serious cleaning.

He leans down and kisses me tenderly. "You're incredible," he murmurs against my lips. "Your surrender...it's beautiful to watch."

I smile weakly, basking in his praise. "I never knew I could be like this."

Leo pulls back slightly, his eyes searching mine. "How are you feeling?"

I take a moment to check in with myself. It's hard to voice my emotions. "I...free."

He traces a finger down my cheek. "That's the power of submission. It's not about pleasure alone, but about trusting another person completely."

"I do trust you." My voice is filled with conviction. "Completely."

His smile widens, and he gives me another soft kiss. "That means the world to me."

He pulls out slowly, and I moan at the emptiness. Leo grabs a napkin from the table, gently cleaning me up. His tenderness touches something deep inside me, and I blink back sudden tears.

"Thank you," I whisper, my voice thick as a fat tear slips down my cheek.

He pauses, looking at me with concern. "Are you really okay, my sweet lass?"

I nod quickly, offering him a watery smile. "I'm happy. I don't know why I'm crying."

His face softens, and he lifts me into his lap like I weigh nothing, wrapping me up tight. "It's normal to have a lot of emotions after an intense scene like that, sweetheart. You did so well."

My body starts shaking as I burrow my face in his neck, breathing in the familiar orange scent that's become my anchor. Leo holds me tighter, one hand cupping the back of my head, the other rubbing soothing circles on my back. "Shh, it's okay, Alice. I've got you. You're safe."

I cling to him as the flood of emotions pours out. I'm raw, exposed, yet utterly safe in his arms.

"That's it, let it all out," he murmurs. "You were brave. I'm incredibly proud of you."

His voice steadies something inside me, and I take a deep, shuddering breath. Leo presses a soft kiss to my temple.

"You're doing so well, sweetheart. This is the hard part, processing all those intense emotions. But you're not alone. I'm right here with you."

I nod against his chest, my tears slowly subsiding. He's right. This is hard, but being in his arms makes everything better.

Leo stands with me still in his arms and carries me into the living room as if I weigh nothing. My legs are still trembling, and the cool air against my sweat-damp skin makes me shiver. When he wraps the blanket around us, I burrow into him like he's the only warm place in the world.

"How about some water?" he asks softly.

I nod, and he reaches for a bottle on the side table. Did he plan this? If he did, it makes me like him even more.

We sit in silence for a while, his arms wrapped around me, my head resting on his shoulder. It gives me time to gather my thoughts.

"Feeling better?" he asks.

I snuggle closer, breathing in orange and comfort. "Yes. Thank you for...for everything."

He kisses the top of my head. "You don't need to thank me, lass. This is what I'm here for, and I need this just as much as you do."

I look up at him, my eyes searching his. "I thought I was here to be your freeuse fucktoy?"

He laughs, and the rumble in his chest makes me giddy. "That too. You are my freeuse fucktoy, but that doesn't mean I won't take care of you."

I sigh happily and kiss his neck. I never expected to be cared for like this.

"Now, how about we get you tucked into bed?" he suggests. "You've had a big day, and you need your rest."

I give him a shy smile. "Only if you come with me."

He smiles back. "That was the plan."

As Leo leads me to his bedroom, contentment settles into my bones. Agreeing to be his freeuse toy until the New Year might be the best decision of my life. But I'm not sure how to explain what I'm doing to other people. I want to talk to Willow, but what would I even say? That I've found something I didn't know I was looking for? That the man I met at a Halloween party has somehow become the safest place I've ever been?

The thought sends a flutter of nervousness through my belly, but I push it aside. Who says I have to tell Willow anything? This could be my secret for as long as I want it to be.

Something has shifted. I'm not just enjoying this arrangement anymore—I'm starting to need it. Need him. The thought should scare me, but when he pulls me closer, all I feel is safe.

Tomorrow's problems can wait. Tonight, everything feels right, and I'm exactly where I want to be.

Chapter 6

The last two weeks vanished in a blur of work and being Leo's freeuse slut. Thanksgiving with him was... educational. Now December's here, and I've finally carved out time for Willow.

Snow crunches under my boots as Willow and I push through the doors of the lingerie store. Winter showed up early this year, and judging by Willow's grumbling, she's not happy about it.

My mind keeps drifting back to Leo this morning and how his eyes tracked my every movement like he was already planning what he'd do when I got back. Willow's voice washes over me, something about her new guy, and I make the right noises at the right times. But part of me watches from somewhere far away.

A month ago, this would have been enough—girl talk, shopping, complaining about work. Now it's like wearing clothes that don't fit anymore.

Not because Willow's changed. Because I have.

And I can't tell her why.

A salesperson approaches. "Welcome! Let me know if there's anything I can help you find."

Willow beams back. "Thanks, we will."

I head straight for the good stuff, running my fingers over silk and lace while Willow makes a beeline for the whites. When she holds up a pristine lace babydoll, I giggle.

"Is that really the look you're going for? You don't want to scare him and make him think you're walking down the aisle."

She mumbles something and shoves it back on the rack.

Deep red. Midnight blue. My arms fill fast, and I smile as I imagine Leo peeling each piece away.

Willow's watching me when I glance up. "What?"

She shakes her head, eyeing my overflowing arms. "How long are you planning on being in the dressing room? I thought this was quick."

My lips curve. "We're not trying any of this on. Pick out as much as you want. My treat."

Her eyes go wide. "Seriously? Did you win the lottery or something?"

For a split second, the urge hits to tell her everything about Leo and the freeuse arrangement. Willow would probably squeal and demand details and be thrilled for me.

But she'd also have opinions and concerns. I'm not ready to defend something I don't fully understand yet.

"I've got myself a sugar daddy." My voice stays light. "He gave me his credit card."

The words feel weird in my mouth. Sugar daddy. He's probably close to twice my age, all that silver hair and experience, and he's choosing to spoil me. Technically accurate, I guess. But it doesn't come close to whatever the hell is happening between us.

At the register, Willow spots my name embossed on the black card. "Hey! You said this was the old geezer's money."

I giggle, nerves and giddiness tangling together. "It is. He got a card made for me."

Her jaw drops. I wiggle my eyebrows. "Don't worry. I plan to pay him back. With interest."

Willow snorts, but curiosity replaces her shock as we head out with our bags. "So you've been holding out on me. You never said how Thanksgiving went with Mr. Moneybags. Here I thought you weren't that interested."

Just thinking about Leo makes me squirm. I think about Thanksgiving and heat crawls up my neck. I'd spent most of it naked. The meal had been an afterthought.

"It's going well," I say carefully. "I don't want to talk about it yet and jinx it."

The lie sits strangely on my tongue. Not because it's untrue. It's going well, but "going well" doesn't capture any of it. Going well is a first date.

What's happening with Leo is something else entirely. Something that scares me because I want it so much.

Willow bumps her shoulder against mine. "Fine. Keep your secrets for now. But you'll spill eventually."

"Deal." I hold out my fist, and she bumps it.

Guilt twists in my stomach. Willow told me everything when her ex cheated—every ugly detail, every crying jag at 2 a.m. She trusted me with her worst moments. And here I am, hiding my best ones.

But how do I explain that I've handed control of my body to a man I met at a Halloween party? That I like it? That the word "fucktoy" makes me wet instead of offended?

How do you explain this stuff? I just hope she forgives me when I finally figure out the words.

When we get to the car, Willow hugs me goodbye with promises to text about her next date.

Willow, work, the apartment I'm moving into after New Year's—that's my real life. The boring one waiting for me when this ends.

I haven't even slept a single night in my new apartment yet, and I'm not looking forward to it. What happens when this thing with Leo is over? What happens when I have to go back to being the person I was before—the one who didn't know what she wanted, who was too scared to ask for it even if she did?

I don't want to be her again.

I'm not sure I even can be.

Later, I'm curled up on the couch with Leo. The Christmas tree casts soft colored light across the room. The fire crackles low. We've fallen into a rhythm over the past few days. Cooking together, relaxing in the living room, and watching the tree. It's less like an arrangement now and more like a life. That thought should probably scare me more than it does.

What actually scares me is how easily I lied to Willow. How natural it's becoming to keep this whole world separate.

My head rests against Leo's chest where I can hear his heartbeat, steady and sure, like everything about him. Neither of us speaks. We don't need to. The silence between us has become comfortable. My fingers trace idle patterns on his chest as I watch the tree lights blink through their slow rotation. Red, then gold, then green, then white. The star on top creates tiny prisms across the ceiling.

This is the kind of moment I used to dream about during those panicked weeks of apartment hunting—not luxury, not even sex, but this. Being held by someone who makes the world go quiet.

Burrowing deeper into Leo's side, I breathe in oranges and spice. Whatever this is, wherever it's going, right now I'm exactly where I want to be.

We stay like that for a long time. The fire pops while the snow outside the window falls gently.

My eye catches on an ornament I haven't noticed before. It's a delicate glass angel, older and more worn than the others. It looks handmade.

"The angel ornament is beautiful." My voice comes out soft as I nod toward it.

Leo follows my gaze. Something in his face shifts, and the easy contentment fades, replaced by something quieter. More distant. The lines around his mouth deepen.

I lift my head to look at him properly. "Leo? What is it?"

He's silent for a moment, eyes still fixed on the angel. When he finally speaks, his voice is rough at the edges. "My mum made that. The year before she died."

My breath catches. I'm curious about his life. There's so much I don't know about him. I wait, giving him space, my hand pressing flat against his chest over his heart.

"She loved Christmas." The words come slowly. "She'd start decorating the day after Thanksgiving. It drove my father mad." A soft huff of laughter, but something hollow underneath it. "The whole house smelled of cinnamon and pine from November through January."

I press closer, letting him know I'm listening. His hand tightens briefly on my shoulder.

"She died when I was fourteen. Cancer. It was quick, at least. Six months from diagnosis to—six months."

'I'm sorry' seems too small. So I just snuggle closer.

He covers my hand with his, pressing it harder against his sternum. "My father didn't handle it well. He was never what you'd call warm, but after she died, he just shut down. Buried himself in work. I'd go days without seeing him, even though we lived in the same house."

Fourteen years old. This commanding, confident man as a grieving teenager, rattling around an empty house while his father disappeared into work. My throat tightens at the image.

"I learned early that if I wanted something to be okay, I had to make it okay myself. Control what I could control. Because everything else..." He pauses, swallows. "Everything else could disappear without warning."

I think of how he plans every scene to enhance my pleasure. The boy and the man suddenly seem the same.

"You don't have to control everything with me." The words slip out before I can stop them. "I mean, you can. I like when you do. But you don't have to."

He looks down at me then. His expression steals the air from my lungs. It's softer than I've ever seen him. Unguarded.

"I know, lass." His thumb strokes across my knuckles. "That's what makes you different."

I don't have words for what that does to me. So I press my face into his chest instead, breathing in his familiar scent.

He's trusted me with something real. Something that cost him. And I'm still keeping this hidden from my best friend.

I push away the guilt before it takes hold. One thing at a time. Right now, I'm here. That's enough.

We cuddle in comfortable silence, and sleep is tugging at the edges of my consciousness when he speaks again.

"My friend Dane is coming for Christmas. He visits every year. We were at university together." His voice has shifted, lighter now, though something thoughtful lingers underneath. "I'd like you to meet him properly."

"I'd like to meet him," I say, and my chest tightens at the thought of Christmas here, with Leo and his friend. I decide to tell him about losing my parents, knowing he'll understand.

"My parents died when I was ten," I say quietly. "Car accident. My aunt took me in after that. My mom's sister. She was amazing, but she passed a few years ago."

Leo's arm tightens around me, and I burrow closer into his warmth.

"I haven't had real family Christmases in a long time," I continue. "It's usually just me and Willow doing something low-key. But this year..." I trail off, looking up at him. "I'm glad I won't be alone. That I get to be here with you."

"You're not alone anymore, lass." He kisses the top of my head my heart warms.

Later, while Leo reads next to me on the couch, my phone buzzes. Willow's name flashes on the screen.

Willow: How's it going with Mr. Moneybags? You've been quiet

Guilt presses hard against my ribs. She deserves better than my deflection.

My thumbs move before I can talk myself out of it.

Alice: Honestly? It's complicated. He's older than I expected to be into. And I'm feeling things I wasn't prepared for. But I'm happy. Really happy. I'm just not ready to explain all of it yet.

The response comes fast.

Willow: I was worried about you. I'm here when you're ready. No judgment. You know that, right?

My eyes sting. I do know that. God, I wish that made it easier to tell her everything.

Alice: I know. Thank you. Love you.

Willow: Love you too, mystery woman.

I set the phone down next to me. It's not the whole truth—not even close—but it's something. A crack in the wall I've been building between my two lives.

Maybe that's enough for now.

I peek at Leo and ask, "Will you read to me?"

Leo smiles. "Of course, my sweet pet."

He starts from the beginning, adjusting his reading glasses. His voice is low, the accent thicker when he reads. I lose track of the words pretty quickly, but it doesn't matter. I'm not here for the plot. Just the sound of him. The fact that he's here.

His fingers thread through mine.

I hold on and let everything else fade.

CHAPTER 7

I've been thinking about it for days.

We're on the couch in our usual spot after dinner. Leo's hand is on my thigh, the fire's crackling, but I can't relax. My heart's beating too fast.

"Something on your mind, lass?" His thumb circles my knee. "You've gone quiet."

I breathe in. Out. I've been carrying this question around for days, and it gets harder to ignore every time he touches me. Asking is harder than obeying ever was, but I want this too much to stay silent.

"I've been thinking about what we did. In the kitchen. On the table." My cheeks flush just referencing it. "The edging."

His hand stills. "Aye?"

"I want more." The words tumble out before I can second-guess them. "Longer. I want to know what it's like to be kept on the brink all day. Until I can't think anymore. Until there's nothing left but..." I trail off, not sure how to describe what I'm craving. The kind of gone where my brain finally shuts the fuck up.

Leo is quiet for a long moment. When I risk a glance at his face, his expression has changed. The warmth in his eyes is gone, replaced by hunger. My heart pounds harder.

"You're asking me to break you, lass." His voice is serious. "To push you past everything you think you can handle. That's not something I take lightly."

"I know. I want it anyway."

He studies me, and I hold his gaze even though part of me wants to look away. Finally, a slow curve transforms his lips.

"There's something else I think you've been curious about." His hand travels higher on my thigh, fingertips brushing the hem of his long shirt I'm wearing. "Something you've been wondering about but haven't asked for yet."

My body buzzes. How does he always know?

"I've seen the way you react when I'm rough with you." His voice drops so low I feel it in my chest. "The way your breath hitches when I hold you hard. The way you wiggle your ass when you're on your hands and knees." He leans closer, lips brushing my ear. "I think my sweet lass wants to be spanked. And I think she's been too shy to ask."

Heat floods me so fast I feel dizzy. He's right. I've thought about it more than I want to admit. I've wondered what it would feel like to be bent over his knee. The image has kept me awake more than one night.

His experience shows in moments like this. He has decades of knowing exactly what he's doing, what I need before I know it myself.

"Yes." The word escapes on a breath. "I want that too."

"Then that's what you'll get." He tips my chin up, forcing me to meet his eyes. "But understand this, Alice. Once we start, I'm not stopping until I decide you've had enough. You'll use your safewords if you need them. Red to stop, yellow to slow down. Repeat them."

"Red to stop. Yellow to slow down."

"Good girl." Two words and I'm liquid. I melt against him like my bones have given up. "Now. We start in the morning. Go to sleep, pet. You're going to need your rest."

His hands wake me.

It's not sexual. His palm travels down my spine as I blink awake. The touch is casual, like he's petting a cat. But every nerve ending lights up in anticipation.

"Morning, lass." His voice is rough from sleep. "Ready for today?"

Words feel too difficult, so I just nod.

He doesn't pounce. That's what surprises me most. We get up, and he makes eggs and bacon for breakfast while I pad around the kitchen naked because he commanded it. He's relaxed and singing under his breath. Brushing against me when he reaches for the salt.

Each contact is brief, almost accidental. His hip against mine at the counter. Fingers grazing my lower back as he passes. A kiss dropped on my shoulder while I pour coffee. None of it is overtly sexual, but I'm hyperaware of every touch, every moment where he could reach for me and doesn't.

By the time we finish eating, I'm wound tight, and he hasn't really done anything.

"Help me with the laundry, pet."

Following him to the laundry room, confusion flickers. This isn't what I expected. But I fold towels while he loads the dryer, and every few minutes he checks on me. Not with words. With his hand between my thighs, pressing against my pussy for just a moment before pulling away.

"Already wet." His voice is mild, like he's commenting on the weather. "And I've barely touched you."

A whimper escapes me, hips chasing his retreating hand. "Leo, please..."

"Please what?" He goes back to loading the dryer like nothing happened. "We have all day, lass. I'm in no hurry."

That's when I realize what he's doing. The anticipation is the torture. Making me desperate before he's even really started. By the time he actually touches me properly, I'll already be half out of my mind.

Holy hell. This is going to wreck me.

By early afternoon, I'm a trembling mess, and he still hasn't given me anything substantial.

We're in the bedroom now. He's positioned me on the bed. I'm on my back, legs spread, completely exposed to his gaze. The sheets are cool against my overheated skin, and I clutch at them like they're the only thing keeping me tethered to earth. On the nightstand, a small velvet bag I don't recognize—something he's set there deliberately.

"Remember," he says, his hand warm on my thigh, "if you can't speak, tap me three times. Or tap the bed. I'll stop immediately. Understand?"

I nod, barely able to focus on his words when all I want is his touch.

"Say it," he commands gently.

"Three taps if I can't speak," I manage. "You'll stop."

"Good girl." His voice is reverent as he settles between my thighs. "Look at you, so desperate already. So ready for me."

Then his mouth is on me, and I cry out at the sudden intensity. His tongue drags through my folds, circling my clit. The pleasure spikes so fast it steals my breath. I'm going to come. After hours of teasing, it's only going to take seconds. I'm already right there.

He pulls back.

"No!" The protest rips out before I can stop it. My hips buck up, chasing his mouth, but he's already moved out of reach. "Sir, please, I was so close."

"I know exactly how close you were." He presses a kiss to my inner thigh, maddeningly gentle. "That's the point, lass."

He does it again. And again. Each time he brings me to the brink with his tongue, his fingers, working me until I'm shaking and desperate, and then stops just before I crest. I'm going to lose my mind. Actual tears prick at my eyes, and I hate how desperate I am. Except I don't. I love it.

All I can do is lie here and take whatever he decides to give me, and that helplessness is doing something to my brain I can't explain.

"Please," I sob. "Please, I can't—"

"You can." His voice is firm but kind. "You can take so much more than you think. And I'm going to prove it to you." He sits back, studying me. "Over my knee, Alice."

My heart slams against my ribs. This is it.

He settles against the headboard and pats his thigh. Crawling toward him on shaky limbs, I position myself across his lap. The position is vulnerable in a way that makes my stomach flip. My ass is in the air, while my face is pressed into the mattress, completely at his mercy. The comforter is soft beneath my cheek and smells faintly of his orange body wash, grounding me even as my pulse races.

His hand rests on my ass, warm and heavy. "Color?"

"Green." My voice is muffled against the sheets.

"Have you ever been spanked before, lass? Properly, I mean. Not a playful swat."

My head shakes against the comforter. "No, Sir."

"Then we start slow." His palm strokes over my skin, soothing and possessive at once. "I'll build the intensity. If it's too much, you tell me. Yellow to slow down, red to stop. Understood?"

"Yes, Sir." My voice comes out breathless, anticipation coiling tight in my belly.

"Good girl."

The first slap is almost gentle. A warm-up. But even that light contact makes me gasp. My skin is so sensitized from hours of teasing that everything registers more intensely.

The second is harder. A sharp crack that echoes through the room, followed by a bloom of heat spreading across my skin. I jerk in his lap, a sound escaping me that's half pain, half something else entirely.

"There it is." Satisfaction roughens his voice. "That's the sound I wanted."

He continues, finding a rhythm. Each impact stings, then blooms into warmth, then fades just as the next one lands. The pain is sharp but fleeting, and what follows it—the rush of heat, the way my pussy tightens with each strike—surprises me with its intensity.

I really like this.

The knowledge settles into my bones as my hips push back for more. Not just the sting, though that sends heat flooding through me. It's the crack of his palm announcing his control over my flesh. It's the way each impact says 'you're mine' without words.

"Color?" he asks again, hand pausing on my heated skin.

"Green." The word comes out desperate. "Don't stop."

His laugh is low and dark. "My sweet little slut likes being spanked. I knew you would."

He rewards me with harder strikes, and something shifts in my head. The pain sharpens my focus when I start drifting, grounds me in my flesh when the pleasure threatens to scatter me. But it also pushes me somewhere floaty and suspended, like the space between awake and dreaming except every nerve is on fire.

When he stops and works his fingers between my legs, I moan at how wet I am. He teases my entrance, circles my clit, and the combination of the residual sting on my ass and the pleasure building in my core is overwhelming.

"Please," I whimper. "Please let me come."

"Not yet, pet." He withdraws his fingers, and I almost scream from the loss. "I haven't decided if you're coming today or not."

Oh, God.

Time stops making sense.

I don't know how many times he's brought me to the precipice now. The afternoon light has shifted, casting longer shadows across the bed, but I can't track minutes or hours. There's only pleasure—his mouth, his fingers, his cock working into me with devastating slowness before he pulls out and denies me again.

He intersperses everything with spanking, the sharp crack of his palm pulling me back when I drift too far. When I'm too tense with anticipation, the rhythm of impact pushes me deeper into that strange suspended space.

My thoughts start fragmenting.

Please. More. Now. Words tumble out without my permission, desperate pleas that don't quite form properly. I'm his instrument, and he's playing me expertly, drawing sounds from me I didn't know I could make. The sheets beneath me are damp with sweat, and the room feels warmer than it should, the air thick with the scent of sex.

"That's it, lass." His voice reaches me from far away. "Stop thinking. Just feel."

Thinking is impossible now. The room has gone soft around the periphery, reality reduced to the points where his flesh meets mine. His voice is the only anchor, telling me I'm good, I'm perfect, I'm his.

His. The word sits in my chest where my thoughts used to be. I'm his. Nothing else matters.

Another crest approaches without release. I sob into the pillow, trembling everywhere, and he strokes my back.

"So beautiful like this," he murmurs. "So completely mine."

Anything. I would do anything for him right now. Anything at all.

In the floating space behind my closed eyes, my mind drifts.

Leo's fingers are inside me, curling against that perfect spot. I'm suspended somewhere between agony and ecstasy, so far gone that thoughts don't form so much as surface—rising like bubbles from deep water.

His hand shifts, and for a disorienting moment I imagine a second set of hands holding me still while Leo takes what he wants. The phantom touch feels so real that I moan, my back arching toward something that isn't there.

Something he said days ago floats up. His friend Dane is coming for Christmas.

The thought shouldn't be erotic. But in my hazy state, my mind transforms it without my permission. What would it be like to have two sets of hands on me? Two voices commanding me? One holding me down while the other takes what he wants?

A moan escapes me, louder than before, and I feel Leo's attention sharpen.

The fantasy intensifies. I imagine two men using me, passing me between them, both of them telling me I'm good.

My pussy tightens hard around Leo's fingers. He makes a low sound of surprise.

"Where did you go just now, pet?" His voice cuts through the haze. His fingers still. "Something made you react differently."

I can't answer. Can't articulate the forbidden thing I was imagining. The shame would surface if I were more present, but I'm too far under to feel anything except the echo of that fantasy and the hunger it's left behind.

He doesn't push. Just watches me with those knowing eyes and continues his torment.

He brings me to the brink again, and this time I scream. Yet I still don't come.

Hours. It's been hours.

The light outside has gone golden, then dim. Every nerve ending is exposed and screaming. There are tear tracks on my face. I don't remember starting to cry, but I can feel the dampness on my cheeks, taste salt when I lick my lips.

My ass is warm and sensitive from the spanking, each shift of my hips a reminder of everything he's done to me. The marks feel like ownership.

Verbal communication is nearly impossible now. The begging has devolved into sounds that aren't quite language. My mind is a blank white space where thought used to live—empty except for feeling, except for him.

Leo's face swims into focus above me. His expression is intense but not cruel. There's something almost soft in the way he watches me shake apart.

"Color, Alice." His voice is firm. "I need words. Or tap if you can't speak."

It takes everything I have to surface enough to speak. I could tap three instead, but I need him to know I want this. The word feels like it's coming from somewhere outside myself, dragged up from deep water.

"Green." My voice cracks on the single syllable. "Please. Please."

He studies me for a long moment. "One more, lass." His voice catches, almost rough, like he's fighting to hold the line himself. His thumb strokes my cheek, wiping away tears. "Give me one more, and then I'll let you fall."

I don't know if I can. I don't know if there's anything left of me to give. But I nod anyway, because he's asking and I would give him anything just to hear him tell me I'm good.

He brings me to the brink with his fingers one final time, and I break.

Not into orgasm—into something else. The tension shatters but doesn't release, and I'm sobbing, clinging to him, trembling everywhere. He holds me through it, murmuring praise and reassurance, and somewhere in the wreckage of my thoughts I understand that this was the point. Not the orgasm. The surrender.

"That's it, sweet girl. You did it. You gave me everything."

His words wash through me like light.

"Now, lass. Come for me now."

His cock's inside me. I don't remember when that happened, time is still slippery. His hand is between us, fingers on my clit. I hear him reach for the nightstand, the velvet bag, and then a vibrator buzzes against oversensitized flesh.

The orgasm doesn't crash. It blooms.

It starts somewhere deep and rolls outward in waves that don't seem to end. I'm screaming—I think I'm screaming—but the sound is distant, muffled by the tsunami of pleasure washing through every cell. My walls convulse, tightening around him. He drives deep one final time, and I feel him pulse inside me, hot and claiming.

"Fuuuuuck." The word is torn from somewhere primal deep in my brain, and he groans and follows me over, pumping me full of hot cum as we shatter together.

Holy hell, it goes on forever. Wave after wave, aftershock after aftershock. All the denied pleasure from the entire day crashes through me at once, and I lose track of where I end and he begins. There's only release, only the overwhelming relief of finally, finally letting go.

When I come back to myself, I'm wrapped in his arms. Blankets cocoon us. The room is darker than I remember, and I have no idea how long I was gone.

My flesh feels wrung out, liquid, not entirely my own yet. But Leo is there, solid and warm.

"There you are," he murmurs when I stir. "There's my sweet girl. You did so well, lass. You were perfect."

Tears leak from my eyes, but they're not sad tears. I don't know what they are. Release, maybe. Everything I held back flooding out now that it's safe to feel.

"That's it," he soothes, his hand stroking through my hair. "Let it out. You're okay. I've got you." He kisses my temple. "You're safe. You were so beautiful, so brave for me. Such a good girl."

He holds me tighter, murmuring praise against my skin, and lets me cry.

The shower water is perfect.

I'm tucked against Leo's chest while the water and steam rise around us. He washes me with gentle hands, checking the skin where he spanked me. My ass is pink but not damaged, sensitive when he touches.

"How are you feeling?" His voice is soft. "Really."

I take stock. Every muscle carries a pleasant soreness. My mind is quiet for the first time in longer than I can remember.

"Amazing," I say, the word barely audible. "Wrecked. But amazing."

He kisses the top of my head. "Good."

Later, after he's changed the sheets, he sits with his back against the headboard with me between his legs. He brushes my hair while I drift in the hazy space between waking and sleep. The bristles move through the strands with careful attention, and the gentleness of the act makes my throat tight.

"Leo." My voice is barely audible. "What are we doing?"

The brush pauses. "What do you mean, lass?"

Turning to face him, I search his hazel eyes in the dim light. "This. Us. It feels like more than an arrangement. It feels real." I swallow hard, forcing myself to say the rest. "I don't know what I'm saying. Sorry."

"Alice." His thumb traces my cheekbone. When he speaks, his voice is raw in a way I've never heard before. "It is real. What we have, it stopped being just an arrangement a long time ago, if it ever was one."

My heart squeezes. "What does that mean for us?"

"It means we take it one step at a time." He leans down, kissing my nose. "It means we see where it leads."

Something warm and fragile unfurls in my chest as I nod. "I'd like that."

"Good." He pulls me close, settling me against his chest.

We lie there in comfortable silence, his heartbeat steady under my ear. Sleep tugs at me when he speaks again.

"Dane arrives in a few days on Christmas Eve." His voice is casual, but something about it makes me more alert.

My pulse kicks. The memory of my earlier fantasy surfaces—two sets of hands—and heat floods my cheeks even in the darkness.

"I didn't know it was so close to Christmas already."

He hugs me. "Get some sleep, pet. You've earned it."

Sleep doesn't come immediately. The thought of being shared lingers. Was that just a thought in the moment? I don't have the answer, but I let the question exist.

"Goodnight, Leo."

"Sweet dreams, lass."

His scent surrounds me, and I let myself drift.

My dreams will definitely be interesting.

CHAPTER 8

Something is wrong.

I know it the moment I surface from sleep. Every muscle carries that expected soreness, but there's something else underneath. An emptiness in my chest that doesn't match anything I've experienced before.

Yesterday was incredible. The most intense experience of my life. I should be glowing.

Instead, I feel like someone scooped out my insides and forgot to put them back.

Gray winter light filters through the curtains. Leo is already awake beside me, propped on one elbow, watching me with soft concern. His hair is mussed from sleep, and the lines around his mouth deepen as he studies my face. The familiar scent of oranges wraps around me, usually so comforting, but right now even that seems muted and strange.

"Morning, lass." His voice is gentle. "How are you feeling?"

My mouth opens to say fine, to tell him I'm wonderful, to thank him for yesterday—

And I burst into tears.

The sobs come from nowhere, wrenching up from some deep place I didn't know existed. I don't understand why I'm crying. Nothing is wrong. Everything was perfect. So why does my ribcage feel like it's caving in?

"I don't—" I gasp between sobs. "I don't know why I'm—"

Leo doesn't hesitate. He pulls me against him immediately, wrapping his arms around me and tucking my head under his chin. His hand strokes down my spine in long, soothing passes.

"Shh, sweet girl. It's all right." His voice is calm. "This is normal. I'm here."

Normal? How is sobbing uncontrollably for no reason the morning after the best sexual experience of my life considered normal? That's the opposite of normal. I'm ridiculous, embarrassed, and I can't seem to stop the tears from coming.

"It's called subdrop, lass." He keeps stroking my back as the tears continue to fall. "After intense scenes, especially extended ones like yesterday, your system goes through a kind of crash."

I hiccup against him, trying to focus on his words through the fog of emotion. His chest is getting wet from my tears, and I should probably care about that, but I can't seem to make myself move.

"All those endorphins and adrenaline you produced, it's like a massive high. And what goes up must come down." He kisses the top of my head, reassuring. "You went very deep yesterday. Your system's working through it now."

Another wave of tears spills over, and shame burns hot behind my sternum. I want to be stronger than this, to handle my own desires without falling apart afterward. The thought makes me cry harder, which only makes me feel more pathetic.

"I'm sorry." The words come out waterlogged and small.

Leo pulls back just enough to tip my chin up, forcing me to meet his eyes. There's no frustration, just understanding. And something that looks almost like pride.

"Nothing is wrong with you." His thumb brushes a tear from my cheek, so gentle it makes my throat tight. "This isn't weakness. This is you working through something intense. It means you trusted me completely. It means you let go in ways you've never let go before."

I want to argue, to insist I'm fine, but another sob breaks free and all I can do is cling to him. His arms tighten around me, holding me together when I can't hold myself.

"Let me take care of you." The words are soft but absolute, no room for argument. "That's my job, lass. Not just during scenes, but after them, too. Especially after them."

I nod against his chest, not trusting my voice. He holds me for a long time, letting me cry without making me feel like a burden. The tears eventually slow, leaving me exhausted and empty, but his arms stay firm around me the entire time.

"That's it," he murmurs. "Let it all out. I've got you."

When the storm finally passes, Leo eases me up from the bed. My legs are shaky like they might buckle at any moment, and he keeps a steadying arm around my waist as he guides me toward the bathroom. I lean into him, grateful for his solid presence.

"Bath first." His voice is matter-of-fact. "The heat will help."

I watch through heavy-lidded eyes as he runs the water, testing the temperature with his fingers before adding a lavender bath bomb. Steam curls up from the surface, and when he helps me step in, the warmth envelops me like a cocoon.

Sinking down until the water laps at my collarbone, I let out a shaky breath. The heat seeps into my muscles, loosening something that's been clenched tight since I woke up. It doesn't fix the vacant sensation, but it softens the edges of it.

Leo kneels beside the tub in a pair of boxer shorts and begins to wash me. His touch is gentle but thorough, tending to me like I'm something precious.

"Let me see your backside, lass."

I shift in the water, letting him examine the marks from yesterday's spanking. His fingers trace over the sensitive spots, and I wince slightly at the pressure.

"They're fading well." Relief colors his voice. "Pink, not bruised. You'll be fine by tomorrow."

He reaches for a bottle of water on the edge of the tub—when did he put that there?—and holds it to my lips. "Drink. You cried a lot. You need to replace what you lost."

I obey without thinking, the cool water soothing my raw throat. He waits until I've finished half the bottle before setting it aside. He planned this. The water, the bath bomb, all of it. Something squeezes in my chest that has nothing to do with subdrop.

There's a film between me and the world. The water is hot, Leo's hands are gentle, and I know all of this should feel good. But I can't quite reach it.

When the water starts to cool, he helps me out and wraps me in a fluffy towel. He dries me off slowly, then disappears into his closet and returns with a soft gray cashmere sweater that smells like him.

"Arms up."

I obey automatically, and he pulls the sweater over my head. It's enormous on me, hanging past my thighs, the sleeves covering my hands completely. He adds a pair of soft flannel pants that I have to roll at the waist, and thick wool socks that bunch around my ankles.

"There." He cups my face in his hands, studying me. "How are you? Scale of one to ten where ten is fabulous?"

I consider. The emptiness is still there, but the world feels a little less muted. I can smell the lavender bath bomb mixing with his normal citrus scent, and my stomach gives a tentative flutter that might be hunger. "Maybe a three?"

He nods, unsurprised. "Let's get some food in you."

In the kitchen, he sits me on a stool at the island and sets about making breakfast. No singing today, I notice. He's focused entirely on me, glancing over every few seconds like he's checking that I'm still holding it together. The kitchen fills with the sound of eggs sizzling and the smell of butter melting in the pan.

Scrambled eggs appear in front of me, along with buttered toast and tea with honey. The smell makes my stomach turn, and I push the plate away before I can think about it.

Leo pushes it back. "Eat, pet." His voice is gentle but firm, that commanding tone that always makes something inside me settle. "You need fuel to recover."

The command loosens something in my ribcage—that familiar comfort of being told what to do. I pick up the fork and take a bite. Then another. The food is tasteless in my mouth, but I keep eating because pleasing him is easier than thinking right now.

By the time I finish eating, something has been nagging at me. The fantasy of being shared by two men. The memory sends a flutter through my stomach, cutting through the numbness for the first time all morning. I remember the certainty and desire I experienced even in that haze.

Leo is washing dishes at the sink, his back to me. I watch the movement of his shoulders, the way his shirt stretches across them, and try to find the words for something I've never said out loud.

"Leo?"

He turns, drying his hands on a towel. "Yes, lass?"

"Yesterday, when I was..." I trail off, not sure how to describe it. Under? Gone? Floating in some space where nothing existed but his voice and the desperate, craving need? "When I was deep. I thought about something."

He moves to stand in front of me, leaning against the counter. His expression is open, attentive, giving me his full focus. "I'm listening."

"You mentioned Dane coming for Christmas. And I started..." My cheeks flush hot. "I started imagining what it would be like. If you—if we—"

The words stick in my throat. I can't quite say it out loud, not yet, not when I still feel so raw and exposed and strange in my own skin.

But Leo's eyes sharpen with understanding. He knows what I'm trying to say.

"Alice." His voice is serious, and he reaches out to take my hand, his fingers steady around mine. "I hear you. And we will have this conversation."

Relief floods through me. He's not dismissing it or telling me I'm crazy for wanting it.

"But not today."

I blink, the relief curdling into confusion. "What? Why not?"

"Because you're in subdrop, lass." His thumb strokes across my knuckles, soothing even as his words frustrate me. "Your walls are down. I won't take advantage of that."

"But I know what I want."

"Maybe you do." He squeezes my hand gently. "And if that's true, you'll still want it when you're steady again." His gaze holds mine, serious and unwavering, with that dominant intensity I've come to crave. "I won't let you consent to something that significant when you're not fully yourself. That's not how this works."

I want to argue, to insist that I'm fine, that the subdrop doesn't change anything. But underneath the frustration is something else. Something that feels like safety.

He's protecting me.

"When you're more like yourself," he continues, "we'll talk about this properly. I promise. But for now—" He lifts my hand to kiss my knuckles. "—just let me take care of you."

I swallow the lump in my throat. "Okay."

"That's my good girl."

Tears prick at my eyes again. Holy hell, I'm a mess today. But his hand in mine is an anchor, and I hold on tight.

The rest of the morning passes in a soft blur.

Leo doesn't push me to talk or to do anything at all. We migrate to the couch, where he arranges blankets around me and puts on a movie I can't follow. The plot drifts past me like clouds, but his solid presence beside me is a comfort I sink into gratefully. At some point I fall asleep against him.

When I wake, he's still there, watching me. His fingers thread gently through my hair.

His voice is soft, relieved. "How are you now?"

I take stock. The emptiness has receded a little, filled in by sleep and comfort and his steady presence. The strange disconnection from earlier has eased. I'm more present, more solid. "Maybe a five?"

His lips curve, satisfied. "Getting there."

He makes me eat lunch. It's soup this time, easy on my unsettled stomach. Makes sure I drink more water, checking in periodically to ask how I'm doing. The questions should feel intrusive, but they don't. They feel like I'm important enough to watch over.

Late afternoon finds us back on the couch. He reads to me again, and it's a light and funny story that makes me smile despite everything. His voice is a low rumble, and I let myself drift without trying to follow the story too closely.

The room is cozy. Snow swirls outside, and the Christmas tree blinks. It's peaceful. The kind of moment I would have killed for back when I was scrambling to find an apartment I could afford, wondering where I'd end up.

Now I'm here. With him. And even though I'm raw and not quite myself, I feel more content than I've ever felt. There's nowhere else I'd rather be, I realize. Just here, tucked against his side, listening to his voice, existing in a space where someone notices when I'm a mess and knows exactly what to do about it.

By evening, the fog has mostly lifted. I can think clearly again. The empty feeling has faded, replaced by something more solid. I'm still a little raw, but I feel like myself again.

I'm grateful for Leo—for knowing what I needed before I did. He's done this before, I realize. Nothing about today surprised him. The thought doesn't bother me. It makes me feel safer. Somehow I picked the right person to trust, even when I didn't know what I was getting into.

Leo sets down the book and looks at me. "You're coming back," he says. "I can see it in your eyes."

"I think so." I face him fully. "Thank you. For all of this. I don't know what I would have done if..."

"You don't need to thank me." He brushes a strand of hair from my face. "But there is something I want to show you. If you're up to it."

Curiosity flickers, cutting through the lingering fog. "What is it?"

He stands and holds out his hand. I take it, letting him pull me up from the couch. My legs are steadier now, and I follow him upstairs without needing to lean on him.

We pass the bedroom where I've been staying less than half the time, then his master suite, continuing down a hallway I haven't explored much. He stops at a door near the end and turns to face me.

"I've been thinking about this," he says, and there's something almost nervous in his voice—an uncertainty I've never heard from him before. "Today seemed like the right time to show you."

He pushes the door open.

Cool air drifts out, carrying the particular stillness of an unused space. The room is empty except for built-in shelves along one wall and large windows that face the backyard. Through the glass, I can see snow blanketing the lawn, the skeletal trees frosted white.

"What is this?" I ask.

Leo flicks on the light, and I blink at the sudden brightness. The room is bigger than I realized, and its high ceilings make it feel even more spacious. My footsteps echo faintly as I step inside.

"It's not anything yet." He leans against the doorframe. "But it could be a studio. If you wanted."

I stare at him. "A studio?"

"You mentioned wanting painting lessons. That you couldn't afford them in college." He shrugs, like this is nothing. Like he's offering to pick up milk on the way home. "The light in here is good. North-facing windows. We could set up an easel, get supplies. Whatever you need."

My throat goes tight. This isn't sex. This isn't part of the arrangement. He's not offering me pleasure or dominance.

He's offering me a future.

"Leo..." My voice comes out strangled. "I don't—that's—"

"You don't have to decide now." He pushes off the doorframe and crosses to me, tipping my chin up with one finger. "It's just something to think about."

But that's exactly the problem. Because thinking about it means thinking about staying. It means imagining a version of my life where I come home to this house, where I paint in this room with its north-facing light, where the arrangement doesn't end on New Year's.

Where I'm his. Not just for a few weeks. For real.

"Thank you," I manage. It's not enough—it's nowhere close to enough—but it's all I can get out past the lump in my throat.

"You're welcome, lass."

He takes my hand and leads me back downstairs, back to the couch. We settle in again, and for a while we just sit there, wrapped up in each other and the comfort of the room.

Later, while Leo reads to me, I can't stop thinking about yesterday. About the fantasy we didn't talk about this morning.

Two men. Four hands. Being shared.

I brace for shame or embarrassment. Maybe the realization that it was just subspace and not something I really want.

But I'm wet instead. My pulse races. The desire is still there, just as strong. Stronger, even, without the fog.

This isn't subspace talking. This is me.

I shift against Leo, and he looks down at me. Can he tell what I'm thinking about?

"Something on your mind, lass?"

My head shakes, not ready to voice it yet. Not until I'm completely steady. "Just grateful. For you. For all of this."

He smiles and returns to reading, but I catch when the curve becomes more of a smirk. He knows. Of course he knows. He's been waiting for me to be ready.

We go to bed early, both of us tired from the emotional weight of the day. Leo tucks me against his side, my head on his chest, his arm wrapped securely around me.

"Thank you," I say into the darkness. "For today."

His hand strokes down my arm, slow and soothing. "Always, lass. This is part of it—the care after. It matters as much as everything else. Maybe more."

I think about that. About how different this is from anything I've experienced before. Past boyfriends would have been confused by my tears, uncomfortable, maybe even irritated that I was ruining the afterglow of something they'd thought was great sex. They wouldn't have known what was happening, let alone how to help.

But Leo normalized it, held me through it without a single moment of frustration or impatience.

"Leo?"

"Mm?"

"Tomorrow." I shift to look up at him, though I can barely make out his features in the dim light. "Can we talk about it tomorrow?"

He's quiet for a moment. His chest rises and falls beneath my cheek in a steady rhythm.

"If you're better and still want to," he says finally. "If it wasn't just the subspace talking."

"I will." The certainty in my voice surprises me, but it rings true.

"Then we'll talk about it after you've slept." His arms tighten around me. "Get some rest, sweet girl. You've been through a lot."

My eyes close, satisfied. Once I'm feeling like myself, I'll tell him what I want. And everything might change.

"Goodnight, Leo."

"Sweet dreams, my pet."

Sleep comes slowly, and the fantasy surfaces again. Complete surrender to two men.

I snuggle into his comfort and something that feels dangerously close to home.

CHAPTER 9

It takes me two more days to feel better, but as soon as I wake up I realize the glass wall is gone. I'm solid again.

And God, despite how hard the drop hit, it was absolutely worth it.

I stretch and smile. My muscles are loose and relaxed. The faint soreness between my legs is a pleasant reminder. Even the marks from the spanking have faded. But the fantasy of two men hasn't faded.

If anything, the waiting has clarified it.

This is what I want.

I find Leo in the kitchen, humming a sea shanty while he makes pancakes. The familiar domestic scene wraps around me as I slide onto a stool at the island, and something in my chest loosens at the sight of him. Salt-and-pepper hair, those strong hands, the lines around his mouth that crinkle when he's pleased.

He looks up and studies my face, and whatever he sees there makes his expression soften. "My lass is back."

"I'm back," I agree, and my voice sounds steadier than it has in days. "I think I'm ready to have that conversation. The one you wouldn't let me have."

He doesn't pretend not to know what I mean. He sets down the spatula and faces me fully, his eyes searching mine. "Are you sure? How are you feeling today. Honestly?"

"Eight out of ten. Maybe eight and a half. The fog is gone."

Relief flickers across his features. "Then tell me, lass."

My cheeks flush, but I don't look away. I've been thinking about how to say this, and there's no point being coy now.

"When I was in subspace and everything else fell away...my mind drifted to Dane coming for Christmas." I pause, gathering courage. My cheeks are burning, and I have to push past the instinct to look away. "I imagined what it would be like to have both of you telling me what to do. Being shared between you."

The words hang in the air. I can't believe I just said that out loud. A month ago, I couldn't have admitted this to myself, let alone to him. But the trust we've built in the past few weeks gives me the confidence to be honest.

"I don't know what it says about me that I want this," I admit. "That the thought of being used by two men makes me—" I break off, flushing harder.

"Makes you what, lass?" His voice has roughened, that Scottish accent thickening the way it does when he's aroused.

"Wet." I can barely get the word out. "It makes me wet just thinking about it."

Leo rounds the island and tilts my chin up until our eyes meet. The hunger there steals my breath.

"It says you're brave enough to ask for what you desire. That's not something to be ashamed of, sweet girl. That's something to be proud of."

Oh thank God. He doesn't think I'm broken or asking for too much.

"Dane is one of my oldest friends," Leo continues. "He's experienced—knows what he's doing in this world—and I trust him completely. I wouldn't share you with anyone I didn't trust to treat you well."

"What's he like?" The question comes out breathless.

Leo's lips curve into a knowing smile. "Different from me. Quieter. More...deliberate." His thumb traces slow circles on my skin. "We balance each other out. Always have."

I wait for more, but he just watches me with those hazel eyes, clearly enjoying my curiosity.

"That's it?"

"For now."

"That's not fair," I protest. "You can't just—"

"I can, lass." He silences me with a kiss. "And I am. Some things are better discovered than explained."

A shiver runs through me. The mystery is its own kind of anticipation.

He presses a kiss to my forehead. "Now, if we're going to do this, we need to talk about boundaries."

He pulls back, his expression shifting to something more serious.

"What are you comfortable with?" he asks. "Both of us at once? One at a time? Are there acts you want off the table?"

I think through it carefully. The truth is, I'm not entirely sure since I've never done anything like this before. But I know what I experienced in that fantasy. The complete surrender.

"I want to try everything," I say slowly. "Both of you at once. Being used by one while the other watches. All of it." I meet his eyes. "But I need to know I can stop if it's too much."

"Always." His voice is firm, absolute. "The safewords still apply. Dane knows the system. He'll respect it completely. I wouldn't have him in my life if he didn't."

"And what about…" I hesitate, suddenly shy. "What about where he can—I mean, both of you at the same time would mean—"

"Are you asking if you can take us both, lass?" The words come out rough, almost a growl. "One in that pretty pussy and one in that tight little ass?"

Holy hell. Hearing him say it out loud makes heat flood through me. I nod, not trusting my voice.

"That's something we'd work up to. Make sure you're ready. Dane is patient—he'll take his time preparing you." His hand slides to the back of my neck, gripping with ownership. "He'll be a lucky man if I share my toy."

The claim in his voice sends a rush of heat straight to my core. "Yes, Sir."

"So you want this? You're consenting with a clear head, knowing exactly what you're agreeing to?"

I look up at him—this man who has taken me apart and put me back together, who held me through subdrop and refused to let me consent until I was ready. I've never trusted anyone the way I trust him.

"Yes, I want both of you."

His smile sharpens with dark promise. "Then, my sweet lass, you'll have us."

My heart stutters. "Really?"

"Dane's flight lands tomorrow. Christmas Eve, remember?" He leans down and captures my mouth in a kiss that makes my toes curl. "My pet deserves whatever she wants for Christmas."

Time stretches impossibly long. I try to read, but the words blur together. I try to watch a movie, but I can't follow the plot. My mind keeps circling back to tomorrow—what it will be like, what they'll do to me. Now that I've really decided, I'm an impatient slut for two cocks.

I'm not going to be able to sleep.

CHAPTER 10

Christmas Eve

After lunch, I shower and take my time preparing. I shave everywhere, smooth my skin with the expensive lotion Leo bought me, and let my hair dry in soft waves. I'm basically prepping myself like a gift, and the ritual of it helps calm my nerves.

When it's time to get dressed, I pull out the red dress from my shopping trip. It's the one I bought knowing Leo would want to rip it off me. It's soft and clingy, shorter than anything I'd usually wear, and it makes me feel sexy and powerful.

No bra. No panties.

Leo leaves mid-afternoon to pick up Dane from the airport. The kiss he gives me before he goes is hard and claiming, a promise of what's to come.

"Be ready when I get back." His voice drops low against my ear. "Dressed just like this. Waiting for us." He pulls back to meet my eyes. "I talked to Dane. He's very much on board with my Christmas gift to you."

Heat floods through me at the confirmation. "Yes, Sir."

Then he's gone, and the house seems too quiet without him.

I'm perched on the edge of the couch, fingers twisting together in my lap, heartbeat hammering so hard I can feel it in my throat.

The Christmas tree glows. The fire crackles, and outside it's snowing. Very Hallmark. Except in the Hallmark version, the heroine isn't sitting here with no panties waiting to be shared by two men.

Instead, my breath comes tight and shallow, anticipation coiling low in my belly.

I tug at the hem of my dress. It rides up another inch every time I shift, a constant reminder that underneath I'm completely bare. The fabric against my skin feels electric, every nerve ending awake and waiting. Tonight, I'm going to get exactly what I've been craving. The thought makes me dizzy.

Can I really handle this? Will I fall apart completely?

The answer rises up from somewhere inside: I want to fall apart. I want to be taken apart by both of them and put back together again.

I trust Leo. And Leo trusts Dane. That's enough.

The rumble of the garage door makes my heart stop.

Footsteps on hardwood. Low voices, too muffled to make out words.

Holy hell. This is real.

Leo appears in the doorway first, and the grin that spreads across his face when he sees me makes my knees go weak. His presence fills the room the way it always does. The man could make me wet by walking through a doorway.

"There's my sweet lass." His eyes rake over my body, hunger flaring in those hazel depths. "And looking delicious."

He moves fast, lifting me from the couch. He forces my chin up, and the kiss steals my breath. I surrender immediately, a moan rising as his tongue slides past my lips. Mint and heat—I want to drown in the combination.

When he breaks the kiss, his eyes are dark with promise. "You look perfect, lass."

Movement behind him catches my attention. Everything else falls away.

Dane steps into the living room.

He's taller than I expected, with broad shoulders that fill out his leather coat and a quiet authority that hits different from Leo's sharp-edged command. His dark hair is slightly mussed, his jaw covered in scruff that only adds to his rugged handsomeness. And his eyes fix on me with a heaviness that makes my skin prickle.

I can already tell he's the slow burn to Leo's blaze.

Both of them radiate the kind of confidence that comes with age and experience. They're men who've lived almost twice as long as I have and know exactly what they want.

He moves closer, his steps unhurried. Controlled grace. The way he watches me isn't the same teasing, claiming pleasure I'm used to from Leo. It's more analytical. Like he's cataloging me. My pussy approves.

Like he's deciding exactly how he wants to take me apart.

He smells like spice and sandalwood, and I have to physically stop myself from leaning in.

"Alice." His voice has a hint of gravel underneath. "Leo's told me a lot about you."

My response catches in my throat. Up close, the reality of him is overwhelming. He's tall, commanding, and those eyes see way too much.

But I manage, "Good things, I hope."

The corner of his mouth twitches. It's not quite a smile, but close. "Very good things."

Leo's hand lands on the small of my back, and I lean into his touch instinctively. My dress rides up another fraction of an inch as I shift.

Dane tracks the movement. He's watching me lean into Leo's touch. When our eyes meet, I feel a jolt of desire. Leo looks at me like he wants to devour me. Dane looks at me like he wants to understand me first.

The difference makes me shiver.

"Leo explained what you discussed," Dane says neutrally. "But I want to hear it from you. Tell me what you want to happen tonight."

My breath hitches. He's not giving me an easy out and letting me say a simple yes or no. He wants me to own it.

I meet his gaze directly. "I want both of you. I want to be shared, used by both of you."

Dane doesn't answer. The silence goes on too long to be accidental. He wants me to hear myself. To understand the weight of what I just offered.

"And if it's too much?" His voice is quiet, but the question lands hard. "If you find yourself somewhere you didn't expect to be?"

My throat tightens, but I hold his gaze. "Then I use my safewords. Red to stop. Yellow to slow down. Or I can tap out."

Approval warms his dark eyes. "Good girl."

The praise from him lands differently than from Leo. And somehow I know he doesn't give it often, but when he does, it means something.

Leo's hand tightens on my hip, and his voice drops to that rough Scottish rumble that always makes my core clench. "Then let's not keep our girl waiting any longer."

He guides me toward the bedroom, Dane close behind. I'm hyper-aware of them both. Each step winds me tighter. My heart's racing, and my pussy aches with an intensity that's still new to me.

At the bedroom door, Leo pauses.

"Last chance, lass. You still want this?"

I look at him—my silver fox, my dominant—then over my shoulder at Dane.

Two months ago, I couldn't have admitted any of this to myself, let alone said it out loud. I was looking for escape, a rough fuck to forget my problems. Nothing more. I didn't know I was looking for this.

"Yes." I turn back to Leo, letting him see everything in my eyes—the trust that's only grown over these weeks, the certainty I didn't expect to find. "I want both of you."

Leo's smile turns wicked. "Then Merry Christmas, pet."

The bedroom door opens. I walk in. Even though I've been here plenty of times, tonight is different. The bed looks massive. My pulse pounds hard enough that I feel it everywhere.

Dane steps in front of me first. "Look at me, Alice."

His voice is quiet, but the command in it is unmistakable. I meet his dark eyes, and what I find there steals my breath.

"You're trembling," he observes.

"I'm nervous," I admit. "But I want this."

Approval flickers in his eyes, subtle but unmistakable. "Good. Nervousness means you understand what you're giving us." His hand comes up to cup my jaw, tilting my face toward the light. His touch is firm but unhurried, so different from Leo's immediate heat. "And what are you giving us tonight, Alice?"

Behind me, Leo's thumb traces slow circles on my spine. They're both waiting for me to say it out loud. To claim this desire with my own voice.

I swallow hard. "Everything."

Leo's groan is low and approving against my ear. "That's my good girl."

But Dane doesn't smile. He holds my stare, his thumb brushing across my lower lip. "Then let's begin."

They guide me toward the bed, and as I move between them, I realize the last knot of fear has unraveled completely. What replaces it feels like jumping off a cliff and knowing someone will catch you.

I'm not scared anymore.

I'm exactly where I want to be and about to get exactly what I want.

My Freeuse Entanglement

Book 3

April Cross

CHAPTER 1

The bedroom door closes behind us, and the click of the latch sounds way too loud.

Leo moves past me toward the bed, and the lamplight catches the silver threading through his dark hair. I have the wildly inappropriate thought that a man old enough to be my father has no business looking that good. Then he's behind me, his hand finding my hip with a possessive familiarity that makes my breath catch. Dane is in front of me, close enough that the sandalwood on his skin hits me in waves, so different from Leo's oranges that my brain short-circuits trying to process both at once.

Two men who both want me. I asked Leo if he'd share me when Dane visited, after I fantasized about two men at once. Leo listened and said, "Dane's someone I'd trust with you, lass. If that's what you want."

I'd never met Dane before today. It hadn't even occurred to me to worry about whether I'd be attracted to him. Turns out the universe decided to hand me two ridiculously hot older men, which is not the kind of luck I'm used to. I'm not about to question it.

Holy hell, my heart is hammering so hard I'm surprised they can't hear it.

"Breathe, lass." Leo's voice is low against my ear. The command settles me the way he always does, and I pull in a shaky breath, even though it doesn't do much to help.

Dane stands in front of me, studying me. The patience in his expression does something strange to my insides. It's not butterflies, more like a slow tightening, a pull low in my belly that makes me want to press my thighs together. He's Leo's college friend, and he just arrived for his annual Christmas visit. He watches me like he has all the time in the world and he's decided to spend it figuring me out.

Does he find me attractive?

"I'd like a few minutes alone with her." Dane's voice is quiet and directed at Leo, but his gaze stays locked on mine. "If that's all right with you."

The request catches me off guard. Leo trusts him and I trust Leo, but what does Dane want to say to me?

"Aye." Leo presses his lips to my shoulder. "I'll be right outside. You remember your words, lass?"

"Red to stop. Yellow to slow down."

"Good girl." He squeezes my hip before stepping away. The loss of his warmth makes me shiver, and I have to fight the urge to reach for him. I'm not sure I realized until this moment how much he's become my anchor, but I want this with Dane.

Two months ago, I was a girl in a cheap duplex who'd never even been to a sex party, and now I'm standing in Leo's mansion on Christmas Eve, naked under this dress, about to let his best friend fuck me.

If someone had told me this would be my life, I'd have laughed so hard.

Leo closes the door behind him, and I'm alone with Dane. I'm hyperaware of my lack of panties and exactly how wet I am already. I might combust as soon as he touches me.

Dane takes a step closer. He's not aggressive or rushed. He moves with a deliberateness that makes me feel like every second is a choice he's making on purpose.

"You're nervous," he says.

"A little." My voice comes out steadier than I expected. "But I want this."

His hand comes up, and his fingers brush the underside of my jaw, tilting my face toward him. His touch is unhurried, nothing like Leo's immediate heat.

"Leo's told me what you like and how you respond. But I want to learn that for myself."

Heat flashes through my belly. He's not going to follow Leo's playbook. He wants to figure me out himself.

Fuuuuck. Okay.

"How?" I ask, breathlessly.

He gives me an almost-smile that I suspect is habitual. "Close your eyes."

I hesitate for half a second, then obey. Everything else gets louder. My breathing is too fast. The fabric of the dress pulls against my breasts, and my nipples harden.

Dane traces his fingers down the side of my neck slowly. It's the lightest drag over my skin as he follows the line of my throat to my collarbone.

My breath hitches, and my skin breaks out in goosebumps where his fingers just were. *How does he do that? Leo's touch lights me up. Dane's makes me ache.*

"You're sensitive here." It's an observation, almost clinical. His fingers travel to the straps of my dress, and he caresses along the fabric without pulling them down.

His thumb brushes the hollow of my throat. "What about here?"

I swallow hard. "Yes."

"Open your eyes."

I do, and his face is so close to mine that I can see the flecks of amber in his dark brown eyes. He's not smiling, but the intensity in his look makes my chest tighten.

"I'm going to kiss you now," he says. "And I want you to pay attention to how it feels and what your body tells you."

Nobody has ever talked to me like this before a kiss. Leo would already be devouring me. Dane is asking me to be present, and somehow that feels more intimate than anything physical.

I nod, not trusting my voice. He's treating foreplay like the main course.

He leans down and brushes his lips against mine. It's barely a touch before he pulls away. My breath catches. I didn't expect that whisper of contact to *ache*. I lean forward without meaning to, chasing something I can't name, and he huffs a quiet sound that might be amusement before he kisses me properly.

It's nothing like Leo. His kisses are fire and possession. Dane kisses me slow and deep, like he has all the time in the world and intends to use it learning me. Every time I try to speed up—seeking friction, pressure, *something* to ease the building tension—he pulls away enough to set the pace again. His hand slides to the nape of my neck, fingers threading into my hair, and the grip is gentle but firm enough that I feel owned. The gesture sends heat pooling low in my belly.

When his tongue slides against mine, I can't stop the moan. He tastes like cinnamon, and I want to climb inside his skin. I curl my fingers in the fabric of his shirt. The muscle beneath is hard and warm, and I hold on like he's the only solid thing in a spinning world while his mouth takes me apart piece by piece.

My lips are tingling, swollen. Every slow slide of his tongue winds me tighter until I'm trembling, until thought goes blank and there's only his mouth on mine.

My pussy throbs, and when he breaks the kiss, I sway toward him. I'm dizzy and disoriented, like I'm surfacing from deep water. He traces my lower lip with his thumb, and his eyes are darker than before.

"Good girl," he murmurs, and a shiver rolls through me. Those two words go straight to the ache between my legs. His gaze sharpens—he felt it. Oh yeah, this is going to be even better than I hoped. I didn't expect him to affect me this much.

His hand stays at the nape of my neck, keeping me close. "When I kissed you, what did you feel?"

My face heats. Nobody has ever asked me to narrate my reactions before. "I felt..." I fumble for the right words while his thumb strokes my nape. "Like you were paying attention to what I like. It made me want to show you more."

His expression softens around the eyes. "That's exactly what I was doing."

My pulse kicks. He's been reading me like a book, and instead of feeling exposed, I want him to keep going.

"Dane." His name comes out breathy, and I try to calm my racing pulse.

"Yes?"

"I want Leo in here." I swallow, making myself say the rest. "I don't want to wait anymore."

His thumb pauses on my neck. For a long moment, he looks at me, and I hold his stare even though my cheeks are burning. Then he releases me and walks to the door, opening it without a word.

Leo is leaning against the hallway wall, arms crossed, and the look on his face when the door opens tells me he's been imagining exactly what was happening on the other side. His gaze finds mine immediately, and the hunger there makes my knees go soft.

"She's ready," Dane says, and the calm authority in his voice goes straight between my legs.

Leo pushes off the wall and crosses the room to me in three strides. His hands frame my face, and his kiss is everything Dane's wasn't—familiar and comforting. His tongue sweeps into my mouth like he's reclaiming territory. I melt into him and whimper against his lips as his familiar scent of oranges wraps around me.

Leo's kiss is a house fire, and I'm clinging to his shirt and grinding against him before I even realize I'm doing it.

"Missed you," I breathe when he pulls away.

"Lass, it's been five minutes." His grin is wicked. "But I know what you mean."

Dane moves behind me. I'm between them again, and the reality of it makes my head swim. Leo in front and Dane at my back, pressing in from both sides.

This is actually happening. Holy hell, this is actually happening.

Leo fingers the hem of my dress. "Let's get this off you."

He pulls it up slowly, and I lift my arms. The fabric slides over my head, and the cool air raises goosebumps across my bare skin. I'm completely naked between them while they're both fully clothed, and the vulnerability makes me catch my breath.

"Fuck me," Leo says, his eyes raking down my body. "Look at her, Dane."

"I see her." Dane's voice comes from behind me, close to my ear. His hands settle on my waist, and the shock of contact against my bare skin makes me gasp. "She's beautiful."

I'm being talked about like I'm a painting they're admiring, and my pussy throbs in response. Their attention is intoxicating. They're still fully clothed while I'm standing here like an offering. Somehow, that's the hottest part.

Leo bends down and takes my nipple into his mouth without warning, and I cry out, my hand flying to his hair. The suction is sharp and perfect, pleasure spiking straight down to my clit. Behind me, Dane's hands travel up my sides, thumbs brushing the outer curves of my breasts while Leo works my nipple with his tongue.

Four hands on me. I've imagined this, fantasized about it, but the reality is more than I'm prepared for. Every touch from a different direction, and I can't predict who will touch me where. Leo's mouth is hot on my breast while Dane's hands explore with that measured patience, mapping every rib, every curve, every shiver. My head falls back against Dane's shoulder, and I close my eyes, soaking in the pleasure.

I might actually die. What a way to go.

Leo releases my nipple and nods toward the mattress. "On the bed, lass. Hands and knees."

I obey without hesitation, crawling onto the bed and positioning myself in the center. The sheets are cool against my palms and knees, and I can feel both of them watching me. The air behind me shifts as someone moves closer.

Dane's hand traces down my spine, and I arch into the touch. "So responsive," he says quietly, and I hear the click of a belt being undone.

Leo appears in front of me, already shirtless, working the button of his pants. When he frees his cock, my mouth waters at the familiar sight of him, thick and hard and straining toward me.

He kneels in front of me. "Open."

I part my lips eagerly, and he slides into my mouth. I groan around him as the salty taste of pre-cum hits my tongue. His hand slides through my hair, holding firm and guiding me as I take him deeper. Behind me, Dane's fingers trace through my wetness, and the dual sensation, mouth full of Leo and Dane's fingers exploring my pussy, makes me dizzy.

I'm soaked. My inner thighs are slippery, and I can hear how wet I am when Dane's fingers slide through my folds. There's no hiding it, and I don't even care.

"Christ, she's dripping." Dane's voice is rougher than before, and hearing that clinical composure crack sends a thrill through me. His fingers circle my clit slowly, and I push my hips backward instinctively, chasing the pleasure.

"My greedy little lass has been desperate for this. Haven't you, pet?" Leo says, his Scottish accent thickening as I swirl my tongue beneath the head of his cock.

I moan around him in agreement, and the vibration makes him groan. His fingers tighten in my hair.

Behind me, Dane pushes two fingers inside my pussy, and the plea-surable stretch makes me gasp around Leo's cock. Dane's fingers are longer than Leo's, reaching deeper, and he curls them against my front wall with an accuracy that makes sparks burst behind my eyes.

"There." Dane's thumb presses against my clit while his fingers work inside me. "Right there."

I'm caught between them, rocking forward onto Leo's cock and then backward onto Dane's fingers, and the rhythm builds quickly. The wet sounds of my mouth on Leo and my pussy around Dane fill the room, and I feel like the most wanton, filthy creature alive. I'm loving every second of it.

Leo pulls out of my mouth, and I whimper. He tips my chin up to look at him, and his eyes are wild. "You ready for more, sweet girl?"

"Yes," I pant, licking my swollen lips. "Please. I need more."

Leo and Dane exchange a look over my head. Something passes between them, shorthand from decades of friendship, and then they move in unison. Dane withdraws his fingers, and I hear the rustle of clothing. Leo circles behind me while Dane comes around to the side of the bed.

When Dane stands naked before me, I get my first real look at him. He's lean where Leo is broad, his chest covered in a dusting of dark hair that trails down a flat stomach. His cock makes my eyes go wide. Long and thick, with a slight curve and veins running along the shaft. The swollen pink head glistens.

"Suck him, lass." Leo's command comes from behind me, and he squeezes my ass possessively. "Show Dane how talented that pretty mouth is."

Dane climbs onto the bed, and when I wrap my hand around his shaft, he sucks in a breath through his teeth. His cock is warm in my grip, and I can feel his pulse against my palm. I look up at him as I lean forward and run my tongue along the underside from base to tip.

His jaw clenches. The control is still there, but I'm affecting him. His hand comes to rest on the top of my head, but he's not guiding me. He's letting me set the pace. Suddenly, I'm determined to break his restraint.

I engulf his cock with my mouth, opening wide to accommodate his girth. The sound he makes—a controlled exhale through his nose—makes me clench. He tastes different from Leo, a stronger musk that isn't unpleasant. The novelty of having someone new in my mouth while Leo watches sends an illicit thrill racing through me.

Behind me, Leo pushes his cock into my pussy in one firm thrust, and I cry out around Dane, eyes squeezing shut as Leo fills me up. The stretch is familiar and perfect, and he doesn't wait, setting a deep, steady rhythm that rocks me forward onto Dane's cock with each stroke.

"That's it, lass." Leo's voice is rough with pleasure. "Such a good girl, letting us use her from both ends."

The words dissolve something inside me. I'm being fucked by one man while sucking another, and all I feel is something right that makes my eyes sting. The girl who showed up to that Halloween party in a Queen of Hearts costume would never have believed this. But I'm not her anymore. Leo saw something in me that night, and he's spent weeks coaxing it to the surface.

I relax my throat and take Dane deeper, moaning as Leo's cock hits that perfect angle inside me. Leo grasps my hips, his pace increasing, and Dane's fingers tighten slightly in my hair, a small crack in his control that makes me burn.

"She feels incredible." Leo's groan vibrates through me. "This tight, wet pussy was made for my cock. Going to fill you up, sweet lass. Fill this greedy little pussy until my seed takes root."

The words hit me somewhere primal and unexpected, and I imagine this is my life forever. Leo fucking me and filling me. I suddenly see a future someday where I'm round with his baby. I whimper as the image sends a ripple of pleasure from my fingertips to my toes.

Holy hell, I should not find that as hot as I do.

My pussy clamps down on him so hard that he groans and digs his fingers into my hips.

"Fuck, you liked that." Leo sounds almost surprised. "My lass likes the thought of being bred."

I can't answer with Dane in my mouth, but my moans say enough. Dane's eyes sharpen, watching my reaction. His thumb sweeps across my cheekbone, and the tenderness of that gesture while I'm being railed from behind makes my chest ache.

Leo's pace turns punishing, and the force of his thrusts pushes me forward each time. Dane matches the rhythm, rocking gently into my mouth while he caresses my cheek. The contrast between them, Leo's rough urgency and Dane's patience, scrambles my thoughts until all that's left is pleasure and surrender.

"She's close," Dane says, and I don't know how he can tell, but he's right. My thighs are shaking, my core winding more tightly with every thrust, the pressure building toward a massive orgasm.

"Aye, she is." Leo pulls back and slams deep. "Come for us, lass. Come on my cock while Dane watches."

The permission breaks the dam. My orgasm crashes through me, and I cry out around Dane's cock as pleasure rips through every nerve. My pussy clenches around Leo in rhythmic spasms, and I hear him curse through the roaring in my ears.

Dane eases out of my mouth, and I collapse forward onto my forearms, gasping and trembling. Leo is still inside me, grinding deep as my walls flutter around him, and then he buries himself to the hilt and groans as he comes. The hot pulse of him filling me draws out another wave of aftershocks, and I whimper into the sheets as my body shudders.

"Good girl." Leo's hand strokes down my spine, soothing even as his cock twitches inside me. "That's my perfect lass."

He withdraws slowly, and I feel his cum and my own wetness slip down my inner thigh. I'm trembling so hard my arms can barely hold me up. But the ride isn't over. Dane hasn't come.

When I look up at him, the hunger in his eyes makes my spent body spark back to life. I can tell his control is hanging by a thread. The raw want on his face makes my pussy clench around nothing.

"Your turn," I manage, surprised I can even form words.

Dane's hand cups my jaw. "Lie on your back."

I roll over on shaky limbs. My skin is flushed and damp, and the cool sheets feel like silk against my overheated body. Dane positions himself between my thighs, and I feel the blunt head of his cock press against my entrance. He's bigger than Leo, and my pussy is already sensitive and swollen.

"Look at me," he says.

I meet his eyes, and he pushes in. The stretch is intense, a slow, relentless slide that forces my body to open around him inch by inch.

I gasp, fingers twisting in the sheets, as he fills me deeper than I've ever been filled. It takes forever. He's so thick that every nerve ending fires, and I can feel every ridge and vein against my oversensitized walls.

Oh god. Oh my god.

"You're so...holy hell." My eyes are watering from the fullness, and my pussy flutters around him. I'm stretched so wide it borders on too much, that knife-edge between pain and pleasure where my body can't decide which way to fall.

"Breathe." He pauses when he's completely inside me, letting me adjust. Leo is watching from beside the bed, his hand on my thigh, his thumb rubbing slow circles that keep me grounded.

My body adjusts, the stretch easing into a deep, throbbing fullness. Every micro-movement sends sparks through my oversensitive walls, and I'm making tiny peeps of pleasure as my body tries to figure out how to take all of him.

When he can tell I'm ready, he pulls out almost all the way before pushing back in slowly. The drag of his cock against my sensitive flesh makes me arch off the bed in pleasure. He finds a rhythm that's nothing like Leo's. Where Leo fucks with fire and force, Dane fucks with intention. Every stroke is designed to hit exactly where it needs to. My mouth falls open, but no sound comes out as my mind is wiped clean of all thoughts.

Leo settles beside me on the bed, his hand finding my breast. He pinches my nipple while Dane fucks me. The combination of familiar and new is so overwhelming that tears prick at my eyes.

"How does he feel, pet?" Leo's voice is a rough whisper near my ear.

"Big," I gasp, arching into Dane's next thrust. "Different. Oh god, so good."

"That's it." Leo's mouth finds my neck, sucking and nipping while Dane's pace increases. "My sweet lass, taking everything we give her."

Leo's mouth on my neck and Dane's cock inside me and Leo's fingers on my nipple. It's sensory overload, and my brain gives up trying to process it and just lets my body take over.

Dane leans down, and his mouth captures mine. He kisses me deep while he fucks me deep, his tongue sliding against mine as his cock fills me completely. The kiss is all-consuming, and I go wild, rocking against him while Leo rolls my nipple.

When Dane pulls away, his composure has finally cracked. His jaw is tight, and his eyes are blazing with lust.

"Come for me, Alice." His voice is rough with the effort of restraint, and hearing that control slip makes me clench around him. "I want to feel you."

He speeds up his thrusts, and I fly apart. My second orgasm tears through me, and I cry out as my walls grip him in pulsing waves. Dane's rhythm breaks, and he slams into me as I drag him over the edge with me. He buries his cock deep and groans, a raw, guttural sound that's the most uncontrolled thing I've heard from him, as he unloads ropes of cum deep inside me.

He relaxes over me, and for a long moment, neither of us moves. My chest heaves, my body thrumming with residual pleasure. When Dane finally looks into my eyes, something unguarded crosses his face before he shuts it down.

"Beautiful," he murmurs and kisses me softly.

He pulls out carefully, and I wince at the emptiness. Between the two of them, I'm thoroughly used and trembling while their cum trickles out of me. The thought makes me flush with a satisfaction that surprises me.

My body is humming. Floating. Every muscle feels like it's been dissolved and remade from warm honey. I got my wish and was fucked by two men. My thighs are sticky, and I feel absolutely, gloriously wrecked.

My brain is still trying to catch up with the rest of me. If this is what asking for what you want gets you, I'm never holding back again.

Leo gets up and disappears into the bathroom. I hear water running, and he returns with a warm washcloth. He cleans me up with care, murmuring praise between gentle passes.

Dane sits beside me and strokes the damp hair away from my face, his touch lighter than Leo's but no less attentive. They've fallen into a rhythm like they've rehearsed it, and warmth blooms in my chest. Three months ago, I was scrambling for deposit money for a new apartment. Now I'm being tended by two men in a house that's started to feel like mine.

"You did beautifully," Dane says, and the sincerity in his voice makes my eyes sting.

Leo finishes cleaning me and pulls the comforter down. "In you get, lass."

I crawl under the covers on limbs that feel like jelly. Leo slides in on my left, his chest against my spine, his arm wrapping around my waist and pulling me close. The scent of oranges and sex surrounds me. His fingers toy with a strand of my blonde hair, winding it around his knuckle the way he does when he's settling in for the night. Then the mattress dips on my right as Dane settles beside me, his hand resting on my hip, his warmth a steady presence along my side.

I'm tucked between two men who just fucked me silly, and I've never felt more whole.

"Thank you," I whisper, already drifting. "Both of you."

Leo's lips brush the nape of my neck. "Merry Christmas, sweet girl." His accent is thick and drowsy, and the reminder that it's Christmas Eve, that this is how I'm spending it, makes me smile so wide my cheeks ache.

On my other side, Dane's thumb traces slow circles on my hip. He doesn't say anything, but the way his hand lingers tells me he's not leaving the bed tonight. Or at least, I hope he's not.

Warm and safe. Held from both sides. I'm already thinking about tomorrow and what else they might do to me.

My dreams are going to be very, very good tonight.

CHAPTER 2

Leo's singing and the smell of bacon lure me to the kitchen before I'm even fully awake.

I stop in the doorway. Leo is at the stove wearing only low-slung pajama pants, flipping bacon with a pair of tongs while belting out the chorus in a terrible pirate voice. His hair is mussed from sleep, and I stand there for a second admiring his broad shoulders. He's ridiculous and the hottest thing I've ever seen at seven in the morning. My brain hasn't even fully turned on yet, but my body perks up.

A pot of oatmeal steams on the burner beside Leo. Ewww, oatmeal. Are they expecting me to eat that?

Dane sits at the kitchen island with a cutting board and a pile of strawberries, slicing them into even pieces. He's wearing jeans and a blue Henley with the sleeves pushed up to his elbows, forearms flexing with each cut. I fucked both of them last night. I might be the luckiest girl in the world.

"What shall we do with a drunken sailor," Leo croons, waving the tongs like a conductor's baton, *"early in the—*"He spots me and grins. "Morning, lass. Merry Christmas."

"Merry Christmas." My voice comes out sleep-scratchy. I'm wearing one of Leo's t-shirts and nothing underneath, and the cotton brushes my thighs as I cross the kitchen tiles on bare feet. The floor is cold, and I curl my toes against it, which is not exactly the sexy entrance I was going for.

Dane's eyes track me, unhurried, and I'm starting to understand this might be the way he does everything. "Merry Christmas, Alice."

Something in his voice makes warmth bloom low in my belly, and I have to look away. Leo hooks an arm around my waist as I pass the stove and pulls me in, pressing a kiss to my temple. The scent of oranges from his skin mixes with bacon grease and coffee, and I breathe him in, my hands flat against his bare chest. I could stay in his arms for hours, but the rumble in my stomach tells me I've got other priorities.

"Hungry?" he asks, his accent thicker in the morning.

"Starving."

"Good. Sit down and let us feed you."

He says it like a command wrapped in kindness, and my body tingles. I take the stool next to Dane, and he slides a mug of coffee toward me without being asked. Black, two sugars. Did Leo tell him how I take it?

I wrap my hands around the mug and take a sip, watching them prepare breakfast. Leo plates the bacon while Dane spoons oatmeal into three bowls and arranges the sliced strawberries on top in a pretty design. Once he adds blueberries and a drizzle of honey, he places the first bowl in front of me. After watching the care he took dishing up the bowls, there's no way I'm going to decline it now.

Leo starts another verse, this one about putting the sailor in the longboat, and Dane shakes his head without looking up. "Your pitch is criminal," he says.

"My pitch is festive."

"Those aren't mutually exclusive."

I laugh into my coffee, and Leo points the tongs at me. "Don't encourage him, lass. He's been judging my singing since university."

"Someone had to," Dane says, and the corners of his mouth twitch.

We eat together at the island, knees bumping, Leo's hand drifting to my thigh between bites. The bacon is perfectly crisp, and Dane's oatmeal is the best I've ever had. I'm not sure if the food is really this good, or if I worked up an appetite last night. I might just be happy, so everything seems wonderful.

They're both in good moods, and breakfast is fun. Leo reaches across me to steal a blueberry from Dane's bowl, and Dane catches his wrist without looking. They bicker about the sea shanties with the comfort of decades between them. They both keep filling my coffee without my asking.

I haven't had a Christmas morning like this since my parents' last Christmas, when I'd watched my dad burn the pancakes while my mom laughed so hard she cried. That was three months before the accident. After that, Christmases were at my aunt's apartment with takeout and the TV on too loud, and eventually, it was me alone in my apartment with snacks and whatever holiday movie looked interesting to stream.

My throat gets tight, and I stare down at my oatmeal, blinking hard. *Don't. Not right now.*

A warm hand covers mine. Leo's thumb strokes across my knuckles slowly, not saying anything. He doesn't have to. I turn my hand over and lace my fingers through his, squeezing, and the tightness in my throat eases enough for me to breathe.

Dane sets a glass of water beside my coffee without a word. He doesn't even look at me when he does it, and that's somehow the kindest thing anyone has done for me in a long time.

I drink the water, and I'm fine.

After breakfast, Leo insists I sit on the living room couch while he and Dane clean the kitchen. I try to ignore the request and get a firm *"Sit!"* from both of them at the same time, which sends me straight to the couch.

The living room is warm, and one of them started a fire already. The Christmas tree glows in the corner, colored lights blinking through their slow rotation. The star casts tiny prisms across the ceiling, and pine mixes with cedar from the fireplace. My chest does a weird fluttery thing that I'm choosing to ignore.

Once the kitchen is clean, Leo drops onto the couch beside me, one arm stretching along the back behind my shoulders. Dane sits gracefully in the armchair. He looks comfortable here and doesn't act like a visitor. It's obvious he visits often.

"Dane has a gift for you, lass." Leo nods at Dane.

Dane reaches down beside the armchair and produces a package wrapped in brown paper, with simple, careful creases. He holds it out to me without ceremony.

Inside is a Mary Oliver poetry book. The cover is beautiful, and when I open it, I find a note written in neat, angular handwriting on the first page: "For the mornings when you need inspiration. —D"

I run my thumb over the ink. I don't know who Mary Oliver is, but the fact he put thought into the gift warms me. This man I've known for less than twenty-four hours bought me poetry for Christmas.

"Thank you," I say. "This is really thoughtful."

"You're welcome." He says it simply, but his dark eyes hold mine, and I can tell the poetry means something to him. I make a promise to myself to read it and see why he chose this gift for me.

Leo squeezes my shoulder and stands. "Alright, lass. Come with me."

The guys lead me down the hallway to the room Leo mentioned as a possible art studio.

Leo turns the handle and pushes the door wide.

The windows are the same as I remember, stretching across the far wall with the backyard buried in snow beyond them. But the room has been transformed. A drop cloth covers the hardwood, and a wooden easel stands in the center, angled toward the light. The shelves along the far wall are stocked with supplies: oil paints, acrylics, watercolors, tubes, and pans, arranged by color. Jars of brushes in every size, from fine detail rounds to wide flats. Palette knives, charcoal pencils, a tin of graphite sticks, rolls of tape, bottles of linseed oil and turpentine.

A stack of canvases leans against the shelves in different sizes, and beside them, a pad of thick watercolor paper and a sketchbook with a leather cover. A wooden palette rests on a small worktable next to jars for water, rags, and a set of palette cups. In the corner near the windows, there's a comfortable reading chair with a side table and a lamp, like he knew I'd want a place to sit in the morning light with a poetry book and a cup of coffee.

Leo did this. When I was shopping at the mall with his credit card and walked past the art supply store and told myself I didn't deserve to go in, he was planning to turn this empty room into a studio for me for Christmas.

I can't move. Can barely breathe. The tears come before I can stop them. Not pretty tears. My face crumples, and I press both hands over my mouth. My shoulders shake because nobody has done anything like this for me since my parents died, and I didn't think someone would ever want to again.

Leo wraps his arms around me from behind, tucking his chin on top of my head and holding me while I fall apart. His chest is solid against my spine, and oranges surround me. He lets me cry until I'm done.

"I've got you, lass," he murmurs into my hair.

I turn in his arms and bury my face against his neck, breathing him in. I don't know how long we stand there, but it's long enough that the tears run dry and I'm left hiccupping against his chest.

"You built me a studio," I say into his neck. "Thank you."

"I converted a room," he says, and I can hear the smile in his voice. "Dane helped me pick out the supplies over the phone. He has strong opinions about brushes."

I look over Leo's shoulder. Dane is leaning in the doorway, arms crossed, watching us. His eyes are soft. He's glad. That undoes me almost as much as the studio.

"Thank you," I say to him and smile.

"You're welcome."

Leo kisses my temple again. "Merry Christmas, Alice."

I glance around in happiness. This is the first Christmas in years that's felt like one.

We eat BLTs for lunch, and Leo puts on soft Christmas music. At some point, I pull on panties and a pair of shorts, which feels almost modest compared to how I spent last night. I curl up on the couch between them with Dane's poetry book while Leo reads on his tablet and Dane watches the fire.

My legs are draped across Leo's lap, his hand on my ankle. I'm leaning against Dane's side, his arm behind me, and I can feel his breathing against my shoulder. I keep sneaking glances at both of them. Leo's jaw, the firelight on the gray at his temples. Dane's long fingers resting on the back of the couch. I want to draw those hands.

I read a poem about wild geese and not having to be good—no kneeling for forgiveness—and something loosens in my chest. I'm sitting between two men who gave me art supplies and poetry and a whole room just because I mentioned once that I used to paint. Now I want to be on my knees for them, not in penance, but just because it feels right and that's enough.

"I want to thank you," I say, closing the book. My voice is steady. "For this morning. For everything."

I slide off the couch and onto my knees between them. Leo's hazel eyes darken while Dane's gaze sharpens. My heart hammers. The hunger in their eyes tells me they understand what I'm offering, and they want it as much as I do.

Leo's jaw flexes. "You don't have to thank us, lass."

"I know I don't have to." I look up at him through my lashes. "I want to."

He glances at Dane, and a silent conversation passes between them. Dane gives a single nod.

Leo slides his hand into my hair, tilting my head back. "Good girl. Now, show us how badly you want our cocks."

My pussy pulses, and my nipples tighten. I'm kneeling on Christmas afternoon with two men looking down at me, and my whole body is buzzing with how badly I want this.

I turn to Leo first because he's the one with his hand in my hair. I run my palms up his thighs, and the muscles tense under his pajama pants. He's already hard, his cock straining against the cotton, and when I wrap my fingers around him through the fabric, he lets out a low hiss between his teeth. Good. I want to hear that sound again and again.

"Impatient," he says, and his voice has gone rough, the Scottish burr thickening the way it does when he's turned on.

"Then let me show you," I say, tugging at the waistband of his pants. He lifts up so I can pull them down.

His cock springs free, and I wrap my hand around the thick length of him. He pulses against my palm. I stroke him once from base to tip, watching the way his abs clench, and my mouth waters.

I lean forward and lick a slow stripe up the underside, base to tip, and Leo groans, a deep, rumbly sound that I feel in my own chest. His fingers tighten in my hair, guiding but not forcing. I take the head into my mouth, swirling my tongue around the ridge, tasting salt and skin.

"Fuck, lass." His hips shift off the couch. "That mouth."

I take him deeper, hollowing my cheeks, finding my rhythm. Leo's big—stretching my lips, filling my mouth—and every thrust sends a thrill straight to my clit. I'm soaked already *because I chose this*. His control cracking while he fights to hold still? That's my power, and it's sexy as hell.

Dane's fingers slide into my hair alongside Leo's, and they both tighten their grip. I could get addicted to both their hands guiding me at the same time.

"You're a good cocksucker," Dane says, and his words ignite me.

I moan around Leo's cock, and Leo swears as his cock pulses like he's about to come. Oh no, he doesn't. I'm not ready for that yet.

I pull off Leo and turn to Dane. His cock is out already. That long, thick cock with the head flushed dark. I wrap my hand around him, and when I stroke him, his breath catches sharply, but his eyes stay locked on mine.

I take him into my mouth, and his taste is earthier than Leo's. I can't take him as deep, he's too big, but I work the base with my hand and suck the head. Dane exhales through clenched teeth. His hand comes to rest on the back of my neck, fingers curling possessively.

"Look at me," he says.

I look up. His eyes burn into mine, his expression fierce with desire but controlled. He holds my gaze while I suck him, and his stare overpowers his cock in my mouth. Heat floods between my legs.

I'm dripping, and neither has touched my pussy. I'm such a slut, I'm seconds from coming just from giving them blowjobs.

"Switch," Leo says, voice rough with need.

I go back to Leo and take him deep. Dane's hand stays on my neck. His thumb strokes the ridge of my spine. I alternate between them and find a rhythm, Leo's cock in my mouth while my hand works Dane. My lips are swollen, my jaw aching in a good way. Soft strains of "Winter Wonderland" drift from the speakers. I lose myself in the surrender and power of kneeling for both of them as I take turns with their cocks.

"I'm close, lass," Leo groans and rocks his hips up to meet my mouth. "Suck it faster. Make me come."

I suck him down as deep as I can. He comes with a curse, his cock pulsing against my tongue, hot and thick and salty. I swallow and work him through it.

When I pull off, I lick the cum from my lips as pure power rushes through me.

My body buzzes when I turn to Dane and take as much of him as I can into my mouth. His hips rock upwards, and his hands move to my head as he takes control.

"That's it," he says, and his voice has turned to gravel as his control frays. "You're such a good girl sucking my cock."

A shiver rolls through me, and I moan around him, working him faster. His breathing goes ragged. I'm surprised when he twists his hand in my hair, pulling my head off his cock.

He quickly stands up, and I realize what he's doing when he starts stroking his cock furiously right over me. I open my mouth, tip my head up, and stick my tongue out.

"You're so beautiful when we're using you," he groans, and I almost don't get my eyes closed in time as he shoots sticky strands of cum all over my face.

I can feel the wetness sliding down my cheek, and I giggle as I wipe it off with my fingers and then suck them clean. I made them both come, and pride warms my chest, like I just won a medal for the best blowjob.

"Did you like that, lass?" Leo asks, and when I glance at him, his eyes glitter with satisfaction.

I sit back on my heels, and I'm so wet I can feel it on my inner thighs. I wipe my mouth with the back of my hand and look at both of them while the throbbing between my legs becomes hard to ignore.

"Yep, so tasty."

Leo pulls me up off the floor and into his lap, cradling me against his chest. "Christ, lass. You're a gift."

I tuck my face against his neck. I'm unsatisfied, and I press my thighs together to get some friction. It's not enough. I want to come so badly my whole body thrums.

Dane rests his hand on my knee and slides his palm up the inside of my thigh.

My breath catches when he says, "Your turn."

Leo shifts me off his lap and onto the couch, laying me back against the cushions. He hooks his fingers into the waistband of my shorts and panties and pulls them down my legs in one smooth motion, tossing them to the floor. The air hits my skin, and I shiver, exposed and wet and so damn ready.

"Oh, my poor pet. Look at how needy that swollen pussy is?" Leo's voice is a soft croon as he pushes my thighs apart and kneels between them. He holds my pussy lips open with his thumbs, and the first stroke of his tongue along my folds almost makes me levitate off the cushions.

"Ohhh, god!" I cry out as he feasts.

I grab a fistful of his hair as he circles my clit with the tip of his tongue before sucking it gently. My thighs are already shaking. I was so wound up from having them both in my mouth that it's not going to take much, and Leo seems to know it because he picks up the pace, his tongue working me in quick, tight strokes.

Within moments, his expert tongue drives me over the edge. I come fast and hard, crying out as my back arches. Leo licks me through the aftershocks of pleasure. When I'm whimpering and shaking, he presses a soft kiss to my inner thigh and sits back.

I'm still catching my breath when Dane takes his place. He kneels between my legs and hooks one of my thighs over his shoulder. I gasp when he sucks on my pussy lips. I'm oversensitive and whimper when his tongue circles my clit.

He pauses, waits, and when I don't push him away, he starts again. Slower this time, but relentless, his tongue tracing patterns against my clit, building pressure in a completely different way than Leo. I flew apart with Leo, but Dane is pulling me toward a deeper, slower wave that's building from my toes.

His fingers press against my entrance, and I moan loudly in pleasure. I can't think straight as the delight builds. He slides two fingers inside me, curling them forward while his tongue keeps its steady rhythm on my clit, and the combination makes my vision blur.

"Dane." His name comes out broken. "Please, I'm going to—"

He doesn't change a thing. He continues with the same pace, pressure, and the same maddening curl of his fingers until I shatter. This orgasm rolls through me in long waves that make my thighs tremble against his shoulders. I hear myself crying out in a crescendo as the pleasure wracks my entire body.

Dane stays with me through all of it, his mouth gentle as I come down, his fingers easing out of me slowly. He presses a kiss to my inner thigh, opposite from where Leo kissed. His lips are wet, his dark eyes heavy, and the satisfied look on his face is so fucking hot.

I'm boneless, and I can't move my legs. What's my name again?

Leo lifts me into his arms and settles me against his chest. Dane drops on the couch next to us and pulls my legs across his lap. Leo grabs a blanket from the back of the couch and drapes it over my bare legs. My mind is mush as I snuggle with them both.

"Merry Christmas, lass," Leo murmurs against my hair.

My "mmm" is all I can respond with, and they both chuckle. My body is humming with a satisfied warmth that makes everything feel soft and far away.

I'm used and cared for. This is the true joy of the season.

CHAPTER 3

The next morning, when I wander into the kitchen, Dane is making us breakfast. It's more oatmeal with sliced bananas, almonds, and blueberries. Hopefully, the tasty oatmeal yesterday wasn't just the happiness convincing me it was delicious, since it seems I'm going to be eating a lot of oatmeal while Dane is here.

I lean against the doorframe, enjoying the backside of a sexy older guy making me food. How did I get this lucky?

"You don't have to hover," he says without turning around.

"I'm not hovering. I'm supervising."

He glances over his shoulder, and the corner of his mouth twitches. "Go sit down. It'll be ready in five."

I plop down on a bar stool at the kitchen island, and Leo strides in.

"Morning, lass," he says, dropping a kiss on the top of my head. He looks impeccable in a crisp white shirt and dark slacks. How does he manage it this early?

Leo pours himself a coffee. "I've got some work to catch up on, so I'll be in my office for a bit. Dane, you're heading out soon, right?"

"Yeah, I won't be gone long. It's just coffee with friends," Dane responds.

"Perfect," Leo says, turning to me with a protective expression that never fails to make me weak. "And you, lass, relax this morning. But be ready when I call for you later. Understood?"

"Yes, Sir," I say automatically, and Leo grins.

"Good girl."

Leo leaves the kitchen with his coffee, taking it towards his office at the back of the house. Dane sits next to me, and we eat in silence for a few minutes. Every brush of Dane's arm against mine sends shivers down my spine.

Dane finally speaks. "So, how are you feeling after last night?"

I blush, remembering how, after dinner, I'd begged them both to fuck me, and I came so hard I nearly passed out. "Good. A little sore, but...good."

Dane's eyes darken. "You're a wonderful fucktoy. I'm glad Leo invited me for Christmas while you're here and that you wanted this."

My pussy clenches at his words, but an odd shyness makes me look away. "Thank you," I whisper.

"Look at me," Dane commands, and I force myself to meet his gaze as he continues. "Never be ashamed of your desires. Embracing them is beautiful."

I nod, not trusting myself to speak. Dane's thumb brushes over my lower lip, and for a moment, I think he's going to kiss me. But then he pulls away, standing up.

"I should get ready to go," he says, his voice slightly rougher than usual. "Finish your breakfast. You need something healthy and filling after last night."

His eyes roam over my body, and my pussy lets me know she's awake. The way he says "filling" makes me think of other ways he filled me last night.

Once he's gone, I'm left alone with a half-eaten bowl of oatmeal and an aching need. Ugh. Why is no one using me this morning? They're making me addicted to them and then leaving me alone. This is torture.

I'm too keyed up to finish my oatmeal, and I toss the rest in the trash. No one will ever know I didn't finish it, and I really did try. It's all Dane's fault anyway for getting me worked up.

I move to my art studio and close the door. Morning light slants through the north windows onto the easel as I squeeze cadmium yellow and cerulean blue onto the palette.

When I pick up a brush, I just stand there.

All I can think about is last night. Leo bent me over the kitchen table after dinner and fisted his hand in my hair before fucking me hard enough to rattle the dishes. Dane watched from the doorway until it was his turn. Dane fucked me slow and deep until I was shaking and begging and the orgasms blurred together.

I drag the brush through yellow paint. One streak across the canvas. It looks like nothing.

I try again, this time a loose curve of blue bleeding into yellow. My hand isn't steady, and my mind just isn't in the mood to paint. There's a pleasant ache between my legs that keeps distracting me every time I shift my weight.

I eventually put the paints away and try to distract myself by reading. It doesn't help. I don't know how many times I orgasmed last night, but I'm greedy and want more today.

I'm pulled from my thoughts by the buzz of my phone. It's a text from Dane.

Dane: Hope you finished your oatmeal and you're behaving yourself.

I bite my lip. What am I supposed to say to that? Before I can decide, another text comes through.

Dane: Remember, good girls get rewarded.

Mmm, I do like rewards. I type out a quick reply.

Alice: Always trying to be good.

That's vague enough without admitting I wasn't good. But shit, do I call him Sir, too? What does someone do when they have two dominant men?

His response is almost immediate.

Dane: That's our girl.

Whoa, *our* good girl? My body zings alive, and I imagine what it would be like being both of theirs for real. Wait, what am I doing? I shouldn't be flirting with Dane like this, not when Leo's just in the other room. But god, the way Dane makes me feel...

Another text comes through.

Dane: Did you finish your breakfast?

Uh-oh. Well, I can't admit it now. He just offered me a reward.

Alice: Yes, Sir.

I mean, I tried. I feel a twinge of guilt for lying.

There's a long pause before his reply comes.

Dane: We'll see about that. Lying has consequences.

My stomach flips at his words. How does he know?

Before I can dwell on it too much, I hear footsteps coming down the hall. Is it Leo? I glance at the clock and realize it's been almost two hours since breakfast—I've been lost in my thoughts and didn't notice how much time had passed.

Dane appears in the doorway of the studio, his eyes dark. Oh shit, he was texting me from downstairs?

"Come with me," he says simply, and I follow him without question.

He leads me to the kitchen, where he pulls out the trash to show me the oatmeal I tossed out. Dane raises an eyebrow at me. "You said you finished your breakfast."

I swallow hard. "I'm sorry, Sir. I...I lied."

Dane nods slowly. "Yes, you did. It would have been fine if you hadn't finished breakfast if you weren't hungry, but it's not okay to lie. Do you know what happens to girls who lie?"

"They get punished," I whisper.

"That's right," Dane says. "But first, you're going to eat something since you didn't finish breakfast and now it's almost lunchtime."

I nod, and he fixes me a turkey sandwich on wheat bread.

"Now eat every last bite, and then we'll deal with your punishment."

I can feel the wetness growing between my legs as I take a bite. Why do I love being controlled like this? I've got a sexy, older guy making sure I eat properly, and it's one of the hottest things I've ever experienced in my life.

Dane watches as I eat, his gaze never leaving me. When I finally finish, he takes the plate and sets it in the sink. "Good girl," he murmurs. "Now, come here."

I stand before him, thrumming. Dane cups my face in his hands, his touch gentle but firm. "I'm going to edge you," he says softly. "And you're not going to come unless I say you can. Understood?"

I nod, my breath catching in my throat. Dane leads me to the living room, sitting on the couch and pulling me onto his lap. I'm only wearing a long nightshirt and panties, and his hands slide under the nightshirt to pull and tease my nipples. When he finally slips a hand between my legs and under my panties, I moan as pleasure swirls in my core.

"Such a needy little thing," he murmurs, his fingers sliding through my folds.

He works his fingers into my pussy slowly, building the pleasure with maddening patience, while he brushes his thumb against my clit. Every time I get close to the edge, he pauses his movements. I grip his shoulders and grind against his hand, trying to get him to finger fuck me harder.

"Please," I whimper after what feels like hours. "Please, I need to come."

"No," Dane says, his voice maddeningly calm. "This is your punishment for lying to me."

He continues his torturous finger fucking, bringing me to the brink over and over again. By the time he finally pulls his fingers out of my pussy, I'm a quivering mess, and I'm covered in a fine sheen of sweat. Oh, thank god, he's going to fuck me now.

"There," he says, pressing a kiss to my forehead. "Your punishment is not coming."

I mewl out in distress. Whaaaat? Oh. My. God. Lust sizzles my brain, and I can't think.

He pulls on my nipple and pinches it until I cry out again, and he chuckles. "I think you've learned your lesson. Remember, honesty is always the best policy. Now tell me what you did while I was gone, since it wasn't eating."

Ugh, time to admit I'm a failure. "I tried to paint. But I didn't know where to start. It's just been so long…"

He tilts his head and says, "What are you afraid of?"

Ouch, that's direct. I open my mouth to deflect with a joke, but he's watching me patiently, and the glib answer dies in my throat.

"That I'll find out I'm not any good," I say. "I've been telling myself I'm someone who paints, but the truth is I'm only someone who wants to paint. There's a difference."

"When did you start wanting to paint?" he asks.

I snuggle against him and sigh. "My mom painted. Watercolors, mostly. She did flowers and landscapes. It was just a hobby, but she loved it. She'd paint at the kitchen table, and I'd sit next to her with my own little set of paints."

My throat tightens. I don't like to talk about my parents much. Most people don't want to know the sad parts of a person's life.

"My parents died in a car accident when I was ten. I went to live with my aunt after, and she was fine, she was nice, but it wasn't…"

I trail off because I don't have the right word.

"It wasn't the same," Dane finishes.

I look at him. He's not giving me pity. Something in his face tells me he gets it.

"Yeah, it wasn't the same."

His arms tighten around me, and we're both silent for a bit, but it's not awkward. It's nice to be held without expectations.

"What about you?" I ask eventually. "Leo told me a little about you, but I don't know much about your life outside of all this."

He's quiet, and for a moment, I think he's going to dodge the question, but then he speaks.

"I was married for four years. Her name was Claire."

Nothing about Dane screams formerly married, but at his age, I shouldn't be surprised.

"What happened?" I ask, then wince. "Sorry. You don't have to—"

"It's fine." He looks toward the window. "Claire wanted the white picket fence. Kids, a golden retriever, dinner at six. And I wanted something she couldn't give me, and I couldn't give her what she needed either. We were honest enough to end it before we destroyed each other."

There's an ache in his voice, not regret. More like the kind of loss that comes from caring about someone you still had to let go.

"How long ago?" I ask.

"Six years. Since then, I've been traveling a lot for work. Different cities, different hotel rooms. I go where the consulting contracts take me."

"And Leo's guest room every Christmas."

His mouth curves. "And Leo's guest room every Christmas. It's good to have somewhere to go for the holidays."

I hear what he's not saying. The consulting and the travel and the not-putting-down-roots isn't all it's cracked up to be.

"You get lonely," I say.

Dane looks at me, and for half a second, the mask slips. His gaze softens, and my breath catches.

Then he straightens, and the mask is back. Before either of us can say anything else, we hear Leo's voice calling me from his office. Dane helps me to my feet, smoothing down my hair.

"Go on," he says softly. "And remember, no coming unless you have permission."

I nod, still trembling from the intense edging session. As I make my way to Leo's office, I can feel Dane's eyes on me, and I wonder what else he has planned for me.

Leo's office is dark wood and floor-to-ceiling bookshelves. A window overlooks the backyard, afternoon light streaming in. His mahogany desk dominates the room.

Leo's sitting behind his desk with his laptop open, looking every inch the powerful businessman.

When I enter, he rises from his chair, his movements predatory. "Someone's turned on. Was Dane playing with you?"

I manage a nod while my body throbs with unfulfilled desire.

"Come around the desk," Leo instructs, his gaze intent. "Bend over, hands flat on the surface."

My heart races as I obey. The wood is cool when I rest my palms on it. Leo caresses my back, tracing the curve of my spine, before he grips my hips, pulling me back slightly. Before I can blink, my panties are on the floor.

"Spread your legs wider, lass," he commands. "I want full access to what's mine."

My cheeks flush, but I comply, the air cooling the damp skin of my thighs. Leo's fingers delve between my legs, exploring the slick, swollen flesh. I moan as he teases my pussy, not penetrating, just circling and driving me mad.

"Leo, please..."

"Patience, lass. You'll get what you need, but on my terms," he promises.

Clothes rustle, and a moment later, the head of his cock nudges my entrance. With one smooth, powerful thrust, he fills me. My body arches, and I cry out in relief and pleasure. Each thrust is deep and makes my head spin. Thoughts of Dane and his vulnerability and the edging blur together with the pleasure of Leo fucking me.

At this moment, I'm completely and utterly Leo's, yet a flicker of guilt lurks in my mind because of Dane. Would Leo care if he thought I was growing feelings for Dane, too?

Leo's rhythm quickens, his grasp on my hips tightening. "Come for me," he growls, the command vibrating through every nerve.

But I'm trapped between desire and denial. Dane's words echo in my mind, *no coming unless you have permission*. My body rebels as if it wants permission from Dane, and I'm torn between the two men, my climax hovering just out of reach.

"Alice, come now!" Leo's voice cracks with urgency, but I'm frozen.

And then, Leo stops moving. In the sudden silence, I realize my mistake. Oh fuck, I was distracted by thoughts of Dane.

Leo lets go of my hips, and his cock slips out of me as he steps back. The absence is a harsh reality.

"Look at me," he says firmly, and I can't tell what his tone means.

Slowly, I straighten, turning to face him. Our eyes meet, and I see a question there.

"What were you thinking of, lass?" Leo asks, his voice softer now.

My heart sinks. I need to tell him and be honest. Good girls don't lie, but how do I tell him I was thinking of Dane?

I open my mouth. Close it. Open it again.

"Alice." His voice drops, patient. "Whatever it is, just say it."

So I do.

"I like Dane. A lot." The sentence comes out in a rush, graceless and blunt. My cheeks burn. "I didn't expect it. I didn't plan for it. And I don't know if that's okay, or if I've broken something—"

"Alice."

"—because what we have means everything to me, Leo, and the last thing I want is for you to think I'm—"

"Lass."

I stop. My heart is hammering so hard I can hear it. Leo's watching me with an expression that's not angry or hurt, but I can't tell what he's thinking.

He wraps his arms around me, and I press my face against his chest, breathing in the scent of oranges and warm skin while I wait for the blow to land.

He kisses my head. "I'm not surprised," he says into my hair.

I go rigid. "What?"

He tucks a strand of hair behind my ear, tilting my face up so I have to look at him. The lines around his mouth have deepened, but not from anger. He's almost smiling. "Dane and I talked about this before he came."

My brain stalls. "You talked about it."

"We've been friends for twenty-five years. Do you think I'd invite someone into our bed without considering all the possible outcomes?" He brushes his thumb along my jaw. "I chose Dane for a reason. Not just because he's a good dom. And not just because I trust him with my life and with you."

His voice goes quieter. "Dane's been alone since his divorce. He doesn't let people in. He comes here every Christmas because this is the only place he has that feels like home." Leo's arms tighten around me. "He needs someone to come home to. And when I saw the way he looked at you on Christmas Eve, I thought, maybe..."

My eyes sting as I stare up at him. "You're not angry?"

"No, lass. I'm not angry." He cups my face in both hands. "What I feel for you doesn't shrink because you have room for him too. Sharing you with Dane doesn't diminish what we have. If anything..." He pauses. "Watching you open up to him makes me want you more. Not less."

The relief hits so hard my knees wobble. I press my forehead against his collarbone, and the knot in my chest finally loosens.

"I was scared to tell you," I whisper.

"I know." He presses his lips to my temple. "But you did it anyway. That's my brave girl."

The praise washes through me, and my whole body goes soft. A shiver rolls through me.

"Leo."

"Yes, lass?"

I look up at him, and the words slip out before I can second-guess them. "I love you. You know that, right?"

His expression shifts, and a vulnerability cracks through. "Aye, lass." His accent thickens the way it always does when he's feeling too much. "And I love you too."

He kisses me softly, but it quickly turns into a claim. His mouth is hard on mine, his hand fisting in my hair.

When he pulls back, we're both breathing harder. My lips are tingling and my whole body is buzzing again.

"My turn to talk," he says. His voice has dropped into that low register that makes my thighs clench. "You're mine. Whatever Dane is to you, whatever this becomes, you're mine. And right now, I'm going to take you to bed and remind you exactly what that means."

My pussy clenches at his words. "Yes," I manage. "Please."

He picks me up and carries me upstairs to his bedroom. The casual display of strength sends a spike of arousal straight through me, and I wrap my legs around his waist. My thighs are already shaking.

He drops me onto the mattress hard enough that I bounce. Before I can catch my breath, he pulls my nightgown over my head, and I almost giggle as I realize my panties are still on his office floor.

My nipples pucker as he stares down at me. There's something different in the way he's looking at me. He's more intense, like the confession about Dane and me telling him I love him unlocked something he's been holding back.

He strips quickly, and I smile when I see he's still hard. I want him inside me so bad my pussy aches.

"On your back. Legs open."

I obey, spreading my thighs, and his possessive gaze on my pussy makes me whimper.

He doesn't tease me, which is good since I'm not sure I could handle any more edging. He covers my body and drives into me in one firm stroke.

I cry out, arching off the mattress before he holds there, buried to the hilt.

"Who do you belong to?" His question comes out rough.

"You," I gasp. "I belong to you."

"That's right." He pulls back slowly, the drag of him against my inner walls making me whimper, and then he snaps his hips forward hard. "Mine. My lass. My good girl. Say it again."

"Yours, Leo. I'm yours." The words tumble out, desperate and breathless, and each one seems to make him more crazed. He drives into me harder, faster, until he's fucking me with a punishing rhythm that consumes us both. Every thrust sends a spike of pleasure so sharp it borders on pain, and I can tell the orgasm is going to be massive.

I brace my hands on the headboard, and his weight presses me into the mattress. His mouth is close to my ear. "Do you know what I think about when Dane has his hands on you?" His breath is hot against my skin. "I think about how you'll still be desperate for more cock when he's done with you. How I'll fuck every inch of you until you can't think of anything but the pleasure."

The thought of being fucked by both of them forever makes my pussy clench around him, and he groans.

He shifts his angle and hits deep inside me. "Squeeze my cock, lass. Show me who this pussy belongs to."

I'm so close. The tension coils low in my belly, and I'm panting against his throat, tasting salt on his skin, my nails digging into his back. He's relentless, each stroke harder than the last.

"Going to fill you up, lass." His accent is so thick now the words almost blur together. "Going to pump this sweet pussy full. Mine to breed. Mine to fill."

Fuuuck, I love it when he talks about breeding me, and I don't care if it's messed up.

"Please," I beg because I need permission. "Please let me come, Leo, please."

"Come." He slams into me one more time, burying himself deep. "Come on my cock. Now."

I explode, trembling with the shock of it. My spine bows with the force, and my pussy clamps around him in waves. He swells inside and groans as he slams into me again, his cock pulsing as he shoots his load into me. Imagining his cum coating me and the possibility that he'd really get me pregnant sends me spiraling higher as another smaller orgasm makes me spasm and rock against him.

When we come down from our high, we're stuck together with sex and sweat. My body is humming, and every muscle has turned to warm liquid. He's still on top of me, and I run my fingers through his damp hair and press my lips to his temple, listening to his breathing slow before I giggle.

I got edged and fingered, then fucked over a desk before admitting my feelings and then got railed into next week. All before dinnertime.

"Is my pet happy?" He rolls off me with a groan, and I giggle again as I snuggle against his side.

"Your pet is very, very happy, Sir."

"Good." He takes my hand and kisses my fingertips. "Now this old man who loves you might need a nap and then a shower before dinner."

"Mmm, sounds good to me."

After we nap, we shower together, and Leo notices I'm quiet.

"You okay, lass?"

"More than okay." I press a kiss to his wet chest.

His hand settles at the base of my skull, thumb rubbing a slow circle, and I melt into him.

"Leo?"

"Aye."

"What you said about Dane needing someone to come home to." I trace the line of his collarbone with my soapy hands. "Does he know you think that?"

"Yes, but he doesn't believe he deserves it."

My chest aches as I think about Dane telling me about Claire and the loneliness I sensed in his words.

"We'll figure it out," I say. "All three of us."

Leo kisses me softly. "Aye, we will."

I close my eyes and let my mind drift as he continues to run a washcloth down my body.

And that's when it happens. The image of a baby in my arms surfaces without warning. Small and warm and heavy in my arms, with a tuft of dark hair that might lighten to silver when it's old. It has Leo's hazel eyes.

I imagine Leo's big hands cradling something impossibly tiny. That rumbling voice going soft the way it does after he's taken care of me, but directed at a small, bundled weight against his chest.

My breath catches. A fierce wave of longing rolls through me. It's not the vague, someday-maybe kind of wanting. It's a visceral, aching, right-down-to-my-bones. I want Leo's baby. I want to be round with it, to feel it kick while his hands span my belly. I want to watch him hold something that's ours.

My pulse races. This was supposed to just be temporary, and now I'm fantasizing about having his baby. He probably doesn't even want a kid at his age. Wouldn't he have one already if he did? Hell, maybe he does have one and he's never told me.

Before I can panic, I press against him and breathe in the orange scent of his body wash. It's too soon to talk about this. We haven't even defined what we are, and then there's Dane. This is technically still an arrangement that has an expiration date.

But the image won't dissolve because this desire isn't going away. I'm just going to have to live with it.

CHAPTER 4

Two days later, Leo has to work again, and he tells Dane to keep me entertained for a few hours. We eat lunch at the kitchen table, and Dane asks me about the store where I work, what I'd want to paint if talent weren't a factor, whether I've read any more of the poetry book he gifted me. The conversation meanders, and I catch myself relaxing.

After lunch, I'm loading the dishwasher while he cleans up the rest of the kitchen. I'm reaching for the last plate when his hand closes around my wrist.

"Alice." His voice drops, and everything shifts.

My thighs press together as my entire body tingles. I'm aware of how close he's standing and the faint scent of sandalwood on his skin.

"Yes?"

"Leo told me you had trouble following a rule yesterday."

My stomach flips. *Oh, shit.* Yesterday, while Dane was out shopping, I came without permission. Leo had laughed it off and called me a greedy little thing, but apparently, the intel had been shared.

"Yes or no," Dane says.

"Yes," I whisper.

He releases my wrist. "Finish the dishes. Then come to the bedroom."

He walks away without looking back. My hands shake as I rinse the last dish and set it in the dishwasher. I press my palms flat against the cool granite countertop and try to slow my heartbeat. The anticipation is already building low in my belly.

Is he going to punish me? This is what Dane does. He doesn't rush the experience, which works me up even more.

By the time I push open the bedroom door, I'm wet and my pulse is loud in my ears.

He's sitting on the edge of the bed, dressed. His posture is relaxed, but his eyes. *Holy hell.* Dark and focused, tracking every step I take into the room. I feel exposed, and I'm still fully clothed.

"Close the door," he says.

I do.

"What's your color?"

"Green."

"Come here."

I cross the room on legs that feel liquid and stop in front of him. He's seated and I'm standing, but somehow, he still feels like the one looking down at me.

"Strip," he says.

I pull my sweater over my head and peel off my leggings. My bra joins them on the floor. When I push my panties down and step out of them, the cool air raises goosebumps across my bare skin and my nipples harden.

Dane doesn't touch me as he looks, slowly, thoroughly, the way someone studies a painting in a gallery. It's more exposing than if he'd grabbed me and thrown me on the bed. Standing naked under his gaze while he takes his time, my skin is burning, and he hasn't laid a finger on me.

"You came without permission yesterday," he says.

"Yes."

"Why?"

Leo wouldn't have asked why. He'd have spanked me and moved on with a grin. But Dane wants me to think about it, and thinking while I'm standing naked in front of him isn't easy.

"It felt too good. I couldn't stop it," I manage.

"Couldn't? Or didn't try hard enough?"

My face burns. *Fuck.* "Didn't try hard enough."

"Honest." His voice warms a fraction. "Now kneel."

I drop to my knees on the soft carpet. Dane leans forward and tips my chin up with one finger, making me look at him.

"This just means you need more practice," he says. "I'm going to take you to the edge, and you're going to count. Every time you get close, you tell me. And you don't come until I say. Understood?"

My pussy clenches. "Yes."

"Yes, what?"

"Yes, Sir."

Approval flickers in his dark eyes. He stands and walks to the bedside table. When he comes back, he's holding a glass with ice in it.

Um...I swallow hard, but I know whatever he plans to do with that, I'm 100 percent on board.

"Get on the bed on your back."

I climb up and lie against the pillows. The sheets are cool and smooth beneath me. My nipples are still hard, and I'm practically vibrating with the thought of cold ice cubes against my skin. This is going to be bad in a wonderful way.

He reaches into the glass and takes out an ice cube. "Color?"

"Still green." My voice comes out breathy.

He touches my collarbone with the ice, and I gasp, arching off the mattress. He drags it slowly across my skin to the hollow of my throat, down the center of my chest. Water trails behind it in thin rivulets that make me shiver. When he circles my left nipple, the cold is so sharp my whole body tenses, and I cry out, fingers curling into the sheets.

"Count," he says.

"One," I whisper, even though I'm not close yet. The cold is a shock, but underneath it, arousal is building. My pussy pulses with every circle of the ice, and the contrast between the freezing cube and the heat between my legs makes my head spin.

He moves the ice to my right nipple, circles it until the peak is stiff and aching, then replaces the ice with his mouth. Hot, wet, his tongue flat against the cold skin. I moan and arch into him because the temperature shift sends a spike of pleasure straight to my clit. My hips rock, and my thighs clench.

"Dane!"

"Shh." He takes another piece of ice and drags it down my stomach, slowly, tracing the lines of my ribs and the curve of my waist. I'm trembling and so wet I can feel it slick between my thighs. When the ice reaches my hip bone, I whimper and squirm.

"Stay still," he growls.

I try, but he slides the ice lower, tracing a path along the crease of my inner thigh, and my hips jerk.

He stops and waits, making me settle before continuing.

This is nothing like Leo. Leo would have me screaming by now. Dane is unhurried, and his patience is worse than roughness because it gives me nowhere to hide.

He presses the ice against my clit.

I shiver and have to stop myself from coming. "Oh god, two, I'm at two."

"Good girl."

A shiver rolls through me, and those two words almost make me come. *Fuuuck*. This is bad. But so so good.

He pulls the ice away and replaces it with his thumb, circling my clit slowly while I pant and grip the sheets. The warmth of his hand after the cold is overwhelming, and pleasure builds in waves. My thighs tense and my hips rock against his hand, chasing the ecstasy.

"Three," I gasp. "Dane, I'm close."

He stops.

I groan, my body arching toward his hand, trying to get more pleasure. *This is cruel. Actual cruelty.*

"Breathe," he says.

I breathe, and the edge recedes, slowly, leaving me shaky and desperate. My pussy throbs with denied release. Everything is swollen and sensitive and pulsing.

He waits until my breathing evens out, and then he starts again.

Ice tracing my stomach, my breasts, circling each nipple until I'm writhing. Then his mouth, hot on the frozen skin, his tongue replacing cold with scorching wet heat. He slides his fingers against my pussy again, pushing two inside me while his thumb rubs my clit. Every touch is amplified, and the pleasure builds faster this time, the tension coiling so tight my thighs tremble.

"Four," I choke out. "Please—"

He withdraws, and I'm breathless. Sobbing. Desperate. I was so close.

"Tell me what you want," he says, his voice calm, like he's asking me to pass the salt.

"To come," I beg. "Please let me come."

"What else?"

I stare at him, panting. "What?"

He leans close, his lips brushing my ear. "What do you need?"

And there it is. He doesn't just want my surrender. He wants what's underneath—the things I barely let myself think.

My eyes sting. Arousal and vulnerability tangled so tight I can't separate them.

"I want to belong somewhere," I hear myself say. My voice cracks. "I want all of this to be real. Not an arrangement. Not temporary. And I want a baby."

Fuck. I can't believe I said that out loud.

Dane pulls back and looks at me. His dark eyes are intense, and his gaze sharpens.

"That's what I needed to hear," he says. He slides his fingers inside me and presses his thumb against my clit, and this time, he's building me with no mercy. Pleasure surges fast, spiraling through me, and my toes curl and my back arches.

"Five," I gasp. "Please, I can't—"

"Look at me," he says.

I force my eyes to his. His face is close, those dark eyes locked on mine, and the intensity of the eye contact while his fingers curl inside me and his thumb circles my clit is almost more than I can take. If he doesn't say it soon, I'm not sure I can stop it.

"Come," he says.

"Oooooh, fuck!" My body goes rigid, and then I come apart, my pussy seizing around his fingers. I'm free-falling from pleasure, and the orgasm tears through me so hard my vision whites out. Pleasure radiates through me. My legs shake, and I'm half-sobbing through it because the release after all that denial is so intense it borders on pain. *Holy fuck.*

Dane doesn't pull away. He works me through every aftershock, his pace slowing as the waves ebb, his other hand pressing flat against my stomach.

When I go limp against the mattress, he slides his fingers free. I'm boneless. My skin is oversensitive, my pulse hammering in my throat while I stare at the ceiling and try to reboot my brain. I'm floating and tingling and don't have a care in the world.

Dane lies next to me and pulls me into his arms. "Color?" he asks.

"Very, very green," I mumble, and the corner of his mouth quirks.

"You did well," he says.

The praise settles into me like warmth from a fire. I roll onto my side to face him, and he brushes a strand of damp hair off my face. This is Dane's version of aftercare.

"Dane?"

"Hmm?"

"That thing you said about going where the contracts take you." I hesitate. "Does it have to be that way?"

He's quiet for a beat. "My work is remote and has been for a while. The traveling is more habit than necessity."

I don't push further. Habit, not necessity. He could stay somewhere more permanently if he wanted.

He pulls the blanket up over both of us and tucks it around my shoulders. I press my forehead against his collarbone and close my eyes, breathing his scent in deeply.

With Leo, I'm consumed. Swept up in his heat, his wildfire energy that burns through every hesitation. With Dane, I'm seen.

I want both of them, as crazy as it sounds with how short a time I've known Dane. I can't imagine giving up Leo, but Dane adds something to the dynamic that I didn't expect. The certainty of my feelings scares me half to death, because wanting two men isn't something I ever imagined for myself. But it feels right, and I'm scared I'm going to lose one or both if I push for this.

Dane wraps an arm around me, and I lie there with my heart hammering and the terrifying knowledge that I'm going to have to say goodbye to him soon.

CHAPTER 5

The next day is almost normal until after dinner, when they finally drag me to the bedroom.

Now we're in bed, and I'm a ball of nerves and lust. Leo's naked and on his back, one arm behind his head, watching me with that lazy half-smile that makes a thrill run through me, straight to my clit. Dane's beside us, propped on one elbow, his free hand stroking the curve of my waist. I'm sitting between them in nothing but the flush creeping down my chest. I'm desperate for them to fuck me.

"You're trembling, lass." Leo smiles indulgently. "Tell us what you need."

We all know why we're here, but they want me to say it.

"I want both of you. At the same time."

There it is. Out loud.

I wait for the panic, but it doesn't come. There's only Leo's warm gaze and Dane's hand on me and the certainty I didn't expect. We really are doing this, and I want it.

"Come here, my pet." Leo reaches for me and guides me over him. "Straddle me."

I swing my leg over and settle onto his thighs. His cock is hard against my stomach, and I'm so wet that I'm already making a mess of him. He slides his hand up to grasp my hips and gives me a reassuring smile.

"Now ride me. Take your time. We're not going anywhere."

I rise up on my knees and reach between us, wrapping my fingers around his cock and lining him up. The head nudges my entrance, and there's no resistance as I sink down slowly. We both groan as he fills me inch by inch until he's buried all the way inside me.

No matter how many times Leo fucks me, that first stretch lights me up from the inside. I press my palms flat against his chest and start to roll my hips in slow, shallow circles. As the ridge of his cock drags against my walls, it's massaging a pleasant spot repeatedly. I might come quickly at this pace.

"Fuck." His grasp tightens on my hips. "You feel incredible."

I ride him slowly in a slick glide as the tension builds. He moves his hands up to cup my breasts and roll my nipples between his fingers. When he pinches them harder, I moan in pleasure.

He growls, "Ride me, sweet girl. Get yourself worked up for us."

For us. Both of them.

My pussy clenches around his cock, and he hisses through his teeth. I lean forward and rock my hips faster. The angle is perfect. His cock hits deep, and my clit grinds against his pelvis on every downstroke. Pleasure builds in slow, heavy waves.

Behind me, the mattress dips, and Dane's hand settles on my lower back.

"Are you sure you want this?" Dane asks in that rough tone I've started craving the same way I crave Leo's growl.

"Yes," I'm panting as I start bouncing on Leo's cock. "Fuck my ass. Do it!"

"Good girl," he responds, and my brain goes fuzzy.

Fuck. I'm such a sucker for their praise. My pussy clenches hard around Leo's cock, and I whimper, grinding down against him as I become lost in the pleasure.

I vaguely hear Dane opening a bottle of lube, and then his slick fingers trace down the cleft of my ass. I shiver as he circles my hole patiently. He's not pushing in and just getting me used to the sensation while I ride Leo's cock.

"Keep going, lass." Leo's voice is strained. His hips rock up to meet mine, and the dual sensation of him filling my pussy while Dane's finger teases my ass makes my head swim. "Let him open you up. You're going to take us both so fucking well."

Holy hell.

I've fantasized about this in the shower. Pressed my thighs together under the dinner table when they both looked at me with lust. But thinking about it and actually being here, spread open on top of Leo while Dane plans to fuck my ass? Very, very different things.

When Dane eases one finger inside, I gasp and stop moving. The stretch burns, but it melts into a pleasure that makes me moan.

"Keep riding him," Dane says against my shoulder. "Don't stop."

I start rocking again. The motion pushes back against Dane's finger and forward onto Leo's cock, and fuck, it's a lot. I drop my forehead to Leo's chest.

"Breathe, lass." Leo strokes my hair. "Push against him."

Dane adds a second finger, and I gasp. He crooks them, and I need him to fuck me.

He adds a third finger and the stretch is intense now. Dane scissors them gently, working me open and getting me nice and lubed up while I rock on Leo's cock. Every movement sends shockwaves through me as sparks of pleasure ripple up my spine.

"You ready?" Dane asks, and all I can do is moan out, "Yes."

I'm so damn ready. Hell, I'm ready for everything, even things I haven't thought of yet. These two guys could do whatever they wanted to me, and I would just beg for more.

"I'm going to go slow," Dane says. He pulls his fingers free, and I whimper at the sudden emptiness. He caresses my spine in soothing circles. "You say yellow, I slow down. You say red, everything stops."

"Okay. I trust you," I pant out as I rock on Leo's cock.

"Lean forward flat against his chest," Dane commands.

I press my breasts against Leo's warm skin, and he wraps his arms around me. His cock inside me is at a new angle, and I moan softly from the pleasure of his small movements.

The lubed-up tip of Dane's cock probes my ass, and my breath catches. Oh god. Here we go.

"Look at me," Leo says. His hand cups my jaw, tilting my face up.

His hazel gaze locks onto mine, and I smile softly at him. I've had his cock inside my ass before, so it's not like this is my first anal experience, but I've never had two guys at once like this.

The pressure from Dane increases, and I tense up, suddenly very aware of how big Dane's cock is. Wait, wait...why did I think this was a good idea?

I'm two seconds from freaking out, and Leo traces my cheekbone with his thumb. "Breathe, lass. We'll make this good for you, I promise."

I exhale, and the love shining in Leo's eyes soothes me as Dane sinks into my ass.

Holy. Fucking. Hell.

The ridge of Dane's cock slides past the tight ring of muscle while Leo pulses thick and heavy in my pussy. For a second, my brain blips out. It's not exactly painful, but it's a fullness so far beyond anything I've ever experienced that my body doesn't have a category for it. He stretches me out, pinging every nerve ending deep inside. My pussy flutters, and I have a wild impulse to start rocking.

Dane pushes deeper, one careful inch at a time. Leo talks me through it. "You're doing so well, lass. So fucking good."

I focus on his voice and the building pleasure as I adjust to two cocks inside me.

When Dane bottoms out, he holds still and his voice is gruff. "Fuck, you're tight. You still good?"

"Yes," I mewl out, giving an experimental wiggle that makes me gasp in pleasure.

Oh my god.

I'm so full I can barely breathe. My pussy clenches, and Dane groans, low and rough, as Leo's hips jerk beneath me. The dual pleasure makes my eyes roll.

"Oh god, oh god, oh fuck!" My voice is so crazed it doesn't sound like mine.

"So good," Dane says, and I feel Leo shudder beneath me.

They move together in an alternating rhythm, and waves of bliss roll through me. They're too coordinated, and it's suddenly clear this isn't their first time. These men have lived a lifetime more than me, and I get to benefit.

Leo grunts, "You feel so good, pet, we might just keep fucking you all night," as he rocks up into me. Dane pulls back—one filling me as the other retreats—and every coherent thought in my head evaporates. The world narrows to just this moment and the unrelenting fullness from their cocks. Each stroke is better than the last, and my toes curl as the pleasure builds. It's a never-ending wave of pleasure from both sides.

I'm chanting, "Oh god," as they fuck me, and I close my eyes and let the ecstasy wash over me.

This is a pleasure beyond anything I imagined. Is this what people mean by a religious experience? Because I think I'm seeing God.

"So fucking beautiful," Dane groans as he fucks me in a steady rhythm, but his ragged tone tells me he's not in as much control as he seems. "You have no idea how gorgeous you look right now."

And I believe him. I'm gorgeous and powerful, taking two men more than twice my age. They're doing this for me because I asked them. They won't do anything I don't like, and if I tell them to, they'll stop. I've never felt more in control than I do in this moment.

I feel myself opening up and surrendering to the experience. This is me. Who I really am. And I'm glorious.

I rock between them, making them both groan as pleasure swirls in my core. The building ecstasy drives me closer and closer to the brink.

Leo's pace picks up as he flexes his hips upwards more quickly, hitting deeper and forcing Dane's cock deeper into my ass. He slides his hand down and circles my clit, and I moan loudly as he creates electric jolts of bliss in my core. My body jerks between them, and the pleasure builds so fast it scares me.

"Going to fill this pussy up," Leo groans. "Both of us, lass. Going to fill you until you're dripping with it. Until it takes."

Fuuuuck.

The breeding talk. Every single time he does it, I want more. I want it in a way that should scare me but doesn't. Not when every part of me is screaming yes.

I'm such a goner for them. Completely, utterly done for.

Dane shifts his angle and hits a wonderful spot that makes me cry out as my body trembles with my impending release. Then they're both moving faster, their rhythm breaking down as they chase their pleasure. The wet sounds of our fucking fill the room as Leo rubs my clit with every thrust. I'm right on the edge, wound so tightly I'm going to snap any second.

"Fuck. Fuck. Fuck," I chant, unable to do anything but rock between them and take their cocks.

"Time to come for us so we can fill these holes," Dane says, and the filthiness of his words and the image of cum rushing out of both holes shocks me into coming.

I explode, and the orgasm rips through me like wildfire. My mind is a swirl of colors as ecstasy floods through me. My pussy quivers around Leo's cock, and my ass clenches around Dane as the bliss continues to spike. The pleasure is so intense I slip into a trance.

And then I'm floating.

Subspace. I know it by now. I let myself sink without fighting. Leo swears in broken syllables, his hips snapping up into me as he paints my inner walls with cum. Dane roars out as he spills thick ropes of cum deep inside my ass.

I'm stuffed full of their cum. Claimed.

I'm floating high as a kite with joy. In the fuzzy warmth, the thought of a baby surfaces, and this time, I don't push it away. This time, there's a baby with Leo's hazel eyes learning to walk across the kitchen floor while he sings off-key. Another kid with Dane's dark intensity, tucked against my chest while Dane reads to us. A house full of noise and laughter and these two men who chose me.

I want it so badly, I ache. Who even am I right now? Who cares?

I almost giggle. I'm floating in a place where time doesn't matter, and I don't know how long I'm slumped against Leo.

When I come to slowly, Leo's softening inside me. Dane has already pulled out, and I can feel cum leaking out of both holes. Yep, this is dirty and wonderful.

Dane stretches out next to us, and he strokes my hair, brushing away tears I didn't even know were falling.

"You're amazing," Dane says softly while Leo kisses my head and adds, "Hey, lass. We've got you."

I can't speak. I can only cry. I'm a mess. A happy, thoroughly fucked mess, but somehow, this feels like the best version of me yet.

They snuggle close and hold me as the tears slow.

That's enough.

The bath is Leo's idea. He runs the water while Dane carries me, and I don't even have the energy to be embarrassed about being scooped up like I weigh nothing. Dane lowers me into the warm water, and I hiss as it hits oversensitive skin. The warmth quickly makes me melt as the heat seeps into my aching muscles.

Leo climbs in behind me, and I lean against his chest. Dane sits on the edge of the massive tub and washes me with the same careful attention he brings to everything. He doesn't seem to miss a single spot, and a small part of me feels like I should be embarrassed when the washcloth is between my legs, but being taken care of like this has turned me into a puddle of goo. I don't think I could complain about a single thing right now.

"You were incredible," Leo says against my hair. "So brave, lass. So perfect."

"How are you feeling?" Dane asks, draping a second warm washcloth across my neck.

"Sore." I manage a shaky smile. "The good kind."

Dane checks me over, but everything is exactly right. I'm a little tender, used. But cared for. I'm probably going to still feel them tomorrow, but I don't even care.

I press my thighs together under the water because even that thought sends heat through me. Thoroughly fucked and already thinking about next time. Yep. That's me.

Leo's fingers find mine and squeeze. "What's going on in that head of yours?"

I think about the babies I imagined in subspace. Before Halloween, I was eating ramen for the third night in a row, wondering if I'd ever belong anywhere. Now I'm in a bathtub with two men who just worshipped every inch of me. The future I keep glimpsing doesn't feel so far-fetched anymore.

It feels like something I could actually have.

"I'm happy," I say. And then, because it isn't big enough, "I'm home."

Leo's arms tighten around me as he kisses the top of my head.

Dane lifts my hand from the water and kisses my knuckles. His eyes are bright with emotion when he looks at me.

Yeah. Home. That's what this is.

After the bath, Leo wraps me in a warm towel and sits me on the edge of the bed. Dane finds the wide-toothed comb and settles behind me. Leo takes my feet into his lap and rubs lotion into them until I'm practically purring. Dane untangles my wet hair with slow, careful strokes.

I might be the most spoiled woman on the planet. I'm not even going to pretend I don't love it. By the time they're done, I'm boneless. Swaying where I sit.

"Come here." Leo pulls the covers aside and slides in, opening his arms.

I curl against him with my head on his chest. The mattress dips as Dane climbs in on my other side. His arm drapes over my waist so his fingers rest against Leo's ribs. We fit together like we've been doing this for years.

"Dane?" I murmur, already half asleep.

"Mmm?"

"Thank you for making me feel safe."

His lips press against my neck. "Always."

Leo rubs my back, slowly. "Sleep, lass. We're right here."

A soft joy makes me smile, and the last thought I have before sleep takes me is that I want this. Not just tonight. Whatever it costs. Whatever terrifying conversations have to happen next. I want all of it.

Go big or go home, right?

Good thing I'm already home.

CHAPTER 6

The register jams for the third time in an hour. I slap the side of it like that's ever worked. It hasn't, but I do it anyway because I'm back at work and my brain is mush, and maybe all the sex has actually rotted something important in there.

Vacation couldn't last forever. Dane's still at Leo's, but stupid real life doesn't wait for me to want to come back to work. The only thing helping is that I texted Willow this morning, and we're having coffee at a local cafe right after work.

"You have to lift the drawer and push it back in," Priya says from the next register. She doesn't look up from the pile of returns she's processing. "Misty from corporate was supposed to fix that last month."

"Misty from corporate has never fixed anything in her life."

I yank the drawer up and shove it into the track. The ancient machine groans to life like it's doing me a personal favor. The customer on the other side of the counter gives me a patient smile, and I ring up her candles and bath set with an apologetic shrug.

Same store, same register, same piped-in music. But I'm not the same person who clocked out weeks ago.

"You look rested," Priya says once the customer leaves. She leans against the counter and narrows her eyes at me. "Like, annoyingly rested. Did you go somewhere for Christmas?"

"Nope, just stayed home."

Home. The word rolls off my tongue so easily now. Leo's house that is starting to feel more and more like the only home I want.

"I had a quiet one," I add and hope I'm not blushing to my roots. Damn fair skin tattles on me way too often.

"Quiet..." Priya's eyes narrow further. "You're glowing. Nobody glows from a quiet Christmas unless there's a man involved."

I act busy, straightening the impulse-buy display near the register. "I don't glow."

"Liar. You're practically radioactive."

I laugh and escape to the stockroom before she can interrogate me further. The stockroom is freezing and smells like cardboard and industrial cleaner.

I press my palms against my warm cheeks. Shit, she's right. I probably am glowing. I'm just so damn happy, it's embarrassing.

I pull my phone from my pocket and see I have two texts.

Leo: Hope work isn't too painful. Dinner will be waiting when you get home. And dessert. The dessert isn't food.

Well, that's just mean. Now that's all I'm going to be thinking about. The second one makes me laugh.

Dane: Leo is attempting to make haggis. I haven't called the authorities yet but I'm monitoring the situation.

I type back to them, Leo first.

Alice: Can't wait. For both.

Then to Dane.

Alice: This sounds dire. Keep a food delivery option on your phone for when we're throwing up and refusing to eat it.

I slide the phone back into my pocket and stand there for a second in the cold stockroom with my heart hammering like an idiot.

I have two men making me food, making me laugh, and offering "dessert" that hopefully comes with a side of orgasms.

My life doesn't make sense anymore, and I don't want it to. This is living the dream.

I grab a box of restock and head back to the floor.

The rest of the shift passes in a blur. The store is having a big after-Christmas sale. I smile, scan, bag, and repeat on autopilot. My body's here, but my head is at home, where Dane's leaving in a few days, and we haven't talked about what happens next.

Willow's already at our usual booth with two lattes in front of her when I get to the cafe. Her phone is face down, and she straightens when she sees me. She's in Full Attention Mode.

Oh god, she knows I'm about to drop a bomb.

"You're late." She stands to hug me, and I notice she's wearing a new vanilla perfume. It's pretty, but it reminds me it's been a couple of weeks since we've hung out, and even longer since we've really talked.

Despite the time apart, everything about her is so wonderfully Willow as she makes small talk. The tightness in my chest that's been worrying me since I messaged her this morning loosens for the first time all day.

"The damn register jammed at work. Twice." I complain as I take a sip of my drink. It's the perfect temperature, and I hum my pleasure. "So how was your Christmas?" I ask her before she can grill me about mine.

I went shopping with her twice before Christmas, and we texted a few times, but I haven't told her much about Leo. All she knows is that I have a sugar daddy. She definitely doesn't know anything about Dane. I'm really not even sure how to tell her I'm fucking two men.

Willow blushes, and it makes me really look at her. If anyone is glowing, it's her. She shrugs, and I can tell she's trying to act casual. "Good. Um, Mike took me to another Freeuse Party... "

Interesting. "Was it as good as the first one?"

She giggles and sets her mug down.

Oh yeah, she's got a story to tell, and I give her a stern look. "Okay, bitch. Spill it."

That breaks open the dam, and her words are rushed. "Oh my god, it was insane. I was wearing this slutty red velvet dress that barely covered my ass."

She pauses and glances around like she just realized we're in a public place. She lowers her voice. "Mike fucked me in front of a guy. It was crazy and hot. Then, when we went upstairs, he shared my mouth with like three guys while he fucked me."

My eyes widen the longer she talks. Suddenly, my two men don't seem so crazy.

She sighs happily. "It was the best holiday ever. Oh, and I might have a boyfriend now." She giggles again. "Okay, now your turn. You've been weird over text for weeks. And now you're sitting here looking like someone who won the lottery and also got really, really good sex."

I open my mouth.

She holds up a hand. "Don't you dare say 'it was quiet.'"

That makes me laugh. She knows me too well.

"Okay." I blow out a breath. "It's more than a sugar daddy situation. It's... a lot more."

Her expression shifts from teasing to attentive in half a second. "I knew it. I knew there was more going on. Tell me."

"He's older. Like, a lot older. And he's..." I search for the right word. Dominant? My owner? The man who edges me until I cry and then holds me like I'm precious? "He takes care of me in ways I didn't know I needed."

The smile on Willow's face is non-judgmental. "Are you safe?"

"Very." That's the truest thing I've said in weeks. "He's good to me, Willow. Really good."

"And you're happy? Like, actually happy, not just good-sex happy?"

I think of Leo singing sea shanties while he cooks. Dane's quiet presence at breakfast. The art studio I cried in on Christmas morning. The way they both hold me like I matter after fucking me silly.

"I didn't know I could be this happy," I say, and my voice cracks a little. "It's the best thing that's ever happened to me."

Willow's expression softens. She reaches across the table and grabs my hand. "Then why do you look like you're about to cry?"

"Because I've been keeping it from you, and I hate it." My throat goes tight. "There's stuff I'm not ready to tell you yet. Not because I don't trust you, but because I'm still figuring out what it all means. And I know that's not fair."

She squeezes my hand. "Alice. You don't owe me every detail of your life."

"But you told me everything about Oliver. Every ugly detail. And I can't even—"

"Hey." She cuts me off. "That was different. I was a mess, and I needed you. You're not a mess. You're glowing like a goddamn lightbulb." She grins. "When you're ready, you'll tell me. I'm not going anywhere."

Fuck. My throat goes tight. I squeeze her hand. "Deal."

She holds on for one more beat before letting go and picking up her coffee. She gives me a wide grin, and the mood shifts like she's flipping a switch.

"Okay. The emotional portion of our program is over. I need at least one physical detail."

Oh no.

"Does his accent get thicker when he's—"

"How did you—" I stop. "Yes."

"Oh my god."

"You have no idea."

We dissolve into giggles, and I'm reminded again why she's been my best friend since childhood. Someday, I'll tell her everything. About Leo. About Dane. About the life I'm building that I never thought I'd have. But right now, this is enough. Sitting with my best friend in this sticky vinyl booth and just being honest about being happy.

My phone buzzes in my pocket, and I pull it out under the table.

Leo: Haggis was a disaster. We're ordering Thai. Dane says to tell you he tried to warn me. Come home soon or Dane might eat it all. He's making no promises to leave you any.

I read it twice. That word. *Home.*

I slide the phone away and smile at Willow.

She gives me a cute grin. "Are you texting him right now? You're totally texting him."

"I am not." I nudge her foot under the table. "Tell me more about Mike. Is he really your boyfriend now, or are you just saying that?"

She launches into it, and I sit back and listen, grateful. Grateful for her, for this, for the fact that she's not pushing. She'll wait.

And when I'm ready, I'll tell her everything.

CHAPTER 7

It's New Year's Eve, and I let the guys plan the evening. Leo's idea includes champagne. Dane said he's in charge of the candles.

After dinner, I decide to take a long shower and pamper myself a little. When I come downstairs, the living room is cozy and romantic. There's a fire going, and candles are placed around the room. Leo is in the kitchen, uncorking a bottle.

This doesn't seem as weird as it would have two months ago, but anxiety has been my constant companion all day. Leo and I agreed on a timeline. I was supposed to be his freeuse plaything through the holidays, and we never actually discussed how long this is going to last now that things have changed.

"There she is." Leo walks out from the kitchen carrying three crystal champagne flutes. "You clean up nice, lass."

His gaze drops to my simple green dress, but the way he's looking at me makes it feel like couture.

"I showered and put on a clean dress. Real high bar."

He grins. "Now come here."

He's so damn sexy it makes my pulse speed up. When I get close, he opens his arms, and I hug him. He's careful not to spill the champagne as he wraps his arms around me. I breathe in his familiar scent and relax a little. It's hard to be wound up around Leo.

He kisses my temple, and his lips linger there. "Happy New Year's," he murmurs.

"It's not midnight yet."

"I'm getting a head start."

I smile against his collarbone. Everything seems so simple with him.

Dane comes downstairs. He's been quieter than usual today, and neither of us has pushed him to talk. He's clearly thinking about something, but he's the type who needs to mull things over before he shares.

I take two of the flutes from Leo and bring one to Dane. Our fingers brush when I hand it to him, and his eyes hold mine a beat too long. I swear I can see a whole debate going on in his head.

"Thank you," he says.

It's just two words, but my body reacts to his gravelly tone as if he's caressing me. Yep, I want them both.

There are still a couple hours until midnight, and we settle on the couch with me between them. Leo's arm stretches behind my shoulders, his fingers playing with the ends of my hair. Dane sits with his ankle crossed over his knee. The TV is low with a New Year's broadcast. Fireworks are already popping somewhere outside. People are eager.

I take a sip of champagne. Past Alice wouldn't be drinking champagne in this gorgeous house.

I suddenly realize I can't do this.

I can't sit here making small talk while the clock ticks down on whatever the hell we are.

"So," I say, and my voice is steadier than I expected. "Tomorrow is January first."

Leo's fingers go still in my hair. Dane's gaze sharpens.

"Aye," Leo says.

"The arrangement was through the holidays. That was the deal." I stare at my champagne because if I look at either of them while they are telling me this is over, I might start bawling. "So I'm wondering what happens now."

"Alice," Dane says, and the way he says my name makes me look up.

His eyes are steady. "I need to say something first."

My pulse kicks hard against my ribs. Oh fuck, this is going to hurt.

He's quiet for a second, and when he speaks, his voice is low. "I came here for Christmas because that's what I do every year. Leo opens his house to me, and I spend a week pretending I have somewhere to belong."

He pauses.

"I didn't expect you."

Oh god.

"Since my divorce, it's just been consulting contracts, hotel rooms, and airports." He's not looking away from me. "I told myself it was freedom. That I didn't need roots because roots were what went wrong with Claire."

His thumb traces the rim of his champagne flute.

"But this week? I woke up every morning with you between us. And I didn't want to leave." His voice drops. "The thought of going back to my apartment made my chest hollow."

"Dane," I whisper.

"I'm not done." His eyes don't waver. "I don't want to go back to my empty apartment and my suitcase. You changed me." He swallows. "I know that's a lot to put on someone I've known for a week, but I've never been good at pretending."

My eyes are stinging. My champagne flute is shaking in my hand. Holy shit.

I turn to Leo. He's watching me with warmth under all that intensity. Fingers are still in my hair. He's not surprised by any of this.

"You knew," I say. "You knew he was going to say this."

Leo's mouth curves. "Dane and I talked. We've been discussing a lot of things while he's been here."

"And?"

He takes the champagne flute from my hand and sets it on the coffee table before taking both my hands.

"Alice." His accent thickens. "The arrangement ended almost as soon as you moved in."

My entire body is buzzing, and I stop breathing.

"The moment I watched you fall asleep in my bed and realized I didn't want you to leave? It stopped being a transaction."

Oh fuck, I'm going to cry. I do my best to blink back the tears.

"Stay," he says. "This is your home, lass. It has been for a while now. What do you say?"

I can't stop the tears, and there's a painful pressure building behind my ribs. I cover my mouth so I don't start sobbing too. Fuck. I'm a mess.

The guys don't say anything as they give me time to process.

"Okay, my turn," I say once I feel it's safe to speak without blubbering. "I want to be here with both of you."

Deep breath, Alice.

"It's not just the sex, even though—holy hell, the sex." A watery laugh escapes me. "I want the singing in the morning and the oatmeal. I want to belong somewhere for the first time in my life."

My voice cracks, but I keep going.

"I want movie nights and arguments about whose turn it is to choose. I want to paint in a studio I never dreamed I'd have."

I take a shaky breath. My face is wet, and I don't care.

"I want you both. I want all of it."

Dane moves first. He kneels in front of me.

And oh. Oh god. This man who has had me on my knees is now on his. That sight nearly breaks me.

He cups my face in both hands and wipes a tear from my cheek with his thumb.

"You can have all of it," he says quietly. "We want to give you everything."

I turn to Leo. The dominant is gone. What's left is a man who looks like I'm a gift he never expected.

"I love you, Alice. And I agree, we want to give you everything and anything you want. You just have to ask."

My voice breaks. "I love you so much it scares me."

His hand comes to the back of my neck. Pulls me forward until our foreheads press together. He kisses me hard. I grab the front of his shirt with both fists and hold on.

When we break apart, I turn to Dane. He's still kneeling on the floor, and his eyes glisten.

I reach for him. My fingers slide along his jaw, over the dark scruff. The muscle there tightens under my touch.

"I love you too, Dane." I say it clearly. Deliberately. The way he would. "I know it's only been a week. I don't care. I love you."

He closes his eyes. When he opens them, there's a wonder in his expression. "I love you, Alice."

I pull him up to the couch, and then I'm wedged between them again, Dane's arm around my waist, Leo's hand on my thigh. I'm crying and laughing at the same time like a complete disaster of a human being.

My two men.

Me. The girl who couldn't pay her rent two months ago is in love with two impossibly sexy commanding men who somehow love me back.

Is this real life? Am I dreaming?

"So what do we tell people?" I manage, wiping my face with the back of my hand. "I have a relationship with bonus content?"

Leo chuckles. "You tell them whatever you want."

"Bonus content," Dane says dryly.

"You're the DLC, Dane. The premium expansion pack."

Leo barks a laugh. Dane makes a sound that might be a laugh or might be resignation. I grin into Leo's chest.

We open a second bottle, and Leo puts on music and hums along while he refills our glasses. Dane tells the story of how they met in college, and

I find out Leo was apparently even more reckless at twenty-two than he is now.

Which is saying something.

"He got into a fight," Dane says. "First week of classes. A guy was harassing a girl outside the library, and Leo walked up and decked him."

"He had it coming," Leo says.

"You broke two knuckles."

"Aye, and he broke his nose. I came out ahead."

I snort. Of course he did.

"And then you became friends?" I ask.

"I took him to the emergency room and waited with him, and he offered me half his sandwich," Dane says. "Then he told me my posture was terrible and I looked like I hadn't slept in a week."

"Both true," Leo says.

"Both true," Dane agrees. "Haven't been able to get rid of him since."

Leo reaches across me to shove Dane's shoulder. Dane's mouth twitches.

I fit here. Between them. With them.

Holy shit, I actually fit somewhere.

At 11:30, Leo pulls me into his lap on the couch. Dane's in the armchair with his legs stretched out, watching us.

"I've been thinking," I say, tracing the collar of Leo's shirt.

"That's dangerous," Leo murmurs against my hair.

I pinch his arm. He catches my hand, presses a kiss to my fingers, and tucks them against his chest.

"When I said all of it earlier?" My face is already getting hot. "I meant all of it."

"Explain," Leo says.

"Yeah." Okay, my face is on fire now. "When you say things during sex. About filling me up." I force the words out. "About it sticking. I want it for real."

It's barely a whisper, but I said it.

Neither of them says anything. Oh god. Did I just ruin this?

I look up at Leo. His hazel eyes have gone dark, but it's not the predatory intensity I'm used to. It's softer, like I've handed him something he didn't dare ask for.

"You want that?" he asks.

"I want the possibility when the time is right." I glance at Dane. "With both of you."

Dane has an expression I've never seen on him before. Stunned is the closest word.

I remember what he told me about Claire and how she wanted him settled and the white picket fence dream, and suddenly, I'm afraid this is the deal breaker for him.

His "yes" comes before I can spiral.

"Yes?" I echo, not sure I actually heard him correctly.

"Yes." He smiles, and his whole face lights up. "With you. Yes."

They really are willing to give me everything.

Leo's arms tighten around me. "We probably shouldn't wait too long to get started on this baby. You're shacking up with two old men."

I laugh and press closer to him while my whole body shudders from relief. "I mean, we might need practice sessions. Lots and lots of practice."

Before anyone can respond, the countdown starts on TV. The crowd on screen is screaming. Confetti is already falling.

Ten. Nine. Eight.

We all stand up.

Seven. Six. Five.

I'm standing between them. Leo's hand on my waist and Dane's fingers laced with mine.

Two. One.

I kiss Leo first. The fire catches the silver in his hair. The laugh lines beside his eyes. The man who gave me a home before I knew I needed one. His mouth is warm, and he kisses me like he's staking a claim. His hand slides into my hair, and when his tongue sweeps against mine, my knees go soft.

Then I turn to Dane. He's tall and still, with that gravity that pulls me in every single time. The man who kneeled at my feet tonight and told me he loved me. His kiss is slow and thorough. His hand cups my jaw while his thumb traces my cheekbone. He kisses me like he wants to memorize the shape of my mouth.

When I pull back, I'm breathless and tingling, standing between two men who love me.

Two months ago, I would've laughed in anyone's face who told me this would be my life.

Two months ago, I was broke, alone, and not sure how I was going to find an apartment I could afford.

Now I have everything I could imagine wanting.

I squeeze Dane's hand and press closer to Leo's side, giving them both my best coy look. "Now, Sirs, are you going to take your freeuse slut to bed and breed her for the first time this year?"

Leo's grin goes wolfish. Dane's eyes darken.

They don't have to be told twice.

CHAPTER 8

They march me upstairs while my pulse is hammering so hard I can hear it in my ears. I just told them to breed me, and they're taking me to bed like they've been waiting for me to say it.

Once we're in the room, I stop in front of Leo's bed. Our bed? God, I don't even know what to call it anymore. All I know is two sexy older men that I love are standing on either side of me, and they're going to make me beg them to fill me up.

Am I insane?

Probably.

Do I care?

Not even a little.

"Dress off," Leo commands.

My simple dress has a zipper down the side, and when I go to pull it down, Dane's hand covers mine.

"Let me."

I'm desperate for them to fill me up. Even if deep down I know I won't get pregnant tonight because I haven't stopped taking the pill, I still want to imagine it's true.

While he pulls the zipper down slowly, his knuckles drag along my ribs, and I shiver. The dress pools at my feet, and I'm standing between them in nothing but black lace panties. I'm not sure why I even bothered with panties since I assumed we'd end up right here.

Leo's eyes drop to my nipples, and they immediately pucker. The low sound from Leo is almost a growl. "On the bed, pet. We're not taking this slow tonight."

Oooh, they won't hear me complain. I crawl onto the mattress, and Dane catches my ankle, not allowing me to go any further than the edge. My knees are on the bed, but my calves and feet hang off. He hooks his fingers into my panties and pulls them down to my knees before I can blink.

I hear them taking their clothes off, and I look over my shoulder to watch how fast they strip. They might be more eager than me. Wet heat flares between my legs. I'm already soaked, and they've barely touched me yet.

Leo sits on the bed in front of me and kisses me hard. His tongue sweeps into my mouth, and I grab the back of his neck and yank him closer. He tastes like champagne. His palm slides down my throat to my breast. When he rolls my nipple between his fingers, I gasp against his lips.

"You want us to fill you up, lass?" he murmurs. "Want us to breed your sweet little pussy until it's dripping out of you?"

"Yes." It comes out desperate and needy. I don't care. "Please."

"Good girl."

Dane's mouth lands on my inner thigh, and I jolt. His scruff scrapes against my skin, contrasting with the softness of his kisses. I squirm as he gets closer to my pussy.

His breath ghosts over my pussy, and I rock backwards like a greedy slut. Which, let's be honest, is exactly what I am right now.

"Oh god," I moan. They better not tease me. I need their cocks.

"What does our breeding fucktoy want?" The rumble of his voice goes straight to my clit.

"Your cock."

He swipes his tongue slowly from entrance to clit, and my whole body shudders.

"Nooo. Oh god, I need your cock."

A splash of wetness leaks from my pussy, and I hear him groan against me. The vibration hits my clit, and I cry out. Fuck, if he keeps doing that, I'm going to come before I get his cock inside me.

Leo strokes his cock in front of my face, and I focus on his hand moving on his shaft. Mmm. My mouth waters, and I almost giggle. Pavlov's slut right here.

"Open," he says.

I obey, and he slides the tip into my mouth. It's salty with pre-cum, and I suck on him gently while he threads his fingers in my hair. He doesn't thrust while he holds my head still, instead letting me suck on him like he's a lollipop.

I moan around his cock while Dane devours my pussy. He works my clit in tight circles with the tip of his tongue and then flat licks before moving to circles again. When he slides two fingers inside me, I clench around them as a jolt of lust ripples through me. He curls them and hits that amazing spot inside me, and my thighs tremble as I whimper softly.

"She's dripping and tastes so sweet," Dane says against my skin.

"Aye, she's ready." Leo pulls his cock from my mouth. "On your back, lass. Spread those legs so we can breed you."

Dane steps back so I can roll over and put my feet flat on the mattress and spread wide. There's zero shame left. I'm a panting, dripping mess, and I want them inside me. I'm such a slut for them, and it's glorious.

Leo takes his position between my thighs, running the head of his cock through my folds, coating himself and teasing me. My pussy pulses, and I whimper.

"Look at me," he says.

His hazel eyes lock on mine. And he pushes inside me with one firm thrust.

"Ohhh fuck!" I can feel every single ridge sliding against my swollen flesh.

He pulls back and drives in deeper. "Fuck, you're incredible. So tight and wet for me."

The pleasure in my core builds fast. His rhythm is rough from the start, and he fucks me like he's staking a claim. Each thrust drives me up the bed until Dane catches my shoulders and holds me in place.

Dane's above me now. He cups my jaw, tilts my face toward him while Leo pounds into me.

"You're so beautiful when you let us use you," he says quietly. "How does it feel to know we're ready to breed you?"

Delight sparks through me, and I moan, "Want it." I'm mentally sinking into a warm, fuzzy place where I just want them to use me and breed me. They can tie me to the bed and just keep pumping me full of cum whenever they want. I'll be their stress relief breeding toy. Whatever they want.

My inner muscles clench around Leo's cock at the thought, and he groans. His pace quickens as he hammers into me. Each time he bottoms out, I'm peeping out tiny moans.

"Going to fill this pussy, lass." Leo's voice is gruff. "Going to pump you so full of my cum it'll be leaking out of you for days."

A massive spike of pleasure rips through me at his words. My spine arches and my thighs tense. Holy shit.

I'm surprised when I hear words tumble out of my mouth. "Yes, yes, yes. Fuck. Fill me."

He groans in pleasure. "Our freeuse breeding pet. Does the pet want my cum?"

"Yes!" I shudder when he hits that magical spot, and I almost come right then.

"Our girl asked to be bred, and we're going to give you what you want." He plows into me as my head spins.

Each thrust from Leo jiggles my breasts, and Dane kneels next to me and rubs his cock on my nipple, almost like he's playing a game. *Tap the Nipple* while he waits his turn.

Leo grabs one of my legs and pushes my knee towards my chest, forcing Dane to stop playing his game.

"Do you want my seed, slut?" Leo growls, and the new angle creates jolts of pleasure from my head to my toes.

"Yes, give it to me. Please, please please."

My entire body is on fire, and he reaches down and rubs my clit in the exact way he's learned makes me come quickly.

"Come on my cock like a good girl, and then I'll give you your treat."

I imagine him filling me with so much cum that it's gushing out of me, and the dirty thought, along with his finger and cock, pushes me over the edge.

"Fuuuuuck," I cry out as a massive orgasm makes my mind blank.

I'm just a fucktoy desperate to be bred as I convulse around his cock. My pussy clenches as hard, rhythmic waves of pleasure rush through me.

Leo doesn't slow down. He fucks me through the climax, and each thrust sends aftershocks spiraling through me.

"Here it comes, lass," he groans a second before he buries himself to the hilt and spasms deep as he floods my channel with his warm cum. I imagine it's rushing out as he fucks it back up into me. The warmth blooming deep inside me triggers a second, softer climax that rolls through me in waves.

I'm whimpering when he slows down and pulls out.

"Good girl," he murmurs. "My perfect lass."

I immediately feel a trickle of cum sliding down my ass crack as he drops my leg back to the bed. My brain is hazy from my orgasm, and when the guys roll me over, I giggle into the bedding from euphoria. My limbs are trembling, and I squeak when Dane pulls me up onto my knees, leaving my face smashed into the bed.

I'm ass up, face down, and I can feel more cum dripping down my inner thighs. And I want more.

"God, look at you." Dane's voice is reverent. He drags two fingers through the mess between my thighs and pushes it back inside me.

I moan at how filthy this is.

"Not wasting a drop. Our slut wants our baby."

My pussy flutters around his fingers as more of my wetness and Leo's cum leak around them.

When he removes his fingers, I don't even have time to complain before he notches his cock at my entrance.

These are my men, and they're breeding me because I asked them to. The idea that I belong to them makes me go half out of my mind as Dane plunges into me straight to my core.

"Oooooh, god!" I cry out from the sharp pleasure.

He's thicker than Leo, and I'm mewling as he pulls out fully, then slams back into me repeatedly. He grasps my hips as he fucks me furiously. I barely have time to register the pleasure before he's hitting that spot deep inside of me that makes my head spin.

I'm sobbing nonsense into the bedding as he fucks me so hard his balls slap against my clit.

"Our breeding good girl," he huffs as he fucks me, and my body vibrates with pleasure.

My thighs tense and my toes curl as I inch closer to my orgasm and I'm crying out with every thrust. "Fuck, fuck, fuuuuck, it feels soooo good."

Leo stretches out beside me and strokes my hair, watching Dane fuck me. I turn my head and try to smile at him, which turns into a gasp of delight when Dane slams into me harder.

All I can do is take it. I close my eyes and imagine I really am getting pregnant from this. Both of the men would be kissing my round belly, and when I give birth, I'd have each of them holding a hand.

My moans grow louder as the fantasy takes over, and it's years from now and we have several kids, still living in this massive house while we're tripping over toys. But it's full of laughter and joy.

I can't take it anymore, and I start begging. "Breed me. Please. Oh god, give me your cum. Need it."

Dane's control snaps. His grip locks on my hips, and he hammers against my pussy hard enough to make me squeal.

"That's it," Leo says against my ear. "Be a good breeding slut and let him fill you up."

Oh god. Oh god oh god oh god.

Tension coils low in my belly, tighter with every thrust. My thighs tense, and the ecstasy builds in layers until I can't take it any longer.

I scream as my entire body is wracked with an almost painful pleasure. It's so powerful I see stars flash behind my eyelids. My body convulses with waves of delight.

Dane groans and slams home one last time, holding still while streams of cum shoot deep inside me. I'm spasming violently, and the orgasm is so powerful my vision whites out. The pleasure is one continuous wave.

My mind splinters, and I don't know where I end and he begins. All that matters is this moment and both my men breeding me.

When I come to, Dane has already pulled out and I'm stretched out on the bed on my stomach. Leo is rubbing my back and crooning endearments in my ear.

The bed dips, and Dane settles in on my other side. He brushes sweaty blonde strands of hair from my face. "Beautiful," he whispers. "You're so fucking beautiful."

"And ours," Leo says.

Dane kisses my shoulder. "Ours."

Leo's voice rumbles in my ear. "We're going to spend the rest of our lives showing you."

All I can do is give a "mmm" in agreement as their mixed cum slides out of my well-used pussy. I want this for the rest of my life.

We lie there. I'm floating. These men are the best things that ever happened to me.

CHAPTER 9

Two days later, Dane is leaving. But he's coming back, and I believe him.

Leo had a meeting to go to that he couldn't reschedule, and when I come downstairs, Dane's suitcase is sitting by the door.

My chest squeezes, and I have to remind myself he's just going to his home base to settle some things before returning.

I find him at the island, slicing a mango. His hair is damp from a shower, and he's wearing comfortable jeans and a shirt. I admire his broad shoulders for a moment and then almost giggle at myself.

He's leaving, and I'm standing here memorizing his shoulders like a lovesick idiot.

"You're staring," he says, without looking up.

"You're worth staring at." I slide onto the stool across from him and steal a piece of mango. "Is this your version of a goodbye breakfast?"

"It's breakfast." He sets a bowl of oatmeal in front of me and adds mango slices. "Eat."

Even on his way out the door, this man can't stop feeding me. I pick up the spoon before I do something stupid like cry over oatmeal.

Because here's the thing. This is a man who told me he loved me on New Year's Eve. Who filled me with his cum and promised to breed me. He isn't leaving for good. He's going back to pack up a life he doesn't want anymore so he can start a new one with us.

We eat quietly, and when he finishes, he studies me until I look up and blush.

"What?" I ask with my spoon halfway to my mouth.

"I need to tell you something before I go."

My pulse kicks. "Okay."

"I told you about Claire."

"Yeah." They wanted something they couldn't give each other.

"I need you to understand something."

Oooh, okay, this is serious.

He continues. "She wanted kids. A family. The whole picture. And I told her I wasn't sure I wanted that."

My breath catches. Um, he's not about to say the same thing to me, is he? Two nights ago, on the couch, when I said I wanted the possibility of a baby, Dane said yes without hesitation.

"I wasn't lying to her," he says quietly. "I didn't want it. Not with her. Not then. And for a long time after the divorce, I thought that meant I didn't want it at all."

His eyes hold mine. "Then you asked me on New Year's Eve, and the word came out before I could think." His jaw tightens. "Because I realized it was never about not wanting a family. It was about not wanting one with the wrong person."

Holy shit.

My eyes are burning.

"You're the right person, Alice," he says simply. "I didn't know I was waiting for you, but I was."

I'm out of my chair in a flash and pressing my face into his chest. His arms come around me, one hand on the back of my head. His heart hammers beneath my cheek.

"Dane." My voice is muffled against his shirt. "If you make me cry, I'm never forgiving you."

"You're already crying."

"Shut up."

He laughs, and it rumbles through his chest and into me. It's the best sound I've ever heard from this man. I clutch the front of his shirt and cry into it and laugh at the same time as he holds me with his chin resting on top of my head.

We stand there in Leo's kitchen—our kitchen—and I let this sink in.

This man, who couldn't make it work before, wants to make it work with me.

"Two weeks," he says against my hair. "Maybe three. I need to deal with the lease. Renegotiate my contracts. The consulting work is location-independent, but there are logistics."

"I know."

"And then I'm coming back to you and Leo."

"I know that too."

"And I'm taking the office across from your studio. Leo already offered."

I pull back. "You two planned this without me?"

"We discussed logistics." His mouth twitches. "You were asleep. We didn't want to wake you."

"Because you'd exhausted me into a coma."

"Accurate." There's no apology in his tone.

I rise on my toes and kiss him, slow and deep. His hand cups the back of my neck, and he kisses me back with all the love he feels for me spilling out.

When we pull apart, his forehead rests against mine. "I'll be back as quickly as I can."

"You better."

He's smiling when he lets me go to get ready to leave. Everything is going to work out. I can feel it.

After he's gone, I wander into my studio, feeling a little lost. The poetry book Dane gave me is on the table by the window, and my heart warms. He'll be back.

I pick out a brush and paint. I don't know what I'm making. Blue first. Sweeping it across the canvas. Then gold bleeding into the edges. Then warm strokes that remind me of skin and sunlight and desire. It's messy and wild and the proportions are all wrong.

I don't care, because I'm finally painting in a house that belongs to one of the men I love. There's a poetry book on the table left by another man who loves me.

I'm so absorbed I don't hear Leo come in. "Lass."

I turn with the brush still in my hand. I'm already a mess, with paint all over my fingers.

He's leaning against the doorframe in his meeting clothes, but he's undone the top button and rolled the sleeves to his forearms. The afternoon light catches the silver at his temples.

"You're painting," he says, warmly.

"I'm making a terrible mess."

"Good." He crosses the room and stops behind me. He looks at the canvas over my shoulder. "It's a start," he says.

"It's awful."

"It's yours. That's what matters."

He wraps his arms around me from behind, and I lean into him. His heartbeat is steady against my shoulder blade, and I'm struck by how right this feels.

"Dane left," I say.

"I know." Leo presses a kiss to my hair. "He asked me to make sure you ate lunch. He's already managing the household, and he hasn't even moved in yet."

I smile. "He talked to me about Claire and how he didn't want kids with her, but he does with me."

"Aye?"

"And you?" I ask. "Are you really okay with all of this? Sharing your house, your life, everything?"

"Alice." He turns me around in his arms, and his voice is rougher than usual. "I spent years building a life that looked impressive and was empty. Big house. Nice cars. Money to burn. Then a lass in a Queen of Hearts costume stumbled into my world at a Halloween party and wrecked every plan I ever had." He tucks a strand of hair behind my ear. "This house hasn't been a home since I bought it. But it is now since you moved in. Do you understand the difference?"

I press my forehead against his collarbone and breathe him in. Oranges and warmth and safety and mine.

"I love you," I say against his chest.

"I love you, lass." His thumb brushes the knot at the top of my spine. "Now. What do you want for lunch?"

I laugh. "You're as bad as Dane."

"Where do you think he learned it?"

A jolt of happiness makes me smile. I lift my head and glance over my shoulder at the canvas, with its wild, messy colors.

This is my life now. Chaotic and mine. Two men who love me.

EPILOGUE

Three months later.

Cobalt blue drags across the canvas in a long, wobbly streak. It's not perfect, but the color is right, deep against the warmer tones underneath. I step back and squint at the whole thing.

Huh. It actually looks intentional.

I've been taking lessons for two months. Now I've got paint under my fingernails more days than not, and my instructor says I have a good eye for light.

I wipe my hands on the flannel I stole from Leo. One of his old ones he never wears anymore. It's covered in paint.

He's never getting this back.

"Alice!" Leo's voice carries up the stairs, and my whole body warms from his Scottish rumble. "Come down here, lass!"

There's something in his tone I can't place, and now I'm curious.

I set my brush in the jar, wipe my hands again—more blue smudges on the flannel, sorry not sorry—and head downstairs.

Leo's standing at the open front door with his arms crossed and *that* grin. The one where the lines around his mouth go deep and his hazel eyes crinkle and he looks like a man holding back a secret.

"What?" I ask.

Then I hear a car door slamming.

I peer around his shoulder, and my heart hammers so hard it might burst through my chest.

There's a vintage car in the driveway. The backseat is packed, and the trunk is open, stuffed with cardboard boxes.

Holy shit. Dane's finally here. He's visited a couple times, but it took him longer to pack up his life than any of us liked.

Dane comes around the side of the car and—okay. He looks different, but it's not physical. He's still tall, still broad-shouldered. Still the kind of handsome that makes my brain short-circuit on a regular basis. But there's something looser about him. Like he finally put down a weight he'd been carrying so long he forgot it was there.

He sees us waiting for him, and the corners of his mouth lift. "I brought more than a suitcase this time."

I look at Leo, and he's still grinning. "Did you know about this?"

"Who do you think helped him find a shipping company for the rest of it?"

I bolt down the front steps. Dane catches me when I throw my arms around him. He holds on longer than I expect. His chin rests on top of my head, and I breathe him in, sandalwood and clean cotton, and my eyes sting.

When I pull back, his expression is soft. This is his expression reserved just for me.

"You're back for good," I say. It's not a question.

"For good," he repeats, and a burst of happiness deep in my stomach makes me giggle.

We spend the afternoon unpacking. Which mostly means Leo gives unsolicited opinions about where everything should go, Dane ignores him with the patience of a man who's been dealing with Leo for twenty-five years, and I sit on Dane's new office floor surrounded by books.

"You own more books than furniture," I say, pulling a worn book from a box.

"Furniture is temporary." Dane takes the book from my hands. His fingers brush mine, and the contact zips straight through me. "Books are the only things I kept from every apartment."

Leo chuckles. "He showed up at college with two duffel bags and a box of paperbacks. Some things don't change."

"And you showed up with a kilt and an ego the size of Edinburgh Castle." Dane doesn't look up from the box he's sorting. "Some things really don't change."

I laugh, finally relaxed for the first time in weeks.

After dinner—Leo made paella, belting out some ridiculous sea shanty the whole time while Dane chopped vegetables—we end up on the couch. I'm tucked between them. Leo on my left, arm slung across my shoulders. Dane on my right, his hand resting on my thigh.

I'm sandwiched between two stupidly attractive men. I've got paint in my hair and a studio upstairs and a life that doesn't make any kind of sense.

I've never been happier.

I'm also not on the pill anymore.

Now that Dane is here, it's time to start trying for real.

I give them both a long look. They're watching me the way they always do, like I'm the center of their universe.

I grin. "Now, Sirs, it's time to take your freeuse slut to bed and breed her for real."

Leo's laugh is a rumble I feel deep in my core, while Dane's mouth curves into that slow, devastating smile.

They don't have to be told twice.

The End

Bonus Story - His for the Holiday

April Cross

Author's Note

So here's a fun behind-the-scenes confession: While I was writing Book 2, I somehow completely skipped over Thanksgiving. Like, Alice went from moving in with Leo straight to being a little slut for Christmas. I didn't even notice until I was writing book 3 and went back to read what happened at Thanksgiving... oops!

But it worked out perfectly because it gave me the excuse to write this spicy bonus story about what actually happened on Turkey Day. Turns out, Leo had plans. Big plans.

So settle in and enjoy the holiday I accidentally forgot to write.

April

Chapter 1

My eyes open to an unfamiliar ceiling, and for a split second I don't recognize where I am. Then the soreness between my thighs reminds me, and I smile.

Leo's bed. Leo's house.

The sheets smell like him—oranges, and something warmer underneath—and I burrow deeper, not ready to face the day. We were up late last night. He'd bent me over the arm of the couch while some movie played in the background, and then fucked me again in the shower before bed. My body feels well used in the best possible way.

The bedroom door opens, and I peek out from under the covers. Leo walks in carrying two mugs, wearing nothing but blue pajama pants that hang low on his hips. The morning light catches the silver at his temples and his salt-and-pepper hair is mussed.

Mmm, he looks yummy. We met at a Halloween freeuse party a few weeks ago, and the connection was so intense that when he asked me to move in as his live-in submissive until the new year, I said yes without hesitation. We're only a couple of weeks into this arrangement, and the sight of him still makes my stomach flip.

"Morning, lass." That Scottish accent does something to me every single time. He sets one mug on the nightstand beside me and the smell of coffee almost makes me groan in pleasure as he settles on the edge of the bed with his own.

I push myself up against the headboard. "Morning. What time is it?"

"Just after nine." He takes a sip, watching me over the rim. That warm hazel gaze tracks my movement as I reach for my coffee, and heat prickles across my skin.

"I forgot what day it was," I admit. The coffee is perfectly sweet with a little cream. He remembered how I take it. Something about that makes my chest tight.

"Thanksgiving." He says it casually, but there's a weight behind the word. "I have plans for us today."

"Plans?"

"Aye." He sets his mug aside and turns to face me fully. He's not just Leo having morning coffee anymore. He's Leo about to give me instructions.

My pulse kicks up, and I wrap both hands around the mug to steady myself.

"Here's how today is going to work," he says, his voice dropping into that commanding register that makes my thighs press together. "You're going to stay naked. All day. No clothes, not even when we're cooking."

I suck in a breath. "All day?"

"All day." His mouth curves. "You'll be accessible to me whenever I want. Wherever I want. If I decide to bend you over the kitchen counter while the turkey's in the oven, you'll spread your legs and thank me for it."

Oh god. My pussy flutters at the authority in every word; the response is immediate and embarrassing. We've played like this before with him using me whenever the mood strikes. But a whole day of it? My head spins.

"What about when we eat?" I manage.

"I'll make sure you get food." Amusement glitters in his expression, but there's an undercurrent of pure intent. "Any other questions?"

All I can think about is how much I want what he's describing. A whole day of being his. No decisions to make, no responsibilities except to please him.

"No, Sir."

"Good girl." He reaches out and tugs the sheet from my grip, baring me to the cool air. My nipples tighten immediately, and his gaze drops to admire them. "That's better. Now, I need to start the turkey, but first—"

He doesn't finish the sentence. I barely get my mug onto the nightstand before he grips my ankle, dragging me down the bed, and then he's covering me with his body.

I gasp as his weight settles over me. The hard length of his cock presses into my thigh through the fabric of his pants, and my hips rock up instinctively.

"Eager little thing." His lips find my neck, teeth scraping over my throat. "I'm going to use this sweet pussy to start my morning right. And you're not going to come."

Wait. "What?"

"You heard me, lass." He pulls back just enough to meet my eyes, and the heat in his expression sends a shiver through me. "Today is about *my* pleasure. You'll get yours when I decide you've earned it."

I'm ready to beg if needed, but his hand is already between my legs, fingers sliding through my wetness, and all that comes out is a whimper.

"Lass, you're soaked." He pushes two fingers inside me, and I arch off the bed, crying out at the sudden stretch. "Your body knows who owns it, doesn't it?"

"Yes, Sir," I pant, clutching at his shoulders.

He fucks me with his fingers, maddeningly slow, his thumb circling my clit with just enough pressure to give pleasure but not enough to get me there. Wet sounds fill the bedroom, and holy shit, they're obscene. I'm already climbing towards release, my whole body tightening with need.

"Please," I gasp. "Please, I need—"

"You need whatever I want to give you." He withdraws his fingers, and I nearly sob at the loss. Before I can protest, he's shoving his pants down and pressing the head of his cock at my entrance. "You need my cock in this sweet pussy."

"Yessss," I moan, and he pushes in with one hard thrust.

I scream from the pleasure of him stretching me out and hitting that spot that makes my whole body light up.

"This pussy feels so good." His accent thickens the way it does when he's turned on.

He sets a punishing pace, drilling into me, and all I can do is take it. This is what I want. To be used like a sex toy and give myself over completely. I'm spiraling towards the edge dangerously fast, despite his warning, pleasure coiling tighter inside me with every thrust.

"Don't you dare come." The words are a growl at my ear. "Not until I say."

I bite my lip, fighting the wave that wants to crash over me. I wrap my legs and arms around him as the headboard knocks against the wall in a steady rhythm.

"That's it, lass. Take my cock like the good little fucktoy you are."

The words shove me right to the brink. I'm trembling, every muscle locked tight, hovering on the edge of a release I'm not allowed to have. He feels enormous inside me, and I can tell by the way his rhythm falters that he's close.

"Going to fill you up," he pants. "Going to pump you full of my cum and then make you cook breakfast with it dripping down your thighs."

Oh god. The mental image is so filthy I almost lose control, but then he's groaning, slamming deep one final time. The hot pulse of cum fills me as he empties himself. The heat of it is incredible and my toes curl.

My whole body vibrates when he pulls out, wound tight from being right there. Every nerve is firing and unhappy.

He stands up and looks down at me with satisfaction, tucking himself back into his pants. "Meet me downstairs. We have a turkey to prep. But don't clean up too much, I meant what I said about my cum dripping out of you."

He picks up his coffee and whistles as he walks out. I stare at the ceiling, pussy throbbing, his cum already leaking out of me onto the sheets. This is going to be a long day.

But as I drag myself toward the bathroom on unsteady legs, I'm smiling. Because for the first time in years, I'm spending the holiday with someone who makes me feel amazing.

And despite the soreness between my thighs—or maybe because of it—I've never been more thankful for anything in my life.

CHAPTER 2

I make it to the kitchen on autopilot, still flushed and aching from being left hanging. Leo is at the counter in front of the turkey in a roasting pan. He's singing under his breath, and the whole scene is so bizarrely normal considering I'm walking in completely naked with his cum on my inner thighs.

He turns when he hears me, and that hazel gaze rakes over my body with appreciation. "There's my obedient lass."

I cross my arms over my breasts, suddenly self-conscious. The kitchen's gleaming surfaces and stainless steel make me feel like a slutty misfit, especially while naked. "I'm just doing what you said."

He smiles and opens a drawer to grab something black. When he tosses it at me, I snag it reflexively. It's a black apron with a ruffled edge. "Put that on."

I hold it up, examining the thin fabric. Does he wear an apron with frills, or did he buy this just for me? The thought makes me smile. "You want me to wear just an apron?"

"That's it." His grin is wolfish. "I want easy access. And I'm going to admire your ass while you're chopping vegetables."

My face burns as I slip the apron over my head and tie it behind my back. The fabric covers my front from chest to mid-thigh, thin enough that my nipples press against it, but my ass is completely bare, and I'm hyperaware of that fact as I move toward the counter.

Leo watches me with obvious satisfaction before turning back to the turkey. "I'm going to get this bird prepped and in the oven. You're on vegetable duty." He nods toward a cutting board already laid out with celery, onions, and carrots. "Dice those for the stuffing."

I grab the knife, grateful for something to do with my hands. The tile floor is cool on my bare feet, and every time I shift my weight, I'm reminded that there's nothing between my skin and the open air behind me.

Leo starts working on the turkey, and after a moment, he begins to sing a sea shanty, something about leaving port. That low rumble fills the kitchen, and I find myself smiling as I chop the celery. This is surreal. I'm naked except for an apron, still denied release, and he's singing about saying goodbye to a lousy ship. Somehow it feels more intimate than anything we've done in bed.

"Do you cook a lot?" I ask, attempting to distract myself from how wet and needy I am.

"Aye. I learned it from my mum when I was young." He glances over at me from his spot beside me at the counter, expression softening. "She believed a man should be able to feed himself and anyone he cares about. It stuck with me."

I file away that glimpse of his past. He doesn't talk about his family much, and he just offered it casually while working butter under the turkey's skin.

"What about you?" he asks. "Do you cook?"

I snort. "Not really. My aunt tried to teach me, but I was more interested in painting. After she died, I mostly survived on ramen and frozen dinners." I pause, the knife hovering over an onion. "This is actually my first Thanksgiving dinner with this much food in years."

My throat constricts when he says, "Then we'll make it a good one."

My eyes start to water almost immediately while I'm chopping. I blink rapidly, trying to see what I'm doing. It's just the onions, I tell myself.

"Breathe through your mouth," Leo advises. "Helps with the sting."

I try it, and he's right, it does help. We work in companionable silence for a while. The kitchen fills with the smell of herbs and butter.

I'm so lost in the rhythm of chopping that I don't notice he's moved until I feel him behind me.

A palm settles on my bare ass and I clutch the knife harder so I don't drop it. "Careful, lass," he says close to my ear. "Wouldn't want you to hurt yourself."

"Then maybe don't sneak up on me while I'm holding a knife," I manage, but the words come out breathy. He's caressing the curve of my ass, dipping lower with each pass.

"You're such a sweet fucktoy." He presses closer, and the hard line of his cock digs into my lower back. My grip on the knife falters.

"Leo…"

"Keep chopping," he commands.

I stare at the carrot while his fingers slide between my legs from behind.

He groans when he discovers how wet I still am. "Christ, lass. You're dripping."

"You didn't let me come," I gasp as he rubs my clit. "What did you expect?"

"Exactly this." He works the bundle of nerves with enough pressure to make me squirm, but not enough to send me over.

"Keep chopping. If you stop, I stop."

I force myself to keep at it, hands unsteady as I try to cut even pieces. The carrot blurs. His fingers are relentless—stroking, teasing, dipping inside me and then withdrawing. I'm quickly spiraling again.

"Such a good girl," his approval hums warm at my ear. "You're following instructions even when you're desperate."

I whimper and slice the carrot. My cuts are getting uneven, but I don't care. All I can focus on is what he's doing between my legs and how badly I want him to fuck me and let me come.

He slides two fingers in, and I cry out, the knife clattering to the counter. Before I can recover, he fists my hair and pulls my head back.

"I said keep chopping."

"I can't—" My voice breaks. "Please, I can't think when you're—"

He withdraws, and the sudden emptiness makes me whine.

"Then I suppose we're done."

"No." I grab for him, reaching. "No, please, I'll be good. I'll keep going."

His chuckle is dark. "We'll see about that later. Right now, I need to check on the turkey."

He steps away like nothing happened, drying his hand on the nearest towel before opening the oven. My legs are like Jell-O and I lean on the counter for support. My pussy throbs with frustration.

This is torture. Delicious, wonderful torture.

I pick up the knife and force myself to continue chopping the vegetables while Leo prepares the stuffing. It's criminal how he's walking around like nothing is wrong as he makes gravy and fetches serving dishes from the cupboards. Every time he passes me, he touches me—a palm on my ass, a trail up my spine, a squeeze of my hip. None of the movements are urgent. Just a constant reminder that I'm here for his use.

By the time I'm finally done with the vegetables, my body is coiled so tight I might shatter if he so much as breathes on me.

"Come here." Leo's seated on a stool at the kitchen island, crooking his finger at me.

I go to him on trembling legs. He draws me between his spread thighs, his hand settling on my hip under the apron. The position puts my breasts level with his mouth, and he takes full advantage as he unties the apron at my neck. When it folds down to my waist, he leans forward and drags his tongue across one peaked nipple.

I moan, grabbing his shoulders for balance. "Please, Sir."

"Please what?" He switches to the other nipple, teeth scraping gently.

"Please let me come. I've been good."

He leans back, looking up at me with heat in that steady gaze. "You have been good. My perfect little fucktoy, walking around naked and desperate for me."

Hope flares in my belly. "So can I—"

"No."

I stare at him, disbelieving.

"The turkey needs another two hours." He says it like we're discussing the weather. "And I'm going to spend that time keeping you right on the edge. By the time we sit down to dinner, you're going to be so far gone you'll do anything I ask."

"I already will," I whisper. "I'll do anything. Please."

His smile is devastating. "I know you will. But I want you mindless. The only thing you'll remember is how to beg."

He stands, spinning me around and bending me forward over the island. The cold granite jolts against my overheated skin, and I moan as he knees my legs apart.

"Hands flat on the counter," he orders. "And don't move them."

I obey, pressing my palms to the smooth surface. Behind me, I hear his zipper, and then his cock nudges my slick entrance.

"You're going to take my cock," he says, "and you're not going to come. Understand?"

"Yes, Sir." My voice is barely a whisper.

He slams into me.

I scream in pleasure. The overwhelming stretch of him after hours of teasing is almost too much. He doesn't give me time to adjust, just starts fucking me, and his hips slap against my ass with each thrust. The granite digs into my hipbones and my nipples drag across the cold surface every time he drives forward.

"Christ, you're incredible." His brogue has deepened. "So fucking tight and wet. This pussy was made for my cock."

I'm already climbing, the pleasure building so fast it scares me. I try to hold back, try to focus on the counter or the old-fashioned kitchen timer ticking in the background, but he fills me too completely for any of that to work.

"Don't even think it," he growls, and I can tell he's reading my body like a book. "You don't come until I say."

"I can't—" Tears prick my eyes. "Leo, it's too much, I can't hold back—"

He slows his pace, shifting to long, deep strokes that make me see spots, each one wringing a moan from somewhere primal. "You can and you will. Because you're my good girl, and good girls obey."

I sob into the countertop, fighting my body's desperate need for release. He fucks me for what feels like forever—deep and grinding, then switching to brutal and fast, pleasure and denial blurring together as he keeps me right at the precipice without ever letting me fall.

When he finally comes, groaning my name as he pulses deep, I'm a quivering mess. He pulls out slowly, and his cum slides down my inner thighs for the second time today.

"Beautiful." He smooths a palm over my ass tenderly. "You did so well, lass."

I can't respond. I can barely think. My chest heaves as my body begs for release, but some twisted part of me is also proud that I held back. That I obeyed him.

He helps me straighten up and turns me to face him. His hand cups my face, expression soft as he thumbs away tears I didn't realize had fallen.

"I know it's hard," he murmurs. "But you're doing perfectly. A few more hours, and I'll give you everything you need."

I lean into his palm, drawing unsteady breaths. "Promise?"

"Promise." He kisses my forehead. "Now, we need to baste the turkey. Think you can manage that?"

I laugh, the sound slightly hysterical. "I can try."

"That's my pet."

He hands me the baster and opens the oven, releasing a wave of heat and the smell of roasting turkey. I try to ignore the slickness sliding down my thighs and the persistent throb between my legs.

A few more hours. I can do this.

Probably.

CHAPTER 3

The kitchen smells incredible from the turkey. My stomach growls, reminding me that the protein bar I ate an hour ago wasn't that filling.

Leo's been keeping me busy for the past hour while we finished the preparations. He gave me small tasks—arranging the rolls on a baking sheet and stirring the gravy—but they were made infinitely harder by the constant need thrumming beneath my skin. Every brush of the apron fabric over my nipples sends a shock through me, and every step I take around the kitchen reminds me of the slickness between my legs.

He's barely touched me since bending me over the counter, and somehow that's worse. The anticipation is its own kind of torture.

"That's the last of the prep work." Leo tosses the dish towel aside and surveys the kitchen with satisfaction while I'm about two seconds from combusting. "We've got an hour before everything's ready."

An hour. I can survive an hour. Probably.

"Which means," he continues, and the shift in his tone makes my spine straighten, "we have time for a Thanksgiving tradition."

I eye him warily. "What kind of tradition?"

"Come here." He settles onto one of the kitchen stools and pats his thigh.

I cross to him on legs that threaten to buckle. He unties my apron and tosses it aside. I'm fully naked again, and the cool air raises goosebumps across my skin.

"Straddle me." He guides my hips as I climb onto his lap. I'm facing him with my knees bracketing his thighs. At some point while I was chopping vegetables, he changed into jeans, and the rough denim drags against my bare skin. I'm suddenly very aware that my bare pussy is pressed against his bulge. "There you go. That's my girl."

I grip his shoulders for balance, my heart hammering. "What are we doing?"

"It's Thanksgiving." His thumbs trace circles on my hip bones. "We're going to practice gratitude."

"Gratitude," I repeat, not understanding.

"You're going to tell me things you're grateful for." His hand drifts lower, fingers trailing down my belly toward my pussy. "For each one, you'll get a reward."

My breath hitches. "What kind of reward?"

Instead of answering, he drags one finger through my folds. I gasp, hips jerking forward. He's barely grazing me, just a light stroke through the wetness, and the contact makes me cry out.

"That kind," he says, smiling at my reaction. "But there's a catch. You have to keep talking. Keep telling me what you're grateful for. If you stop—" He withdraws. "I stop."

I blink as the rules click into place. Talk coherently while he takes me apart. "That's evil."

"That's the game, lass." Amusement flickers across his face. "Unless you'd rather just wait another hour with no touching at all."

"No, I'll play. I'll do it." The words come out fast and eager.

"I thought you might." He settles back in the chair, one hand resting on my thigh while the other draws lazy lines on my hip. "Whenever you're ready."

I exhale slowly and try to think. What am I grateful for? The question feels absurd when I'm sitting naked on his lap, my entire body humming with desire.

"I'm grateful for…" I start, then have to pause when he brushes over my clit. Just a whisper of contact, barely there. "For the apartment. The one you helped me get."

"Mmm." He circles my clit once, twice. "That's a good start. What else?"

The pleasure makes it hard to form words, but I force myself to focus. "The credit card. Being able to buy things without—" I gasp as he increases the pressure slightly. "Without worrying about my bank account."

"Very practical." He dips lower, teasing my entrance. "More."

My mind is starting to blur at the edges. I'm grateful for… what? I scramble for anything to say, anything to keep him touching me.

"The sex club." The words tumble out. "Taking me there. Showing me that world."

He slides one finger in, and I moan, clenching around him. "You liked that, didn't you? Being watched."

"Yes." I rock my hips, trying to draw him deeper. "I liked it. I didn't think I would, but—"

"Keep talking." A second finger joins the first, stretching me in the most delicious way. "What else?"

My thoughts scatter. He rubs my clit while his fingers curl inside me, and the combination tears through me so hard I can't breathe. "I'm grateful that you—that you push me. Make me try things I wouldn't try on my own."

"Like what?" He's working me slowly now, in and out, a lazy rhythm that builds pressure without release.

"Like the freeuse stuff." The words are getting thready. "I never knew—god, that feels good—I never knew I wanted to be used like this. Available. Owned."

The word hangs in the air between us. Owned. He goes still, and for a moment I'm terrified I've said too much, crossed some line we weren't supposed to cross.

But his eyes darken with possessive hunger that sends a jolt of lust straight through me. "Owned," he repeats, rough. "You like belonging to me, lass?"

"Yes, Sir." It comes out as a whisper.

He rewards me with a hard thrust of his fingers, and I cry out, tightening my grip on his shoulders. My hips are moving now, rocking against his hand, chasing the pleasure he's been withholding since morning.

"More," he demands. "What else are you grateful for?"

I'm losing the ability to think. The pleasure is building, my body tightening, everything coiling low in my belly. His thumb circles my clit relentlessly while his fingers work inside me, driving me higher and higher.

"I'm grateful for—" My voice breaks. "For the way you take care of me. After. The baths and the—the holding me and—"

"The aftercare," he supplies, and there's warmth underneath the command now.

"Yes." My eyes sting with tears, though I couldn't say why. "No one's ever—I've never had someone—"

I can't finish the sentence. The sensation is too much, cresting toward a peak that will get me in trouble. My thighs are trembling, my whole body wound like a bowstring.

"Don't stop," he warns. "What else?"

"I'm grateful—" I'm panting now, barely coherent. "I'm grateful for you. For this. For not spending today alone with a frozen turkey dinner and reruns on TV. For feeling safe for the first time in—in years. For—"

My voice cracks, and to my horror, actual tears spill over from everything hitting me at once—the vulnerability and how fucking intimate it is, telling him why I'm thankful while he edges me.

Leo's expression shifts. The predatory edge softens into tenderness that makes my chest ache. He withdraws his fingers and cups my face with both hands, still warm and damp from touching me, tilting my head to meet his gaze.

"Alice." His voice goes soft. Like, really soft. I've never heard him sound like this before. "Look at me."

I blink through the tears, meeting that steady amber gaze.

"You're not going to be alone anymore." He says it like a fact. "Not today. Not on any holiday, if I have anything to say about it."

My ribs expand around a feeling too big to name. I surge forward and kiss him, hungry and messy, tasting salt from my own tears. He kisses me back just as hard, one hand fisting in my hair while the other wraps around my waist, hauling me flush against him.

When we break apart, we're both breathing heavily.

"I still haven't let you come," he murmurs against my mouth.

A broken laugh escapes me. "I noticed."

"Soon." He kisses my cheek. "At dinner. You've more than earned it."

I groan, dropping my head to his shoulder. "You're going to kill me."

"Never." He caresses my spine, soothing. "But I am going to wring every ounce of pleasure from your body before this day is over. When I finally let you come, it's going to be the best orgasm of your life."

I press closer. "You mean that?"

"On my life." He pats my ass. "Now up you go. I want you to set the table."

I slide off his lap, boneless, feeling like I've just run a marathon. My body still thrums with unspent need, but there's a warmth spreading through me now that has nothing to do with being turned on.

He said I wouldn't be alone anymore. He said it like he meant it.

This is supposed to be temporary—a holiday arrangement, a few weeks of exploration before I go back to my regular life. But standing naked in his kitchen while we prepare tasty food, that future feels very far away.

"Alice." Leo's voice cuts through my thoughts. He's watching me with knowing eyes. "Table. Now."

"Yes, Sir."

As I gather plates and silverware, I catch myself smiling. My body is spent, my emotions are a mess, and I'm about to sit down to Thanksgiving dinner more turned on than I've ever been in my life.

But I feel like I'm exactly where I'm supposed to be.

Chapter 4

The table looks beautiful. I've set it with the good china Leo pointed me toward—delicate white plates with silver edges, crystal wine glasses, cloth napkins in burgundy that match the centerpiece of autumn leaves and small gourds. It's elegant and festive, and I feel ridiculous standing naked next to it.

Leo carries in the turkey on a platter, golden brown and glistening. The smell makes my mouth water, though I'm not sure if I'm hungrier for food or for the orgasm he's been dangling in front of me since morning.

Both. Definitely both.

He sets the turkey down and glances at the table with approval. "You did well, lass."

"Thank you, Sir." The praise settles warm in my chest despite everything.

He draws out a chair—my chair, I assume—and gestures for me to come closer. I cross to him, expecting to sit, but he shakes his head.

"Not there." He sits down first, then pats his thigh. "Here."

"You want me to sit on your lap? For dinner?"

"I want you close." Heat simmers behind his steady gaze. "Is that a problem?"

It shouldn't be hot. It's weird and probably unsanitary. But my pussy buzzes at the command in every word, and I find myself moving toward him without conscious decision.

He takes hold of my hips and guides me down onto his lap, positioning me sideways so my legs drape over the arm of the chair, my side resting against his chest.

The position is intimate in a way I wasn't prepared for. His arms come around me, one resting possessively on my stomach, and his heartbeat thuds against my shoulder blade. His cock presses into my ass, thick and impossible to ignore through his jeans.

"Comfortable?" he asks, and I can hear the smirk.

"Not really." It comes out breathier than I intended. "That's kind of the point, isn't it?"

"Good girl." He reaches past me to serve food onto the plate—turkey, stuffing, mashed potatoes with gravy, green bean casserole. The movements press his body into mine, and I'm hyperaware of every point of contact.

When the plate is full, he spears a piece of turkey with a fork. Instead of handing me the utensil, he brings it to my lips.

"Open."

I part my lips, and he slides the fork in. The turkey is flavorful and perfect, but I barely taste it because his other hand has started wandering idle paths across my bare stomach.

"Good?" he asks.

I nod, chewing. The whole thing is so weirdly domestic and so filthy at the same time that my brain short-circuits. He's feeding me

Thanksgiving dinner while I sit naked on his lap, his erection pressing into me. He touches my body like he owns it.

Because he does. At least for as long as I'm his freeuse toy.

He feeds me another bite—this time of the stuffing. The wandering touch drifts higher, grazing the underside of my breast. I swallow hard.

"More?" He's already loading the fork with mashed potatoes.

"Yes, please."

The potatoes are creamy and buttery, but I lose the flavor entirely when he pinches my nipple. Not hard, but enough to send a spark straight to my clit. I gasp around the food, and cough.

"Careful." I swear I can hear the smile in his tone. "I want my mouth on you, but not giving you mouth to mouth."

"Then maybe don't—" I start, but he pinches again, and the words dissolve into a whimper.

"Don't what?" He offers me a green bean from the casserole, innocent as can be. "I'm just making sure my sweet girl is comfortable."

I shoot him a look as I take a mouthful of green bean casserole. He grins, unrepentant.

The meal continues like this. Bite after bite, fed to me while he touches me everywhere except where I need it most. He teases my nipples until they're peaked and aching, strokes the insides of my thighs close to my pussy and then retreats. Every time I think he's finally going to give me relief, his knuckles trail up my spine instead, and I shiver.

I can't taste anything. The food is probably delicious since we put hours of work into it, but my entire world has narrowed to his hands on my body and the relentless throbbing between my legs.

"You're getting distracted," he observes, offering me another sliver of turkey.

"Hard to think," I manage, "when you keep—oh god."

His fingers have finally slipped between my thighs, sliding through the wetness there. He doesn't enter me or touch my clit. He's stroking through my folds, spreading the slickness around, and making me squirm.

"When I keep what?" He sounds genuinely curious, the bastard.

"Teasing me." I shimmy my hips, trying to get his fingers in the perfect spot. "Please, Leo. Sir. I can't—"

"Can't what?" His hand withdraws, and he brings glistening fingers to his mouth. He sucks them clean while I watch him over my shoulder and my pussy clenches around nothing. "You can't enjoy a nice Thanksgiving meal with me?"

"That's not—" I make a frustrated sound. "You know what I mean."

"I do." He picks up the fork again, loading it with stuffing. "Open up."

I eat the stuffing because I don't know what else to do. My body is keyed up so high I might vibrate apart. I'm about to lose my mind.

"Please." The word escapes before I can stop it. "Please, Sir. I've done everything you asked. Please let me come."

He sets down the fork. For a long moment, he's quiet and when he speaks his voice drops low.

"You have been good. My perfect pet. Letting me use you. Playing my games."

My pulse jumps with anticipation. "So can I—"

"Not yet." He picks up a small plate I hadn't noticed—pumpkin pie with whipped cream. When did he slice that? "Dessert first."

I nearly scream. "Leo—"

"Ah ah." He scoops up a bite of pie and holds it to my lips. "Be patient. We're almost there."

I eat the pie, barely registering the taste. All I can feel is the rising neediness as his cock presses against my ass.

"Do you know what I'm thankful for?" he asks, feeding me another bite.

I shake my head, not trusting myself to speak.

"I'm thankful for you." His lips brush my ear, and goosebumps race down my neck. "For your trust. For your willingness to let me push your limits. For the way you look at me when you're burning to come and trying so hard to be good."

My eyes sting with unexpected tears. What is it about this man that makes me cry at the worst possible moments?

"I'm thankful," he continues, his hand sliding down to my pussy, "that you said yes to this arrangement. That you're spending today with me instead of alone."

He finds my clit, and I jerk in his arms, a broken sound escaping my throat.

"And I'm thankful," he murmurs, circling that swollen bud gently, "that I get to be the one who takes you apart."

"Please." I'm past shame. "I need this, I need you."

"Shh." He kisses my temple, never stopping his maddening rhythm. "I know. I've got you, lass. Just a little longer."

He feeds me the last of the pie with one hand while the other is between my legs, keeping me on the razor's edge. I'm trembling so hard I can barely swallow.

When the pie is gone, he sets down the fork.

"Now." His brogue is thick. "I think it's time for my dessert."

Before I can blink, he's lifting me, carrying me toward a free part of the dining table. My back hits the wood, cool against my overheated skin.

I look up at him. I'm laid bare like an offering, and his expression makes my breath catch. There's tenderness and a fierceness I don't have a name for.

"You've earned this," he says, unbuckling his belt. "You've been so good. Now I'm going to reward you."

Mmmm, this is it. Finally.

My thighs fall open without any instruction, and his laugh is dark as he looks at my puffy, swollen pussy.

"That's my sweet girl. My perfect pet. Let's see how many times I can make you scream."

The dining table is hard beneath my back, and the food is half eaten, but I can't care about anything except the man standing between my spread thighs, looking at me like I'm the real feast.

"Beautiful." He removes his shirt, revealing the broad chest I've spent nights exploring with my hands and mouth. "Spread out for me like a buffet."

Oh fuck. I whimper, reaching for him, but he pins my wrists and holds them above my head against the table.

"Keep these here, my pet." His gaze bores into mine. "Don't move them unless I say. Understand?"

"Yes, Sir."

"That's my girl."

He releases my wrists and trails his fingers down my arms and sides. I arch off the table, desperate for contact, but he just smiles and keeps his unhurried exploration going.

"You're a good girl." His fingers skim my hip bones. "Hours of edging. Hours of being my obedient little fucktoy without getting to come."

"Please." The word comes out wrecked. "Leo, please, I can't—"

"Shh." He leans down and kisses my inner thigh. I nearly jackknife off the table. "I know, lass. I'm going to take care of you."

His mouth moves higher, breath ghosting over my pussy without making contact. The anticipation is almost worse than the denial. I fist my hands, fighting the urge to grab his hair and shove his face into my pussy.

"You smell incredible." Another kiss, just beside where I'm desperate for him. "I've been thinking about this since this morning. Watching you walk around naked in my kitchen, dripping for me, begging so sweetly." His tongue flicks out, a teasing lick that barely grazes my outer lips. "Knowing that when I finally tasted you, you'd fall apart."

"I'm already falling apart," I gasp. "Please, please, please—"

He licks me.

One long, slow drag of his tongue through my folds, from my entrance to my clit, and I scream. The sound echoes off the dining room walls. I barely recognize my own voice. After hours of denial, the direct contact is almost unbearable, and the pleasure is so intense it borders on pain.

"Just like that." The words vibrate against my pussy as he speaks. "Let me hear you."

He devours me. There's no other word for it. His tongue works my clit in a relentless rhythm while he grips my thighs, holding me open. Wet, obscene sounds fill the room as he eats me like he's starving, and I'm writhing on the table, sobbing from pleasure.

The orgasm builds with terrifying speed. After being edged since dawn, my body is primed, taut as a wire, ready to explode at the slightest provocation. I can feel it cresting, that familiar tightening low in my belly.

He pulls back.

"No!" My denial is a wail. "No, please, I was right there."

"I know." He kisses my inner thighs again, waiting for me to come down. "Not yet."

"You said—" I'm crying now, hot tears streaming down my temples into my hair. "You said I could come. You said it was time—"

"And it is." He lifts his head, meeting my eyes with a fierceness that knocks the air from my lungs. "But first, I want you to understand something."

He hooks his hands under my thighs and pulls my ass to the very edge of the table. He's still in his jeans and he grinds his covered cock against my pussy. The denim is rough on my oversensitized skin, and I writhe and moan in pleasure.

"This isn't just about making you come." He rocks against my pussy. "It's about showing you what you deserve. Someone who pays attention to every reaction, every sound you make. Someone who takes the time to learn your body."

Fresh tears streak down my face. "Leo—"

"You're not just a quick fuck, Alice. You're something to be savored."

I can't speak. My throat is too constricted, my heart too full.

His gaze is blazing. "Now," he says, leaning back down until his face is hovering above me. "Let's try this again."

Jesus. His mouth returns to my pussy, and this time there's no teasing. He sucks my clit between his lips, tongue flicking in a rhythm that whites out my vision. Two fingers slide inside me, curling, and I'm gone as the pleasure builds so fast I can't breathe.

"Come for me, lass." The command vibrates against my clit. "Come all over my tongue."

I come so hard I see stars.

The orgasm hits me like nothing I've ever felt. It's a full-body earthquake that rips through me until even my fingertips are buzzing. I scream his name, clenching around him as wave after wave keeps rolling through.

He doesn't stop. His mouth keeps wringing every last tremor from my body until I'm sobbing and pressing my hands against his head because I can't take any more.

He lifts up just long enough to speak, lips glistening with my arousal. "One more."

"I can't."

"You can." His fingers curl inside me and pleasure zings up my spine. "Give me another one."

He drops his mouth back to my clit, and somehow, impossibly, the pressure starts building again. I didn't even know my body could come so hard and then immediately start racing toward another peak. But he's relentless, sucking and licking and finger fucking me. I'm helpless to do anything but take it.

The second orgasm crashes over me while I'm still twitching from the first. This one is different. It's deeper, slow waves instead of one big explosion. I moan his name over and over, hands fisting in his hair.

When he finally lifts his head, I'm a boneless heap and the world has gone fuzzy.

"So good for me." He kisses his way up my stomach. "Such a good girl."

"That was…" I stop. My brain isn't working.

"We're not done yet."

He flips me over, and suddenly my cheek is pressed to the table, my feet are on the floor, and my ass is in the air. I hear the drag of his zipper and the rasp of denim before he's nudging against my opening, thick and insistent.

"Tell me what you want." The command is rough and barely controlled.

"You." I push back, desperate. "Please, I want you."

He slams home.

I cry out as he fills me, the pleasure almost blinding. He's right there on the first stroke, and a bolt of pleasure rips through me. After coming twice, I'm so sensitive that every inch of him feels magnified and almost too much.

"Fuck, you're tight." He grasps my hips firmly to pin me in place. "So fucking perfect, lass."

He fucks me in long, hard strokes and all thoughts dissolve. The table creaks as he drives deeper and each thrust makes me moan.

He groans, "Take it. This pussy is mine."

I take it. I couldn't do anything else if I tried. My fingers curl around the edge of the table, and I let myself be fucked. Be used. Be his. The tension builds again and I'm spiraling towards a pleasure I've never experienced before.

"Touch yourself." His breath catches. "Make yourself come on my cock."

I loosen my grip on the table and find my swollen clit. The first touch makes me jerk, and a few urgent strokes later, I'm coming again—clenching and screaming into the table while Leo pounds into me.

"Christ, Alice," he groans. "Time to fill this pretty little pussy."

He buries himself to the hilt with one last punishing thrust, and I feel him pulsing, hot spurts of cum painting my inner walls. The sensation triggers another aftershock, and I'm shuddering with him, milking his cock while we both ride out the wave.

When it's finally over, he collapses against my back, both of us breathing hard. The table is a mess, sticky with food and god knows what else. I couldn't care less.

"Holy hell," I manage when I can form words again.

His laugh is breathless. "Aye. That about sums it up."

He pulls out slowly, and I gasp at the emptiness. Then he's gathering me up, lifting me from the table like I weigh nothing, cradling me to his chest.

"Where—" I start.

"I'm going to run you a bath and get you warm," he says gently.

CHAPTER 5

He carries me into the bathroom and sets me on the edge of the tub while he fills the tub. The water is perfect, and he adds lavender bath salts.

I sink into the tub with a groan of relief, immediately feeling the soreness start to dissolve. Leo strips off his clothes and slides in behind me, pulling me back against him. His arms come around me, holding me secure.

"You did so well today," he murmurs into my hair. "So fucking beautiful when you come. I could watch you fall apart forever."

My vision blurs with happy tears. "I didn't know it could be like that."

"Like what?"

I search for the right words. "Intense. But also... safe."

His arms tighten around me. "That's exactly how it's supposed to feel."

We stay there for a long time, soaking in the warm water while he holds me. Eventually, he helps me out and wraps me in a soft towel, then carries me to the bedroom. He dresses me in one of his t-shirts that smells like him and tucks me under the covers.

He sets water and snacks on the nightstand, then gets into bed beside me and pulls me close, one arm wrapped around my waist, his heartbeat steady under my ear.

"Drink," he says softly.

I sit up just enough to drink, gulping down half the glass. My throat is raw from all the moaning and screaming, and the water soothes the burn.

"There's also a protein bar if you wake up hungry."

"Okay," I yawn. "But what about the turkey?"

He chuckles. "I'll go down in a few and put it away. Just sleep."

I smile and close my eyes. The orgasms were worth the wait.

When I wake up, I'm snuggled against Leo's chest, and I'm surrounded by warmth and the scent of his orange body wash mixed with the lavender bath salts. His breath is steady, and I sigh in contentment. He's here.

Best Thanksgiving ever.

I close my eyes again and burrow back into Leo's chest. Tomorrow we'll clean up whatever is left of the mess and heat up the leftovers. He'll probably start all over again and find new ways to drive me crazy. And I'll love every second of it.

But right now, I just want to stay here. Wrapped up in him. Grateful.

It's enough.

The End

I'm a writer of spicy stories... okay, I'll be honest, most of my stuff is ghost pepper spicy. I started writing wife sharing stories under Lacey Cross before branching out to longer romantic erotica. I write power play stories with guys who demand to be in control.